Born in Coventry two years before the start of the Second World War, Christine was the youngest of three children, her two brothers being several years older. To be safe from the bombing in Coventry, a city that was to experience huge amounts of damage, she was sent away to Yorkshire, to live with an aunt and uncle in Bradford, where she stayed for the duration of the war.

After the war she returned to live with her family, returning with a noticeable Yorkshire accent, which even now after many years of living in Cornwall, can still be detected.

Married to her beloved Jeffrey and with two children, they moved house several times until fate intervened and they finally moved to Cornwall in 1983, not to retire but to work. Thirty years later Christine and her husband are now both happily retired.

While her husband is busy in the garden she spends her time writing, something she's always done but not seriously until she retired from work. Since then it's become an addiction that cannot be cured!

Willelm D'Anville

C.M. Bryden

Willelm D'Anville

Vanguard Press

VANGUARD PAPERBACK

A CIP catalogue record for this title is
available from the British Library.

ISBN 978 178465 109 1

*Vanguard Press is an imprint of
Pegasus Elliot MacKenzie Publishers Ltd.*
www.pegasuspublishers.com

First Published in 2016

**Vanguard Press
Sheraton House Castle Park
Cambridge England**

Printed & Bound in Great Britain

This book is dedicated to the memory of all of those who perished during the Revolution in France.

Acknowledgements

My thanks to the many historians who have written about the French Revolution, thus inspiring me to write this story.

Special thanks to Ann Kenwright, for the beautiful watercolour and ink picture of the *Mary Anne* on the cover, and for her continuing friendship. Also to my friend and fellow writer, Stewart Akass, for his willing support and for the time he has spent guiding me through the minefield and mysteries of computer techniques, a task I fear that will be on going.

To my readers, I hope you enjoy this story and I would be honoured to receive your reviews and comments. Thank you!

Contents

Prologue

Henri, Marquis D'Anville

The day started well enough, it being Sunday and a day of rest and prayer. I would normally have attended church with my wife, Angeline. To our sorrow, since the revolutionary forces had taken control of the country, organised religion was no longer allowed. Neither had I made any plans to attend to my work at the bank, founded by my ancestors. I merely intended to enjoy my day at leisure, after my wife and I had eaten le petit déjeuner.

Afterwards, while my wife amused herself with her embroidery, I planned on riding my horse through the surrounding countryside. To my dismay, I found there to be an air of general unrest, with scattered mobs of peasants milling about in noisy groups when I would have expected them to be in their homes. Unfortunately, there had been a great deal of unrest in the country over the past few years, mainly caused by a countrywide famine due to adverse weather conditions and the country's spiralling financial debts, a problem that the King and his ministers seemed incapable of solving.

Fortunately, the weather had improved somewhat since the spring, and there was evidence of the newly planted crops once more beginning to grow in the fields, all of which boded well for the future.

True Frenchmen like myself and my fellow aristocrats, being wealthy, were immune to the grinding poverty of ordinary citizens. Although we were not ignorant of what was happening in the country. Like many others, we thought that the King would eventually solve his country's problems, which in turn would quell the unrest. We had no thoughts that he too would sadly lose his life before peace would once again be found in the kingdom. Neither did we know that a new order would soon be in control.

Too late to save us, this ignorance was something I came to regret. Like many others, I found myself to have been misguided but there was nothing I could say or do that would alter the future as the days of my life were already numbered.

Sadly, my ignorance was caused mainly by an inbred belief that my illustrious rank in society was mine, and mine alone, and that there would never be freedom of equality in the lower echelons of society. Not that I believed the poorest of citizens were not worthy of enjoying civil and human rights that I, and those socially like me, had enjoyed and taken for granted for many years. I had never thought equality would ever become a fact of life for the masses; therefore, I paid scant heed to the miscreants as I rode my latest acquisition, a thoroughbred horse, across what had once been, for some years, barren fields of countryside.

As I rode, for no more than an hour, I enjoyed the feel of fresh country air on my face, which, after a week of incarceration at the bank left me feeling refreshed and invigorated. I was unaware as I rode that my time as a privileged aristocrat was rapidly running out, or that on my return home I would be greeted by my hounds running loose in the grounds. It was this one act, along with the insolent attitude of the servants, in how they responded to my polite request that they lock up the animals, and serve refreshments to my wife and I, that surprised and alarmed me the most!

My wife, hearing me admonishing the servants, joined me in the main salon, where I could see she too was upset, even more so when I remarked on the lackadaisical behaviour of the outside staff. Her demeanour, unlike her normal kind and gentle manner, changed as she told me she too had received much the same treatment from her maids, which in itself was unusual, for we had always treated those who worked for us with the utmost courtesy and kindness, considering them to be part of our family; but today, for reasons which we both found hard to fathom, we were being ostracized and rudely ignored.

The rest of the morning passed with nothing happening to alert us to the events that would occur later in the day. Had there been any signs of impending trouble, we would have fled our home earlier, and taken refuge with friends in the country. As it was, the house remained quiet until early in the evening, when our lives took a turn for the worse.

We were sitting together in the salon, talking and enjoying each other's company, when a commotion could be heard coming from the hallway.

Suddenly, there were sounds of banging on the main door, noises so loud they no doubt could be heard throughout the rest of the house, and then the voices of strangers could be heard, shouting orders to our servants, calls to 'stand aside', as the door was thrust open, and then the sound of boots, scuffing across the stone floor of the hallway as unwelcome intruders marched noisily into our home.

At the first sounds I leapt to my feet, as did Angeline, both of us suddenly afraid of what was about to happen. We stood and looked at each other, our eyes mirroring each other's fear and shock.

I could see Angeline was trembling, with the colour abruptly fading from her beautiful face as the door to the main salon was suddenly thrust open. She clutched at my arm in her distress as, in the next minute, several men all wearing the uniform of the revolutionary army marched in to confront us, along with a smaller group of citizens who, from their dishevelled and disparate apparel, appeared to be part of the newly formed militia; all, no doubt, recruited from the local peasantry. Armed with heavy wooden staffs or pikes, their obvious intention seemed to be looking for trouble and blood; it was at that moment I realised, with sickening horror, that it was our blood they were after!

Two of the men roughly grabbed hold of me as another pair, to their everlasting shame, did the same to my wife; manhandling and bundling us into the hallway, past some of our servants, who were standing in a huddle as we came out of the room. Some, I could see, were openly showing their delight at our distress, whilst others were smirking and looking acutely embarrassed at their part in our discomfort. We were then taken out to the courtyard, where yet another crowd of peasants, whom I knew to be from the locality, had gathered to watch the events that were about to happen.

We had no time to speak to our staff or to gather any personal belongings, except for those we already wore, before we were being lifted and tossed headlong into a waiting tumbril. From its filthy condition, I could see that it would last have been used to transport animals to market. It was then I finally realised for certain, by our inhumane treatment, that we were now considered no better than farmyard animals, our previous social standing meaning nothing.

I was despondent, my senses telling me I was looking for the last time at the house that had been my home for nearly fifty years. It was a grand house, one of style and substance, built by my ancestors nearly two centuries earlier. Finally I knew; if I was expecting justice from those in charge, I was going to be sadly disappointed. We staggered and reeled in the tumbril as it took off down the cobbled street and I finally realised it must have been someone quite close to me who had betrayed us, someone who believed that we deserved to lose our heads, even though we had always been loyal to our King and country.

Who would have thought so ignoble an end would come to a man who was well known in the city as a banker and an upright citizen? Was there to be no justice for us? I fear not!

My dearest wife, in her distress and fear, clutched hold of me as we stood together in the tumbril. Her beautiful face was now showing signs of her distress. Her once lovely pale blue silk gown was torn, and splattered with blood, from the cuts she'd received from the many stones thrown at her by the angry mob as we were taken from our home.

I'm sorry to say I fared no better. My fine Sunday coat was bloodied from a missile thrown at my head by one of the watchers. Thankfully, the blood had begun to congeal.

We stood close together, my dear wife and I, clutching at each other, fearful of what was about to happen, afraid to voice our fears as we were taken from our home and driven through the cobbled streets of Paris, to La Force, that most notorious of buildings, which we realised was to be our destination.

On our arrival, we were again roughly manhandled as we were pulled out of the cart, with little care as to our welfare, before we were pushed and thrust inside the entrance to the prison.There, a surly and uncouth man, dressed in the filthy garb that passed as the uniform of a revolutionist, was waiting to score a line through our names on a sheet of parchment which he held in his dirty hand.

I could see my name, and that of my wife, headed the list of aristocratic names. It was obvious, from the toothless grimace that passed for a smile, that our jailer was definitely a man who enjoyed his work and, even more so, he was enjoying the power he had over us at that awful moment in our lives. He was a man I would not have employed to brush my dogs, let alone work amongst people who were his betters, aristocrats such as myself, who were now gracing the prison, human beings who would in the future be grateful for any small mercies he might show them. Yet even I could tell this wasn't going to be, for how could anyone give thanks for such awful treatment as we were going to experience?

This was to be the most dreadful moment of my life, when I finally realised these peasants were the ones now in control of France; uneducated people I would never trust to care for the country, or its citizens, but I was powerless to change what I knew was about to happen. This is where my regrets very nearly overwhelmed me. I feared for our lives, quite sure that we would never survive to see the next year if just walking into this place and experiencing one day as a prisoner was a foretaste of what was about to happen to us in the future.

My body was strong, as was my resolve, and I was determined I was not going to let these animals, humans that go by the name of 'man', to get the better of us. I knew I had to be strong, both physically as well as mentally, and think not only for myself, but also for my beloved wife, knowing she would be unable to withstand the rigours of prison life without me at her side.

My thoughts at that time were not only for my wife and myself, but also for our dearest son, Willelm, our only child. Thankfully, he had not been at home on the day of our arrests, but had been staying in the country with his tutor, where he was finishing his studies, before returning home at the end of the month to start his working life with myself in the family bank. My unspoken thoughts at this time were, that at least he was safely out of the city and, hopefully, if he could evade capture, his life would be saved.

I thanked God for my foresight in making arrangements for such an event, and now I hoped all would go according to my plans, for I knew I would no longer live to see them come to fruition.

And so began the miserable days of our captivity, each day passing with a grinding slowness as we slowly starved to death, as the small amount of food we had was finished. Food was purchased for us by one of the guards, having sold our good outer clothing and the few jewels my wife had been wearing on the day of our capture; less, of course, a deduction for his trouble. Money that went into his pocket along with the money he'd collected from our friends, who were all in the same miserable condition.

Unfortunately for us, the food he'd purchased, or obtained by other means, was rotten, not fit for pigs, let alone humans, and even that small amount we had to get at before the rats sharing the cells could snatch it away.

By now, to add further to our physical discomfort, the prison population had doubled, as more of our friends and acquaintances were captured and thrown in to join us. Having no means of a further bribe, we had to rely on these friends, but even their supplies were soon diminished, leaving us all to slowly starve.

There was no way of escaping from La Force and, therefore, it was beyond our imagination as to how we could be saved. Only a miracle could save us, but we all knew praying for such an event as that would be useless; we were incarcerated in La Force until death, by starvation, or, God forgive, the guillotine! It was a case of which came first?

As the hours passed into days, we gave up counting. Our minds numb with fear and hopelessness, mentally paralysing us in our misery, so much so we were no longer able to determine what would happen to us, until the dreaded morning arrived when, along with many of our friends and acquaintances, we were dragged from our cells and taken to the Palais de Justice where we were to stand trial before the Committee of Public Safety and where a travesty of a trial took place.

Within the next few hours we were all swiftly condemned to death as enemies of the fledging republic, victims of a reign of terror sweeping throughout the country.

Unfortunately for us, we had no lawyer to help us. And who could possibly blame him or her for not wanting to take on a case as hopeless as ours?

My wife and I knew when we were first captured we would undoubtedly have to face a trial where we knew we would surely be found wanting. We also knew what our sentences would be, and our expected fate. And so it happened, exactly as we had imagined. Our day of judgement had arrived.

Along with our friends and acquaintances we were then taken from the court, once again packed into tumbrils, before being driven to one of the many squares in the city to where guillotines had been quickly assembled and where they were already doing a brisk business in despatching the heads of those found guilty.

One by one, in quick succession, heads of the accused would be despatched in front of a large waiting audience, consisting mostly of old men, except for the tricoteuses, those old hags who sat knitting, only putting their work to one side when yet another aristocrat climbed the wooden steps to their appointment with death. Bystanders would be applauding and jeering, their faces covered with joy as each aristocratic head was swiftly removed from its body and then, along with other common citizens of Paris that were watching, they would laugh, joking with each other at the demise of yet another good and honourable man, or woman.

Our lifeless bodies, like many before us and, no doubt, like many hundreds more that would follow, would then be taken to the city boundary and thrown into deep pits, where they would be covered in lime and left to rot. There would be no last rites spoken over our bodies, or a religious ceremony spoken on our demise, merely a rough committal into unconsecrated ground by strangers, those who had no care or thought for our dignity, let alone our illustrious past.

We knew only too well that our bodies would not be committed to the family mausoleum, with its honourable coat of arms of the D'Anville family, a place where the bodies of our ancestors had rested for many years, or even a simple grave in the grounds of our family home in the Breton countryside. Neither would there be a lasting memorial, carved onto stone, as our ancestors enjoyed, to extol our virtues for those that follow to read. Neither would there be any other earthly reminders of our existence. unless Willelm, our only son and my heir, should survive this terrible time. This was our final shared hope, as we climbed the wooden steps onto the bloodied

21

stage to face the guillotine, where the last few minutes of our lives are to be played out. Sadly, we will be no more. Our lives will be over. With great sorrow, and with no one to save us, we are resigned to our tragic fate.

I was allowed to briefly kiss my dearest wife before we were led up the steps to the guillotine and now, all that is left for us to do as we wait for the evil contraption to finally dispatch us to our maker, is to pray to God that he will have mercy on the souls of Henri, Marquis D'Anville and his beloved wife Angeline; that he will keep our dearly beloved son, Willelm, safe from harm, and that he will have a good life and never have to suffer the same fate as his parents.

Now, all I can do, before I lay my head on the block, is to say a final silent prayer, asking for God's blessing, and then I must close my eyes and wait for my end.

And so it came to pass that on the 16th July 1789, on a fine summer's day, two days after the Bastille had been stormed, a good and loyal Frenchman and his beloved wife, lost their lives. Their deaths taking place in an unnamed Paris square, in front of a disreputable mob of citizens with nothing better to do with their time than to watch as Henri, Marquis D'Anville and his honourable wife Angeline, lost their lives. Two people, both unfortunately descended from a long line of aristocratic men and women, who had fought in past wars on behalf of France over the centuries, services that had been repaid by grateful monarchs with titles, land and wealth; wealth that Henri, Marquis D'Anville, and his ancestors, had used to better the lives of those who served them. Their deaths were witnessed that day by the ordinary people of Paris, who knew no better but who had the good fortune to be born simple folk; unlike *the deceased, who had the misfortune to be born into lives of wealth and privilege.*

The last earthly memory, Henri, Marquis D'Anville had, as he went to meet his maker, was the sounds of jeering, and applause ringing in his ears, from those citizens of Paris who had sat watching as Madam Guillotine did its infamous work. The guillotine, an ancient invention from England that the powers that be in France had decreed should be the weapon of execution for those it decided could no longer be allowed to live as aristocrats. Not even the great bell of Nôtre Dame could mask the noise of the citizens as they cheered and clapped, watching the heads of Henri and Angeline D'Anville, (as well as those of their friends and acquaintances who were killed upon the same day) as they rolled into simple wicker baskets, having been swiftly dispatched from their bodies.

Is this what is meant by Liberté, Égalité and Fraternité?

Chapter 1
Willelm D'Anville

Willelm D'Anville would always remember the 4th August 1789. It was memorable for two reasons: firstly because it was his eighteenth birthday and secondly, he had just received news that his beloved parents were both dead and, because of that, his life changed direction.

He had been staying with his tutor, Henri Masson, at his teacher's home in the Normandy countryside, many miles from his own Paris home, completing his studies before joining his father in late August as a beginner in the Paris bank founded by his ancestors.

Henri Masson was in his late thirties; well educated and well travelled and, at that time, unmarried. Willelm's father had known him for many years, through some of his friends, who had used his services as a teacher for their young sons and daughters. He now lived with his aged mother in what had once been the steward's house of a large estate (his father being long since deceased, after many years service as the estate steward, which allowed him the privilege of his widow retaining the house, until her death.) His mother, consequently, was surviving on a pittance of a pension and whatever Henri could earn tutoring the sons of wealthy men, such as Willelm's father.

Henri was well travelled, having ridden across France and Italy in his younger days, teaching wherever went. He was also well versed in the classics of Greece and Italy, and could speak several languages but, on his father's death, had returned immediately to care for his mother who, being quite elderly and infirm by then, was now in need of him. Therefore, the money Willelm's father paid for tutorage was a godsend in keeping them in some comfort.

Willelm had been looking forward to working with his father at the family bank ever since he had been a child, much to his father's delight, but to his mother's dismay, as she had dreamt of him becoming an academic. She saw Willelm as a man of great learning, but that was not to his liking. He much preferred his own vision of his future that of working in the family bank with his father.

In reality, Willelm knew hardly anything of any great consequence about the world of banking, or world finance, except for that which he had gleaned from his father, knowing nothing at the time of how money could be used for evil, as well as good. Not that he intended erring on the side of the Devil when the day came for him to step down from his father's carriage and walk at his side into the illustrious building (which, in Willelm's eyes, was a temple for the worship of gold), becoming the latest in a long line of the D'Anville family to serve France, as had his ancestors – but this time, as a banker, not as a soldier of fortune.

So far, as befitting the only son and heir of a Marquis Willelm's education had been well rounded and, as was the custom in those days, he had been taught at home; first by his nurse, who taught him the basic good manners and behaviour expected of a young aristocrat, followed afterwards by a succession of governesses who taught him how a young man in society should behave and then, as he grew older, a further succession of educated strangers came to his home, but this time in the guise of tutors, such as Henri Masson, teaching him the intricacies of Mathematics, Greek and Latin, as well as the languages and customs of Italy and Spain.

The language of Brittany came naturally to Willelm, for this was where he had spent his early life, living in one of the most beautiful houses in the Breton countryside. But it was at the family home in Paris where, aged thirteen, he learnt to master the language of the English.

It was about this time his father first began his business association with a Cornishman, Captain Martin Sawyer, a master mariner who was not only the master, but also the owner of the *Mary Anne*, a lugger that he won in a gambling game from a Dutchman called Jaden Grist.

The *Mary Anne* was renamed so after Martin Sawyer's English-born mother. It was a fast and easily manoeuvrable ship that responded well to the deft touch of its captain, sailing regularly between England, Le Havre and Calais, as well as to Roscoff in Brittany, and to other foreign shores, even crossing the Atlantic to the Caribbean, where Captain Sawyer traded in exotic spices as well as other goods that at the time fetched large quantities of gold for him, and for those men who, like Willelm's father, had had the intelligence and foresight to understand the world was wide open for such trade, happily investing their wealth in the Cornishman's expertise.

To begin with, as Willelm's father and Captain Sawyer talked, they were unaware that the lad listened into their many conversations, where they spoke in English, his father being fluent and so, not only did Willelm learn the language of those who lived across the Channel, but also the language of world trading, it was then his appetite for business and travel was whetted.

But I digress.

Early on the morning of 4th August 1789, a fateful day as far as Willelm was concerned, a rider arrived at Henri Masson's home, bringing a missive from Captain Sawyer. A letter that not only contained news that shocked, but also devastated the lad. Immediately, all the plans he had made for his future evaporated, dissipating into thin air, just as the mist in the nearby valley disappeared when the sun rose high in the sky. Willem had heard the sound of a horse and rider stopping outside the house. As he was busy preparing for the day ahead, ready to work on some Latin Henri had decided, the evening before, that he needed to know, he paid no heed whatsoever to whoever had just arrived until he heard Henri call for him to come downstairs immediately. As Willelm stood in front of him, so Henri thrust a letter into his hand. The young man broke the seal and started to read.

After a few moments, he found it impossible to continue. His hands were shaking so much, he found it hard to hold onto the document; his eyes were so full of tears that he could barely make out the words.

Henri, his dear friend and companion as well as his tutor, seeing the expression on his face, knew the letter must contain dire news. Taking it upon himself to remove it from the young man's hand, he read the contents before reading it out aloud to Willelm and his own mother who, alerted to a stranger arriving, had just made her way into the room.

The letter, from Captain Sawyer, told in great detail of how he had recently been informed, by a business associate, that Willelm's parents had been arrested at their house in Paris, and had then been taken brutally, by those who considered them to be enemies of the new regime, to La Force.

To Willelm's horror, Henri continued to read the words Captain Sawyer had written, simple words that told how on that awful day, his beloved mother and father, along with several of their friends and acquaintances, had all been taken to the notorious prison in Paris, where they'd been incarcerated and badly treated. And then how an unjust trial had followed, where, without exception, they had all been declared guilty of crimes against the state, with no one to speak on their behalf to refute the accusations made against them. The letter then told of how the Bastille had been stormed that same day by the revolutionists; as far as he knew, no one had been killed in that incident, as the majority of those arrested for being aristocrats were already ensconced in other prisons in the city.

Henri continued reading, adding to Willelm's despair as he read out the details Captain Sawyer had taken great pains to describe of what had happened after the trial. How Willelm's parents had been taken to a public square in the city, where they had been dragged, unceremoniously, with no care for their age or standing, onto a makeshift stage and where, in front of a jeering crowd, they had been beheaded by the infamous blade of the guillotine, a despicable contraption of horror. The young man found it hard to comprehend how his parents must have suffered at the hands of their fellow countrymen and women, or the injustice of their sentences.

The letter continued. There had been no dignified burial for Willelm's parents, or their friends, whose only crimes against the new republic were those of being born to wealthy and privileged members of the hated aristocracy, all killed merely because of an accident of birth. Because of this, all aristocrats were deemed to be traitors to the revolutionists cause and, as such were dispensable!

Stunned and reeling from the dreadful news, Willem took the letter from Henri's hand and silently read it for himself, unable to believe what was written, his tears falling unchecked.

Henri, being his good friend, didn't need to make any comment, for he had immediately understood the young man's grief. Taking him in his arms, he tried to comfort him and, once the enormity of what had taken place had sunk in, he allowed Willelm to sob uncontrollably, until his tears finally slowed, leaving him with his head reeling with the awful thoughts of what had happened to his beloved parents and what action he should take next. Feelings of deep grief filled his breast at what had happened, feelings that were never to leave him.

Looking back, years later, on the events of that morning, Willelm could remember saying to Henri that he must return to Paris to deal with his father's affairs. However, at the thought of returning to his Paris home, Willelm's composure had broken and, unsuccessfully, he had tried to hold back his tears. It had taken several minutes before he had managed to do this and to find his voice, and then finally, when he did, there was an edge of bravado to it that he'd found from somewhere deep within him; maybe it came from the years of training by his parents, who believed aristocrats have a responsibility to those below them in rank, that those of high birth should never waver, or show weakness, when faced with disaster.

Willelm was to remember how cold he'd felt that day, as if the blood running through his veins had suddenly turned to iced water from the burden of his loss and the bleak future that now faced him.

As he stood in front of Henri and his mother, Willelm read the captain's letter again. In his mind's eye, he saw the image of his parents as he had last seen them, an image that would remain etched on his memory forever.

He could see them many years later, in his mind's eye; his mother and father, standing close together at the door of their Paris house, waving goodbye as he set off for the country, his mother waving her silk handkerchief with a glint of tears in her eyes as he rode away, his father waving his hat.

As he read the Captain's words, Willelm tried not to think of how they must have looked as they were taken to the guillotine. Instinctively, he knew they would have held their heads up high, for they were proud people: proud of who and what they were. As he thought of that moment, Willelm fell, sobbing this time into the arms of Henri's mother, his heart broken, knowing his carefree childhood and youthful days were over and that his manhood had arrived with a vengeance on that day, the anniversary of his birth. Just eighteen years of age on that very day, Willelm was no longer the carefree youngster he had once been. He was now a man.

Henri tried hard to persuade him not to leave. 'It's too dangerous,' he said. 'You should stay where you are safe.'

But Willem was adamant. He had to go and see for himself the state of his home as he had a firm duty to his parents, and to his heritage, to see that their home was safe and that the servants were well taken care of. Henri did, however, persuade him that the Paris house would no longer be a place to show himself, telling him that, in all probability, it would already have been confiscated by the revolutionists. After some thought, Willelm agreed. But what of the house in the country? The beautiful old chateau in Brittany where he had grown up and which had been in his family for four hundred years, would that have been taken as well?

He had to go there! News of his parents' capture and deaths surely would not have reached as far as Brittany just yet! Or had it? Also, Captain Sawyer's ship would be waiting for him in Roscoff, many miles away from Henri's home and, the sooner he left, the better!

It took very little time for Willelm to pack the few possessions he owned into a canvas bag; a few spare items of clothing and a notebook he used as a journal, along with a small religious keepsake from his mother (a relic he'd kept close to his heart since he'd been a young boy).

He strapped the bag onto Henri's horse, having exchanged the thoroughbred he had ridden from his father's Paris stables for a workaday animal, knowing full well if he were to be found riding such good horseflesh as his it would certainly point him out as an aristocrat and, with this sad thought, he made Henri's horse ready for the journey.

There was very little food available those days, even in the countryside, but Madam Masson kindly gave him what little she could spare from their meagre supplies: tearful, because she could spare no more, but Willelm assured her the amount would be more than sufficient to last for the journey that he knew would take several days; for this was going to be a journey like no other he'd so far taken.

He would have to crisscross the country, avoiding the towns and villages in Normandy he would normally have brazenly ridden through, for now there were barriers everywhere, impeding the people from moving freely about the country. It was common knowledge throughout France that there were customs posts everywhere, the authorities looking to stop salt and tobacco from being smuggled, as well as other goods in short supply.

Willelm knew that he would have to avoid these barriers at all costs if he was to evade capture and, with the amount of food inside the canvas bag, he knew that he would be able to reach his destination without having to betray his presence by searching for food. For that, he was thankful.

Next, he donned a set of clothes belonging to Henri. Fortunately for him, his tutor was of a similar height and stature. By exchanging his well-bred, rich young man's clothes for a set of workaday ones, he looked less like an aristocrat and more akin to that of a country farmer, hoping his disguise would help him to evade capture by an eagle-eyed customs officer.

His favoured dark blue velvet jacket, with its silk frogging and silver buttons that he dearly loved wearing, he traded for a well-worn, dark brown Linsey-woolsey coat, with a matching waistcoat and a plain linen shirt, along with a pair of well-worn dun-coloured breeches. He wore his own stockings, of course, for they were old.

Henri then passed him an equally well worn, but faded, black felt hat instead of his fine tricorne which would have immediately pointed him out as an aristocrat. At least the hat covered Willelm's fair hair which, after some discussion with Henri's mother, the young man tied back from his face with a black silk ribbon. However, nothing he wore could hide the fact that he was well born and of high birth, for his heritage was bred into his features as well as in his posture and bearing.

It was to be hoped, by the time he reached his destination, that Willelm might well have changed somewhat; if not, his refined looks could possibly be the first cause of any betrayal.

Henri's words 'bonne chance' resounded in his head, for the tutor had spoken of his suspicions that Willelm's home would probably be under surveillance. If so, the young man's life would be in great danger and Henri left unsaid his thought that Willelm could expect nothing less from his captors other than to receive the same fate as his parents if he was recognised and caught. But Willelm already knew what his fate would be. Tutor and pupil were of one accord as to what would happen, should Willelm be so unfortunate as to get himself captured.

Again Willelm thanked Henri, and his mother, for their advice and past kindnesses, promising to contact them when he was safe with Captain Sawyer, but this was one promise he failed to keep, realising later it would give his whereabouts away to the authorities and, quite possibly, would bring harm to anyone who had known him or his family. It was to be many years before Willelm found out what had happened to them after he'd left.

In less than an hour, the young man was mounted on his borrowed horse, knowing he had to leave straightaway and make his way to the family's chateau home in Brittany, where he then had to do as his conscience deemed fit. Once that was salved, he would then make his way to Roscoff, where he would seek out Captain Sawyer, as the sailor had asked in his letter, placing himself, and his future under his care.

With Henri and his mother's farewells ringing in his ears, Willelm dug his heels into the horse's flanks and, in fear and trepidation, he started out on his journey towards an unknown future, not knowing if he would ever see them again.

Chapter 2

En route

Willelm rode away, taking the shortest route and skirting the nearby village, keeping well out of sight of any villager who might recognise him as they went about their business. Fearing capture at every turn, he reined the horse into a trot, afraid the noise of a galloping animal would draw attention to himself and increase the chances of discovery. Even with his precautions, he could still hear the sounds of men in the distance, shouting and calling out to each other as they searched the village, seeking out those they deemed to be against the new regime then dragging them out of their homes and, for all that Willelm knew, immediately clubbing them to death, thereby avoiding the bother of a trial and the subsequent beheading (which was, by now, the normal practice for anyone betrayed as a dissenter to the new regime and, indeed, for most of those arrested). It was a terrible time for everyone and, quite rightly, it was called The Terror by those living through one of the worst times in French history.

Even with his senses on high alert, his first day riding away from Henri's home passed easily enough, especially after he had left the locality where he could well have been known. Before nightfall he managed to find shelter, of a sort, in a wooded area just outside a small village, where the trees were dense enough to hide the horse and himself.

He could hear a stream trickling nearby and, after leading the horse to drink, he let it graze for a while at the edge of the wood, ever watchful of those who would seek to do him harm. The next morning, after only a small amount of fitful sleep, he quickly made himself ready, intending to be on his way before daybreak. This time though, he went on foot. Leading the horse, he silently skirted the sleeping village and, only when he was out of sight of any habitation did he remount and ride on his way, but this time at a gallop, or it would take many more days than he wanted to reach his destination. The second and third days passed in much the same way as the first and he began to relax a little, but the vigilance never left him.

On the third night, the horse and Willelm sheltered in another wooded area and again his sleep was disturbed: several times by the sounds of wild boar grunting, as well as the noises of other wild animals, as they roamed and foraged through the woods.

He woke early the next morning with a start, his senses on full alert, afraid the animals, or their hunters would return. An early autumn mist was seeping eerily through the woods and then, suddenly, he heard the sounds of men approaching where he lay.

Afraid of being discovered, he crept forward on his hands and knees to where his horse stood pawing at the ground, throwing his jacket over its head to soothe it, afraid it would snicker and draw attention to their presence. Thankfully, the men veered away from his hiding place as one of them shouted for the others to follow him. With his legs trembling and his heart beating furiously in his chest, Willelm waited awhile before he walked the horse on through the trees, stopping every now and again to listen for the men's return until, hearing no more, he once again began to relax; his heartbeat returning to normal, he mounted and rode on.

About half a day's ride from his home, he passed a village where he had friends, and one in particular, a young girl called Marietta. They'd grown up together, although she was two years older and, after Henri Masson, she was the only other person that he trusted. He wondered for a short while if he should take a chance and see her. Or would it be too dangerous? But his heart ruled his head that day and he walked his horse onwards. Choosing a narrow lane as he got nearer, he reined his horse onto a grassy verge, thus avoiding the main entrance to the *manoir* that was Marietta's home.

Once he reached the environs of the house and, after tethering his horse out of sight in a thicket, Willelm crept silently through the gardens, hoping her father would not be at home, for the young man knew that he was the commanding officer of the newly formed militia in the area, in control of much of this part of France. As he had known Willelm's mother and father, he might well have been one of those who had denounced them as enemies of the state.

Willelm knew that he was taking a huge risk in exposing himself in this way, but his desire to see Marietta won over his doubts and he continued on his way.

It was as Willelm had hoped. There were no signs of people, or horses, or of Marietta's father being at home. He breathed a heartfelt sigh of relief and walked onwards, his legs trembling. With all of his senses on full alert, he was ready to run if someone should round a corner and accost him, wanting to know his business at the house.

After entering the house through an open door at the back, he found his way easily enough into the kitchen, which thankfully was free of servants.

From there, he crept silently into the main part of the house, where he could hear muted voices coming from a room he knew to be the main salon, immediately recognising the voices as those of Marietta and her mother, talking and laughing together.

Again, and silently, he made his way across the stone-flagged hallway, towards the salon. He hid, just in time, behind a large tapestry wall-hanging as a manservant came out of the room and made his way towards the kitchen, bearing a tray upon which Willelm could see the remains of a small repast. Willelm's heart was by now beating so loud, he was quite sure it would be heard, as well as the rumblings of his stomach, for it had been some considerable time since he'd last eaten.

Willelm knew that he would be discovered if he stayed where he was for much longer and, for some time, he debated as to whether he should return to his horse and be on his way. Suddenly, he heard the salon door opening.

He peered through a small hole in the fabric and saw Marietta's mother leave the room and walk into the hallway.

He caught his breath, holding it in as she passed close to where he was hiding, afraid she too would hear his heart beating. Thankfully, she was quite oblivious to Willelm's presence as she made her way across the hall and up the stairs to the second floor.

Staying hidden, he waited until he heard a door open on the landing and then closing as she'd entered into what he assumed was her boudoir. Without any further ado, he took the opportunity to get out from behind the dusty tapestry. Walking quickly and silently, he headed across the hallway, carefully opening the door to the salon where he entered, quietly closing it behind him.

Marietta was alone in the room, standing before a full-length window and looking out at the garden. She turned as she heard the door opening, gasping in surprise as she immediately recognised

Willelm, even in Henri's old clothing. Smiling broadly, she ran lightly across the elegant room towards him, her delight in seeing him obvious.

He held his fingers to his lips to silence her and then, holding out his arms, she ran into them, where he held her in an affectionate embrace for some considerable time, loving the way her growing body felt against his.

'Willelm,' she whispered, 'what are you doing here?' Her face coloured at the intimacy of their embrace.

'I'm on my way home,' he said. 'My parents have been arrested and killed.'

She cried out, shocked at his words, placing her hands over her mouth to stifle her gasp. Her face paled and, even as Willelm watched, her blue eyes filled with tears.

'Oh, Willelm!' she cried. 'What are you going to do?' She wiped away her tears with a fine, lace-edged handkerchief after he had told her what had happened.

'I'm going to see the state of my home,' he said. 'I need to make sure the servants are safe, and then I will go away. There can be no future for me here in France, now my mother and father, and no doubt all my aged relations, are dead!'

They held each other close. Willelm could feel the softness of her body as she clung to him, as well as smelling the sweet scent of her hair, its colour as dark and as seductive as the night, to a young man unused as he was to females.

'You must go,' Marietta said, after they'd clung together for some minutes, her voice suddenly filling him with the need for urgency, knowing that he was in great danger. 'My father is in the village with his men, but will return shortly and he mustn't find you here.'

Willelm understood immediately. Her parents and his might have been neighbours but they had not necessarily been close friends and now was not the time to put his trust in them, sure they would denounce him if given the chance.

Marietta's father had once been a minor dignitary in the town, in line now for something better once the new order changed. Until then, he was in command of men from the village, among them one young man called Jean-Luc Dupont, a young man a little older than Willelm. The pair of them had known each other for many years, for, Jean-Luc too had grown up in the village. Willelm disliked him intensely, a feeling almost certainly returned; the young aristocrat had always considered the fellow to be uncivil in his attitude and having no social graces at all.

Willelm also thought him to be coarse and rude. However, perhaps that was because Jean-Luc saw him as a threat, being a close friend of Marietta, who was young, attractive and a woman he wanted to possess above all others.

Willelm wondered what Marietta's mother thought of her daughter's friendship with Jean-Luc, and whether she really approved of him as a prospective suitor, especially as he was the antithesis of what most mothers would like for their daughters. However, that was just Willelm's opinion and, of course, by this time he was no longer living in the neighbourhood and had no knowledge as to whether Jean-Luc had changed or not.

Breaking away from Willelm's embrace, Marietta caressed his face, her fingers tracing the outline of his cheeks, as though entrusting their shape to her memory. Her eyes were filled with tears.

'Willelm,' she said, with great feeling, 'it's not safe for you here.' Her concern for his welfare was all too obvious. 'You must leave before someone sees you, but we will meet again, of that I'm sure.'

With that, she kissed him, fully on the mouth, as a woman would kiss a man she loved. From that moment on, Willelm knew Marietta would always have a large part of his heart, even though another man wanted her as his wife.

Suddenly, he heard voices outside the room. It was Marietta's mother speaking to a servant and, not daring to risk capture, Willelm silently opened the window and carefully climbed out onto the terrace, leaving Marietta to close it quietly behind him.

She watched from the window as he moved away from the house and slid silently into the shadows; his last sight of her, as he made his way to where his horse was patiently waiting, was her hand, raised in a farewell salute.

When Willlelm next looked back at the house, once he had mounted his horse, she was gone; leaving him to wonder if and when they would ever meet again, not knowing the bond they shared would be tested by events over which they had no control; this was 1789 and France was already a country in turmoil, where families and friendships were fast being destroyed by the indiscriminate use of the guillotine, as Willelm already knew to his cost.

That night he spent the hours of darkness huddled in a corner of a derelict barn, with Henri Masson's horse lying beside him, the last of his meagre food supply eaten and with my stomach noisily rumbling.

Early the next morning, well before dawn broke, he had saddled the horse and was silently making his way, knowing it would only be a short while before he came to the edge of his father's estate, where he knew he would be safe; at least for a while, as he knew every part of its land, for hadn't he played there often as a child?

As he rode nearer to the chateau, he kept to the woods, mindful of the unrest plaguing the country, well aware there were many in this region that would delight in seeing the heir to the D'Anville title and its estates captured and guillotined, as had happened to his parents. It was then he realised, with his father dead, he was now the rightful Marquis D'Anville!

Suddenly, as he rode through the trees, he could hear the sounds of men nearby, shouting out orders to their companions and his heart started pounding in his chest, his mouth became dry with fear, an emotion he was experiencing daily and one he wished would be no more.

As he urged his mount onwards, he wondered what would happen if Jean-Luc should be amongst the men searching the woods, and what would he do if they came face to face? Would Jean-Luc kill him at first sight and ask questions later? Willelm thought so, and, with his own self- interest foremost, he decided to be extra vigilant from then on. It was then that he heard noises coming from the opposite direction. He knew at once it was the sounds of armed revolutionists, a band of marauding peasants going about their mischief. He knew it was not in his best interest to alert them to his presence and, with this in mind, he went fearfully on his way, knowing he was too well known in the area and would make a fine prize for anyone who captured and denounced him.

Bypassing the small village, and the cottages of those who lived and worked on his father's estate, Willelm dismounted from Henri's horse and walked the animal through the woods, opposite a high wall that skirted the estate. He edged his way through the trees, the horse walking calmly beside him, occasionally nudging him with its velvet muzzle, perhaps seeking its own comfort in feeling a familiar hand.

Willelm came to a halt as soon as he could see that the ornate iron gates leading to the house were open. Waiting a while, his fear of the unknown made him nervous. The long carriageway was enticing, but he cautiously ignored this entrance, even though he knew it would take him directly to the front of the house. Instead, he continued walking through the wood, his eyes and ears alert for any sign of activity that would put him in danger, knowing that further along he would be able to cross the lane safely and enter the estate from a little used side entrance, and this he did.

It took only a few minutes before he arrived at the rear of the chateau where the imposing building sat in a pool of sunlight, its old stonework glittering, belying its great age, his heart aching at the familiar sight, especially knowing it might well be the last time he would see what had once been the jewel in his inheritance.

Keeping a tight hold on the horse's reins, he walked down the narrow bridleway which he knew would take him directly to the stables.

There were no signs of horses or cattle in the fields nearby, or in the yard; nor of any human activity at all as he approached, and neither were there any signs of grooms or stable hands going about their business. He felt uneasy at the quietness of it all. It frightened him, seeming to be strange and unnatural, used as he was to his parents' country home being a working estate, where many of the local villagers worked and, not for the first time, he wondered where everyone had gone. It was as if they had all been spirited away.

Once in the stables, he removed Henri's jacket and hung it on a nail. He then unhitched the canvas bag, hiding it out of sight at the back of the stable, amongst other tackle, before he released the reins from the horse, allowing his borrowed steed to move unencumbered and to rest for the first time in days. Little did it know that its journey was not yet over.

Willelm too began to relax as it became obvious he was completely alone on the estate, there was no one about, not as far as he could see, but he wasn't about to shout and scream, just in case...

Knowing he had to take care of the animal first of all, for without it he would not have reached this far and he had more miles still to travel. With no groom available to do his bidding, he took up the tools and cleaned and brushed the horse himself, feeding it a little of what remained in the stable and then, once satisfied he had done all he could, he quickly rinsed his face and hands in the water trough before donning Henri's old jacket once more and making his way across the cobbled courtyard to the house where, as at the stables, there were no signs of life. There were no outside servants to be seen, nor signs of anyone working in what had once been the vegetable garden, denuded now of any produce.

He walked quickly across the courtyard and opened the door at the back of the house, which he knew would take him into the kitchen, but that too was strangely silent, where normally it would have been busy at this time of day, with servants bustling about, but there were no signs of people, nor signs of food being prepared, or cooked, and then he understood why. The doors of the huge wood-fired ovens were standing open and unlit, with not a single pan or dish to be seen in the kitchen, or in the larder, that adjoined it. Both places were completely empty.

Willelm could see the cupboards and shelves had been ransacked, and all that remained of the Sevres porcelain his mother had treasured were a few broken dishes that lay on the stone floor. It was though they'd been dropped, and then left where they lay, in someone's haste to leave the house. As he went from the kitchen into the main part of the house, Willelm found that to be empty as well, with not a stick of furniture to be seen anywhere.

The ancient interior walls of the house, once covered in old and precious tapestries and paintings that had been his parents' prized possessions, had been stripped bare, with only dusty outlines to show where they had once hung. Thick drapes that had once kept out the winter draughts were no longer hanging at the windows and, as he walked slowly through the house, he saw every room told the same chilling story. His home had all but vanished. All that was left were the stones of the chateau itself. Perhaps they were to be the only memorial to his dearest parents, until someone razed them down to ground level to re-use in another place.

Empty as it was, every room in the old chateau echoed with memories of his past life, especially in the nursery, where much of his childhood had been spent; it was there his memories came flooding back, making his heart ache with its longing for what was past and gone.

He explored the rest of the rooms, all empty and silent now, except for the ghostly sounds of his past. Everywhere was devoid of the possessions that a family who had been in residence for over two hundred years would have gathered, but he could still hear his past life echoing in his head. The chateau might have been empty of possessions, but nothing could take away the images he had in his mind.

So vivid and poignant were they it brought tears to his eyes, especially the images he had of his mother, singing and laughing as she went about her business, and then the sounds of her servants, chattering, as they carried out her bidding.

Willelm went into the room his father had once used as his office, its fine wood panelling defaced by whoever had stripped the room bare of the D'Anville family memorabilia; there was evidence that someone had hacked away his father's mementoes of his and his family's military past, but nothing could take away Willelm's memories, for the empty room was still redolent of his father's masculine presence and, in his mind's eye, the young man could still see him seated at his desk, his attention taken by the ledgers that had been so much a part of his life.

In his imagination, Willelm could even smell the aroma of the tobacco his father had favoured, just as he could smell the perfume his mother had used when next he ventured into her room. It was there his heart ached the most, and where his eyes filled with tears, as he looked at where once the lovely trinkets his father had bought her over the years would have lain on the top of the beautiful cabinets, or on the small and fancy tables that used to litter the room, but were no longer there. It was in her boudoir, his mother's own favoured place, away from the bustle of the main rooms that he wondered, and asked himself, not for the first time, where had it all gone? Who, he wondered, was now wearing the beautiful jewels and the sumptuous silk brocade and lace dresses she had favoured? He could only guess at the answer.

As he looked out of the windows, especially those set at each corner in the turrets of the roof, he knew there was nothing left for him here. It was time to leave, to be on his way, but to where? He knew that he was supposed to meet Captain Sawyer in Roscoff, but what then, where would his life end? And what was in store for him in the future?

The chateau, empty as it was, was full of memories, as well as the ghosts of his parents who, as far as he was concerned, would haunt the chateau forever, even devoid as it was of all the possessions that they had once owned. Their presence was in every stone of the ancient building, as it was in the surrounding fields, now devoid of animals, and that saddened him even more, as he wondered where his father's treasured herd of cattle had gone. Common sense told his that they were probably already eaten and, where once the views from the chateau windows would have been of a bucolic pastoral scene, with animals grazing, and where crops would have been growing in the fields, waiting for the harvest, now there was nothing but the fine green haze of crops that might, or might not come to fruition; it broke his heart.

There was only the eerie sound of silence as he looked at the estate; it was as if even the birds had flown away to go somewhere else, to where there's life and hope.

A sense of foreboding struck his heart with a chill, for he knew it was time for him to leave. There was no point in being there any longer. As for the servants, they too had all gone; Willelm knew not where and, sadly, neither did he care. His grief at the loss of his parents was too raw to worry about those who would wish him harm, should they have known of his return.

He knew that he would have to leave them to their fate, for there was no longer anything he could do for them. They had made their choice and now he had to make his own.

As he walked through the empty rooms of what had once been his home for one last time, Willelm was full of despair. Knowing he might never return and that he must make plans for his own survival. His only other relatives, aunts and uncles, were ancient and, like his parents, most probably by now were all dead, murdered, as his parents had been, for being aristocrats.

Heartbroken and desolate at these unhappy thoughts, he sat on the cold stone of the stairs in the hallway, his tears falling in copious amounts until he realised he had to go forward with his own life, as his parents would have wished. He was not only alone, but also young and inexperienced, with very few practical skills. How, he asked himself, was he to survive in a country that was at war with its own inhabitants? Especially as he now realised that being fluent in Greek and Latin would be of no use to him. He needed other skills, if he was to be housed and fed, but that was for the future.

With the resilience of youth, Willelm knew he had to dry his eyes and stop pitying himself. He had to take stock of his life and leave the place where he was born, for there was nothing left for him now. He had to make his way to the port of Roscoff, where he would seek out Captain Sawyer. His father had trusted him and he had to do the same.

It felt strange to be riding through countryside devoid of crops and animals, all because of several years of bad weather. So much damage had been caused to farming that Willelm could see why famine had ensued, causing not only great hunger and starvation for the citizens, but unrest as well, wreaking havoc on the lives of all, rich and poor alike, with the King and his ministers either unable, or unwilling, to solve the problems besetting the country, leaving the citizens to take the law into their own hands, which then left them deciding a monarchy was not for France.

Taking advantage of the situation, the poor took control until, suddenly, France was ready and ripe for a new regime. But this new regime, where imprisoning and beheading the rich, and anyone else the good citizens believed, rightly or wrongly, to be against their new way of thinking, became endemic; merely a symptom of the many troubles in the land, where, eventually, it will turn the country into a republic.

There will be many more deaths and much destruction before peace reigns again, but Willelm knew nothing of this as he went on his way, knowing he was going to leave the country of his birth. Closing his mind to what was about to happen to the country was the only way he would survive and, with a new determination taking hold of him to do whatever it took to make his parents proud, he gathered some strength from his past upbringing and heritage and, with his memories tucked safely to the back of his mind, he went away from his home to face an uncertain future.

He was only a couple of miles from the port of Roscoff. At that time, it was a small port that had managed to continue its trade with foreign ships, in spite of the troubles and a war that was soon to be started between England and France.

With Henri's horse calmly carrying him onwards, Willelm went on his way to find Captain Sawyer, the horse contentedly trotting around the edges of fields where the first signs of crops would soon be growing again, but it was too late to stop what had already happened.

Still being cautious, he skirted the villages, aware that at any minute he might be spotted by a local who might see him as an easy way of raising an income, until, suddenly, the horse stopped in its tracks and Willelm was very nearly catapulted over its head.

The young man gradually righted himself, unaware of why the animal had decided not to continue. Digging his heels into its flanks, he urged it forward, but the animal stubbornly refused to move and then he understood why. With his heart in his mouth, Willelm leant forward, his head leaning against the horse's neck, holding onto its mane as he listened, too afraid for a few moments to move.

Too close to where he sat astride his horse, Willelm could hear the sounds of men, shouting and calling to each other, and then, worse than that, the noise of guns being fired, again too close for his comfort. Alarm bells started to ring in his head and he quickly dismounted, sliding off the horse, holding onto its reins and keeping a firm hand on its head, soothing it, before gently pulling on its reins as he led it forward, walking slowly towards a small copse of trees he could see ahead, knowing the last thing he wanted was to be caught, especially so near to his destination.

Being arrested and imprisoned was not on his agenda, and neither was having his head swiftly removed from his body!

Once hidden amongst the trees, the horse seemed eager to be on its way, but again his whispered words soothed and calmed it, or perhaps it too had suddenly understood its life was in as much danger as its rider, for any animal found wandering in the countryside would make a welcome meal for those who hadn't tasted fresh meat in many a month.

Together, the horse and Willelm patiently waited, until the sounds of men shouting and guns being fired subsided.

Once he was sure they had gone in the opposite direction, the young man remounted and rode onwards, heading towards the sea, where he hoped a new life would be waiting for him.

A couple of hours later, he knew his journey must be nearing its end, after many days of riding through woods and across open countryside, all the time avoiding the countless tolls and internal customs barriers set up throughout the country, at the same time, hoping against hope, he would not be seen and captured.

After a while, he could see several crumbling old barns that from a distance appeared empty, all standing at the edge of a decrepit and ancient farmstead.

He urged the horse forward, heading towards them and then, breathing a sigh of relief when thankfully he finally reached them, he found they were indeed empty and, joy upon joy, there were no signs of men working in the nearby fields, or of animals grazing nearby.

From then on, Willelm knew that he must travel the rest of his journey on foot; it was no longer safe to be riding a horse, for, if found, it would indeed point him out as someone who should be stopped and questioned. If that happened, it would certainly be the end of his journey and possibly his life as well.

After removing the canvas bag hanging from the saddle, he changed into his last clean shirt. Then, tucking his journal into the inside pocket of Henri's old jacket, he hid the bag and the saddle, along with the reins, deep within a nearby hedge, where he hoped they wouldn't be found for a long time (their very presence would alert those seeking the likes of himself to look further afield, quite possibly giving trouble to the farmer if found).

With the horse at last unfettered, Willelm turned to the animal, stroking its velvet muzzle, sadly whispering into its ears, 'bonne chance,' before he turned it loose, smacking its rump in an effort to send it away to fend for itself, at the same time hoping it would survive, for it had been a worthy companion.

It turned and looked at him, a sorrowful expression in its deep brown eyes, snorting as though in reply, before trotting away to where it found a small area of greenery, the welcome sight of grass of more interest. Paying Willelm no more heed, it put its head down and started to graze, its work for him done.

Satisfied with his efforts, the young man walked away empty-handed from the barn, down a path he knew would lead him to the harbour, for he could smell the scent of the sea.

He knew this port well from his younger days of going out fishing with his father and the local fishermen.

He walked down the steep path to where it soon opened onto a well-used lane, one that he knew led directly to the harbour, already bustling with the noise and activity as the local seamen went about their daily business.

He could easily make out the fishermen from the small port, identifying them by the distinctive smocks they all wore. Mostly, they were busy with either mending and tending to their nets or else with cutting up bait for their lobster and crab pots; generally, they were getting their fishing tackle and boats ready for the next day's work.

Willelm envied them their simple lives, at the same time knowing how hard it was to make a living from the sea that, for many, proved to be an unpredictable taskmaster.

His appearance, as dishevelled as it was, caused no one to look at him twice, for which he was grateful. Had anyone recognised him, he knew it could well have led him into trouble with the authorities, but his newly grown whiskers made him look older than his years and actually gave him confidence. So much so, he considered himself no different from the men who casually glanced his way as he walked on by, with Henri's old felt hat pulled well down over his eyes.

For the first time in days, he felt able to walk in a fearless manner as he sought out Captain Sawyer's lugger from amongst the many craft moored in the harbour.

Willelm could see there was a large four-masted merchantman anchored just outside the harbour that, from its name, he took to be Dutch, no doubt soon to be on its way to the East Indies. His only hope now was that he would find the man he was seeking before the military found him and took him before the magistrates, those men of some standing, who had once thought themselves to be above such atrocities, but were now, like the ordinary peasants, eager and baying for the blood of innocent people to swell the river of blood that had already flowed. The very thought made Willelm shudder and lower his eyes. He trusted though that on that day, God was on his side, looking after his body, as well as his soul!

As he walked along the harbour, looking for the *Mary Anne*, he could smell the different aromas of the port, mainly fish of course, mingling with those of ropes and tar, and even the food being cooked in the many galleys on board the ships, berthed and waiting for the tide. He looked keenly at all the craft moored in the harbour, all appearing ready to sail, without seeing the *Mary Anne*, until suddenly, across the harbour, on his left, he noticed an old stone building. This he knew to be a tavern, from its familiar swinging sign hanging over the door, proclaiming it to be a house that sold food and drink to travellers.

It was bustling with activity and he could see sailors, some wearing the distinctive headgear and footwear of Dutchmen, coming and going through its door, laughing and joking with each other, their hands full of flagons he took to contain wine, or even ale, for there was the distinctive smell in the air of brewing coming from the region of the tavern itself, and then he remembered from his younger days that this place had a brewhouse at the back!

Trying to appear calm and unconcerned, Willelm walked across the rough stones of the hard to join those already enjoying a drink outside the tavern door. Several sailors moved aside to let him pass and, as he stepped inside the old stone building, he found it hard to adjust his eyes, for at first sight it was like entering a dark and menacing cave. Its rough stone walls were dingy and discoloured by years of grime and smoke from an open fire that smouldered across the other side of the room. Even now, it was filling the air with fumes that most of those inside managed to breathe in without coughing, but the smoke made Willelm splutter.

It took a few moments for his stinging eyes to focus on what was in the room. Suddenly, he could see the room was full mostly of sailors and some who, from their speech and garb, he took to be Cornish.

Singling out one particular group of men, Willelm made his way across the crowded room, intending to speak to them. He spoke in French at first, thinking it a better policy, asking if anyone of them knew the whereabouts of Captain Sawyer, the master of the *Mary Anne*.

They all looked at him with suspicious eyes, turning their heads away and ignoring him. Realising he had made an error of judgement, Willelm persevered and asked another group of sailors the same question; this time directing his question in English to one young man in particular, who looked at him quizzically. He said nothing, but turned and looked at the others. It was then they all muttered something to each other that Willelm didn't quite hear and, before he could repeat his question, another sailor in the group, one who appeared to be the oldest, moved away from them and, taking his arm in a firm grip, he bustled the young man out of the tavern and onto the cobbles of the harbour, whispering in his ear as he did so that he should say no more.

Before Willelm knew what his intentions were, they were heading at a fast pace along the harbour until they reached a ship that, as they got nearer, the young Frenchman could see had the name *Mary Anne* picked out in gold on its bow. Rather flamboyant, he later remembered thinking, for a wood and iron ship.

Even though it was getting late, and not long before darkness descended, Willelm could see the ship was armed to the hilt, swivel guns ready for any action that obviously wasn't going to be peaceful.

Without further ado, the seaman pushed him up the gangplank and onto the deck, and then, with a low whistle, he bent down and removed a hatch cover and pushed him forward, indicating that he should climb down the ladder to the deck below where a fairly large man, dressed in a fine blue frock coat with silver buttons, the uniform of a captain, stood waiting for him.

Willelm recognised him immediately as Captain Sawyer, his father's friend and business associate, a man whom he had known for many years. The young man nearly burst into tears in his relief that he had at last found the man who had sent him the letter. Seeing his distress, the Captain placed his arms around the lad's shoulders and held him close, as a father would do to a beloved son, thankful he had at last found the young man he'd been instructed to save.

Once their greeting was over and Willelm had wiped his eyes, they climbed up the ladder onto the deck, which, to the young man's relief, was now filled with the rest of the crew, most of whom he had already seen in the tavern. Once they were all assembled in an orderly line, the Captain made Willelm known to all the men.

'This young man will, from now on, be sailing with us,' he said to all those gathered before him. 'His name is Billy Sawyer and he is to be our new cabin boy and general dogsbody!'

The young Frenchman was shocked. Why had the Captain changed his name? Then he realised it was better that no one on the *Mary Anne* knew who he really was, for his own safety as well as theirs. He didn't know if he liked the name but, like skin, everyone soon gets used to things changing and surely it was better to be known as Billy Sawyer and to be alive, than Willelm D'Anville and the target for someone with an itchy finger on the trigger of a firearm, or on the pommel of a sword in its scabbard.

With Captain Sawyer's introduction made, 'Billy' was told to keep away from any ropes and gear (the necessary detritus of all sailing ships) that might be lying loose about the decks of the ship as it got ready for its departure, one that for the young man couldn't come fast enough.

Left to his own devices, and with the tide and wind rising, the Captain called for the crew to unfurl the sails and get ready to lift the anchor; within an hour of her new crewman being found and taken aboard, the *Mary Anne* was on its way out of the harbour, the sooner the better as far as the young Frenchman was concerned.

It wasn't too long before the lights of Roscoff harbour were mere specks in the distance and they were sailing in open water, Billy relieved to be away from a part of France where he was well known.

He knew not where they were headed: but with the wind filling the sails, and the ship making a decent speed, he began at last to feel that his life was changing, and for the better.

He knew then that being anywhere in the world would be infinitely better than being locked up in a French prison before being guillotined just for being the son of an aristocrat.

And so began his new life. No longer was he to be known as Willelm D'Anville, the legitimate son and heir of a French aristocrat, but 'Billy Sawyer', cabin boy and general dogsbody.

The Captain had already placed Billy Sawyer's name on the ship's muster list as his son. In the meantime, the crew had been instructed to teach him the ways of a cabin boy and dogsbody, two occupations that would quickly transform him from being an aristocrat to that of a young seaman. These became his working roles on the *Mary Anne* as it was bound for someplace where he thought that he would be safe. Well, at least that was what he thought!

Chapter 3
Cornwall

It was a moonless night when the *Mary Anne* sailed into the waters of Talland Bay, in the east of Cornwall, where it was to anchor. Captain Sawyer, a master of his craft, skilfully avoided the rocks that spelt danger to an unwary mariner, but this captain knew these waters, as well as the lugger and its crew of strong Cornish and Devon men. Even so, knowing these waters better than anywhere else, the crew still heaved a sigh of relief, glad to have finally reached their destination, for a storm had raged as they'd sailed from Guernsey, its last port of call. It had been a miserable journey, even for the old-timers amongst the crew, men, one would have thought to be immune to seasickness, after a lifetime of sailing in rough seas, but this was not so.

With the *Mary Anne* safely anchored in the bay, Captain Sawyer ordered Jed Pengelly, the first mate and his second in charge, to light a lantern. Once this was lit and burning brightly, the Captain took hold of it: waving it in the direction of the steep cliffs, hewn out of the granite over the centuries by the forces of nature, cliffs the Captain knew to be ahead, but at that time he couldn't see.

It was some minutes before an answering flash of light was sighted. With a grunt of satisfaction that all was well on shore, the Captain ordered some of the crew to lower the ship's rowboat into the still raging water, and then to climb down and hold it steady, ready for the goods from France to be lowered and stowed aboard; hurrying those men he thought to be a little tardy with their efforts, for there was very little time left before dawn would break, by which time the *Mary Anne* would have to be on her way.

The storm hampered the men in their work and it took some time before the hold was empty, except for the last few items of several oilskin packages, and a heavy wooden sea chest.

Soon, all the cargo had been lowered. Once all the goods aboard had been stowed and covered with tarpaulin, the Captain beckoned a young man, standing nearby, watching the crew with interest, to come forward.

Without hesitation, at the Captain's bidding, the young man staggered over the rocking deck to stand at the Captain's side.

'Billy, I want you to join the men tonight,' the Captain said, pointing to a rope ladder which was swaying precariously in the wind.

Billy wasn't so sure he wanted, or even needed such an experience but, being obedient to his master and extremely nervous, he approached the rope ladder which was rocking dangerously against the side of the ship.

Billy felt as though his heart would burst with fear. Not for the first time in his life, he felt sick and very afraid of what lay ahead. Holding his fear in check, he climbed down the rope ladder to join the other crewmen, who were all eagerly awaiting the Captain's order to shove off and make for the shore; the sooner that they unloaded the goods, the sooner they would return to the ship and be on their way to their next destination.

The Captain, with a wry smile on his weather-beaten face, watched nervously as Billy scrambled down the ladder and jumped into the loaded rowboat already sitting low in the water, weighted down as it was by its cargo.

The crew good-naturedly teased Billy as he took his place next to the first mate, all aware of his fear, having experienced the same many times, but now were keen to get the rowboat on its way before it overturned and the waves sent them, and the cargo, crashing down into Davy Jones's locker at the bottom of the sea.

This voyage had not been Billy's first experience of sailing, but sailing on the *Mary Anne* was quite different from the fishing boats he'd been on with his father when a small child. But this was no pleasure ship; it was a working vessel, fast and manoeuvrable, as well as armed, and fitted out for sailing the high seas, and for transporting trade goods, as well as contraband goods smuggled in from France and the Channel Islands. Having had some of its storage converted just for that purpose, there were secret compartments that the custom officers had so far never found when searching the vessel, as happened sometimes when the ship docked in certain ports in England and the Caribbean, another favourite place for the *Mary Anne* to visit.

As he sat in the rowboat that night with the rain lashing down, Billy pondered his role on board the *Mary Anne*, a role that had come about only by a quirk of fate; it was an occupation vastly different from the one he'd thought previously destined for him in France, which is where he should have been now, with his family, working under the watchful eye of his father; not working as a cabin boy cum general dogsbody aboard the *Mary Anne*. Billy, however, knew that he owed his life and his present freedom to the Captain, and so his present discomfort was nothing compared to what might have been.

Sitting in the ship's rocking rowboat, as the waves tried to get the better of the craft, waiting for the order from the Captain to move away from the anchored mother ship, Billy thought back to his previously well-ordered life and how it had changed. Changed forever, since he'd left his tutor's house many weeks ago, his student days over but not forgotten.

Seeing the rowboat loaded and ready, the Captain gave his signal for the men to release the holding ropes and push off with their oars into the darkness of the night.

A few minutes later, he heard the oars of the rowboat swishing through the waves that threatened at any minute to swamp the boat. The captain knew his men well, and soon the oars were working in unison, tuned by years of practice. Within a minute or two, they were rowing powerfully through the rough sea towards the shore.

Moving smuggled goods from ship to shore was always a dangerous event, but the storm raging that night was the crew's saving grace, for the Excise officers were none too keen to take to the sea in their lightweight cutters when storms raged. Even so, there were exceptions to this; it was not a given!

Therefore, those who were involved in smuggling never considered any time safe for the landing of contraband goods. Pitfalls to be expected on every journey, be it the weather, or the sudden appearance of the Excise cutter coming round the headland, making its way towards them, and this night's work was no exception.

The Captain's biggest fear that night had been just that. If not running into the men who patrolled the rugged Cornish coastline, in a ship equally as fast and armed as his own at sea, instead there was always the chance they would be waiting on the cliffs. He also knew, if that happened, the crew of the *Mary Anne* would stand no chance if they were found on land.

Knowing this well enough themselves, the crew tried to keep the noise of the oars as quiet as possible, as well as their laboured breathing, for they were afraid for their lives. If the customs officers heard so much as the swish of an oar breaking through the waves, or any other sound, all would be lost; the cargo, the profit, even themselves, for they would all be taken away to the assizes and tried. There, for sure, they would all be found guilty and hanged in Bodmin as the criminals that they were.

Soon, all that the Captain could hear was the sound of waves breaking against the bow of the *Mary Anne* as she waited at anchor, the storm force of the wind and the raging of the waters in the bay pulling the ship on its anchor cable. With the rain pelting down, Captain Sawyer knew he would have to put his fears aside and have patience and faith in his crew.

Shaking his head, he went below to wait for the rowboat to land on the rocky shore and then, once the goods were unloaded, for his men to return, all except for one.

Meanwhile, the crew, pulling hard on the oars, could at last hear the sound of the sea changing as the waves broke on the nearby shore. With the rain at last starting to ease, the boat was suddenly hurled headlong through the surf, scuffing its bottom on the shingle beach, before scudding to a halt, narrowly missing a huge granite rock on the shingle that had fouled many a previous landing; the rowboat came to a stop in front of a band of Cornishmen, all waiting patiently with packhorses and ponies, ready to carry the goods inland; their animals pawed at the gravel as they waited, snorting and shaking their heads, impatient to be on the move as their breath misted in the dark.

With the boat safely ashore, the crew, along with Billy, jumped out and together they hauled the rowboat in as far as they could, before unloading the goods the Cornishmen had waited so long to see.

Billy was handed a large oilskin-wrapped package, one of the first items from the load. He was then pushed towards the waiting horses, where he was told to put the package into a basket slung over the back of a waiting animal. He made several journeys, back and forth, repeating his task, until all the oilskin packages (that he later found contained bolts of Lyons silk and lace) had been stowed and covered with pieces of canvas to hide them.

While he'd been kept busy, so had the crew. Along with the men from the village, they'd carried the rest of the goods from the boat and strapped them securely to the backs of the animals. The goods in the tubs, Billy later learnt, was tobacco. Then there were kegs, full of fine wine, as well as ankers of the much-prized French brandy, all joined by sacks of sugar and coffee from the West Indies. They were destined for Truro and London, these luxury goods that were much in demand and appreciated by the gentry; for those with a purse full of gold to pay for them, as these goods were sure to command a high price when sold to the gentlemen in both cities, especially those not so keen on paying the high taxes that the Treasury demanded for such luxuries if the goods arrived legitimately.

Once all of the waiting animals were loaded, with the village men shouldering the remaining kegs, one by one, the motley crew started to move off the shingle in single file. The men urged the pack animals towards the cliff path; the hooves of the animals were covered in sackcloth to muffle any sound.

As silently as they could, the village men, some with their sons and grandsons helping and along with some of the village women as well, made their way up the steep and rocky path. The band of men and animals headed inland, along another well-worn path on top of the cliffs, and thence to the village. Some of the men and animals would be going further afield, along the coast, even across the moors, to hiding places previously arranged for the goods to be stored, until it was safe for them to be moved to the waiting customers.

As soon as the Cornishmen and women, and their loaded animals, were on their way, the *Mary Anne's* crew made ready to return to the ship.

Billy stood on the shingle, waiting patiently for his turn to jump aboard, but, to his surprise, as he went to go forward, Jed Pengelly clutched him by the shoulder and held him back. 'Captain says you're to go with the men back to the village, to make sure the goods get hidden away safely.'

Billy shook his head, he didn't understand. Why did he have to go? He was young and agile for sure, but certainly no match for any excise man who might be on the cliff path that night waiting to apprehend smugglers heading towards the village, and neither did he know anyone in Cornwall!

'The *Mary Anne* will sail without me if I have to follow the horses and wait to see if all the goods get hidden,' he complained to Jeb. 'I'll be left behind.'

This last was said in such a tone that Jed felt sorry for the boy, but orders were orders, and the lad had to do as he was told.

'Aye, boy, but that's what the captain wants. You're to go back with James,' he said, pointing with a grubby finger towards a man, barely visible, standing in the dark shadows of a recess in the cliffs with his laden horse. 'That's him over yonder, waiting for you. You're to stay with him and his wife, Sally, until we come back. You'll be safe there.'

'But that will be months away,' said Billy. 'What am I to do? I don't know anything about the English.'

'James will look after you and you're in Cornwall now,' said Jed, impatient to be on his way. 'He'll be the one to teach you all you need to know about the Cornish and their ways.'

He laughed, until suddenly he caught sight of the horrified look on Billy's face (had there been any light, he would have seen Billy's face had turned ashen).

'Don't you be afraid! He's a kinsman of the Captain. His own boy drowned some time ago and Sally will enjoy spoiling you. It will take her mind away from her own pain and loss.' Purposely not saying it might well ease Billy's own heartache too, him being privy to the boy's circumstances. 'Now, be a good lad and do as the Captain says.'

As an afterthought, the first mate reached into his jacket and fumbled for a small oil-skinned wrapped packet, which he thrust into Billy's hand, 'and Captain says this is for you. Now, off you go lad and remember, we'll be back soon.'

Billy put the packet into his coat pocket and then, with mixed feelings, he watched as the rowboat was pushed back into the surf, and the remaining crewmen jumped aboard, leaving him behind.

The crew were soon rowing speedily away now the rowboat was empty of its cargo, heading to where the *Mary Anne* lay at anchor, its sails already unfurled, ready and waiting for the crew to be back on board before the anchor could be lifted, fulfilling the Captain's plans to be on their way well before dawn broke.

Apprehension was the uppermost emotion Billy was experiencing as he stood abandoned and alone on the shingle beach, with a stranger and his loaded horse waiting patiently for him. Billy was fearful of what lay ahead for him; it wasn't just being left alone in a strange country that worried him, even though it was a place he knew very little about. He might be able to speak the language but he was still a Frenchman, alone in a country that was nearly at war with France.

Alone, and feeling desolate, Billy watched as the rowboat headed through the waves towards what had once been his safe haven, his new home, and the crew his new family. His eyes welled up with sudden tears as he saw the flash from the lighted lantern on board the ship as it guided the rowboat's passage. Using his sleeve, Billy wiped his eyes on the rough material of his sea coat, ashamed and humiliated that the man, designated to be his minder, might see his distress.

When next he looked towards where the ship had been anchored, the rowboat had disappeared into the darkness, the guiding light from the lantern extinguished, the night swallowing not only the boat, but also its crew. With a deep sigh and a shrug of his shoulders, he was starting to accept that his life was now under someone else's care.

With the optimism of youth, Billy thought about his future. He might be in the hands of a Cornish smuggler, but better that than in the hands of those in France who operated the guillotine: a piece of metal invented and designed to kill with one cut, that to some people, given the chance, would be delighted to use on him! Billy turned, and went to where James was patiently waiting.

After shaking his hand, Billy followed James off the shingle beach, where they joined the other Cornish folk, young and old, already walking as silently and sure-footedly as they could along the rough cliff path. The folded sackcloth tied about the animal's hooves did the job intended but everyone's eyes peered through the darkness, looking for a glint of a musket or sword, their ears tuned in to every sound of the night; all of them hoping not to hear the tread of footsteps (other than their own), or the shouts of the Excise officers as they suddenly appeared in front of them, demanding that they stop, and then the skirmish that would surely follow.

Billy walked by the side of the horse he had loaded, the animal's body close to his. He could feel its warmth through the coarse material of his sea coat and took some comfort from it, holding on tight to a length of rope that served as its rein, his head full of remembered days: days that now seemed a long time ago in the past, when he had ridden his own fine horse through the French countryside for pleasure. He had sat upon the finest handmade saddle money could buy, made from the best leather available, with reins made by the same craftsman (unlike those he had held in his gloved hands when he'd ridden Henri's horse across the countryside, escaping from those in revolt and who had taken his parents away).

As he walked silently at the side of this Cornish workhorse, Billy looked towards the sea, but it was still too dark to see any sight of the *Mary Anne* in full sail as she made her way to wherever Captain Sawyer had decided they would next visit.

Billy's mind strayed to his past, something that happened often when he needed comfort; remembering the last time he'd seen his parents on the morning he'd ridden away from his Paris home, riding on the back of one of his father's thoroughbred horses, as he went to stay with his tutor in the country.

That morning his mother had been wearing a new, wide-brimmed, straw bonnet with sweet scented flowers tied with coloured ribbons threaded about its brim, with one ribbon tied in a fetching bow under her pretty little chin. She'd been gaily waving her handkerchief as he rode away, unaware it would be the last time she would ever see her beloved son and then, in his mind's eye, he could see the face of his father, waving his best hat, a black three-cornered affair he usually only wore for court occasions. Billy smiled to himself as he remembered. His father had been smiling too, a broad smile Billy knew so well; a smile that crinkled the skin at the corner of his eyes, but in reality hid his sadness at his only son's departure.

Billy was unaware, as he rode away that morning, that, within a few short weeks, his parents would be arrested and held imprisoned in La Force, and that he would never see either of them smile again. The last news of his parent's fate had been in the letter he'd received from Captain Sawyer of the *Mary Anne* that was now on its way to he knew not where.

By this time dawn was starting to appear on the horizon and, most of the penurious band of men, with their heavily laden packhorses, had reached the centre of the village where the goods were to be unloaded, and then hidden in all the usual secret places.

Billy was tired to the point of exhaustion, but in no time at all, with James struggling to carry the wooden chest (the last item taken from the rowboat) they were soon climbing a short flight of stone steps leading to the door of a cottage, built into the side of the granite cliff.

James told Billy to open the door and enter. Doing as he was told, Billy stepped into the cottage, closely followed by James, huffing and puffing on his heels. After placing the chest on the stone floor, he quickly closed the door firmly behind them, ready to greet his wife, Sally, who'd been anxiously waiting for James to appear.

The nights when the village men were out waiting for a ship to anchor, and disgorge its cargo, was always a worrying time for the women waiting at home, and this night was no exception.

Sally looked up as the door opened, giving a gasp of surprise as she saw a stranger enter the room. Pulling her shawl close about her shoulders, she picked up a solitary candle in its holder from the table.

Holding the candlestick high, she peered at Billy, appraising him through the dim light of the candle that was spluttering from the draught of the door. Its flickering light, and the glow of the embers off the fire, were all that served to light the small room.

Once his eyes had grown accustomed to the gloom, Billy could see the room held a simple scrubbed table, laid ready and waiting, with thick pottery bowls and simple wooden platters, stacked ready to use; he could smell something tasty cooking in the black pot hanging over the fire, its aroma tantalising him, making him realise how hungry he was, suddenly remembering his last meal had been many hours earlier, whilst on board the *Mary Anne*.

After a brief introduction from James, with the simple explanation that the young man would be staying with them for a while and, before he knew what was happening, Billy was clasped in Sally's arms, clutched to her ample bosom as she hugged him so tight it left him breathless. Suddenly, she held him away from her, lifting the candle that she might look more carefully at him, intrigued as to why this young man was in her home and why he was to stay with them. With her questions unasked, Sally helped Billy remove his outerwear: the old seaman's coat, heavy from the rain that had lashed down earlier, she hung behind the door and then his sodden boots she upended to remove any seawater from inside them, before placing them by the fire to dry. She then pushed him towards the table, where she bade him to sit on a wooden settle propped against the rough-hewn wall of the stone cottage. Within a few minutes, a thick pottery tankard, containing a steaming hot toddy, was placed on the table in front of him. Sally indicated that he should drink. This was quickly followed by a bowl of thick fish stew from the black pot, along with a slab of coarse bread, Billy had watched being cut from a loaf that had sat on a wooden platter in the middle of the table. He noticed James received much the same treatment, including a rough hug. It was the sight of two people greeting each other so lovingly that brought tears to Billy's eyes and, for a few moments, he thought of his mother and father, and their affection for each other and for himself. Trying hard not to let his emotions show, which was easier said than done, he thanked providence the light in the room was so dim that Sally and James might not have noticed, but Sally did!

After saying a silent grace, Billy ate and drank his fill of the simple fare, a meal that was to become one of his most memorable food memories and a significant introduction to the new life he was about to start in Cornwall.

Muttering his thanks to Sally, he mopped up the last of the stew with the bread until, warm and replete, he began to feel his eyelids closing, as sleep tried to overtake him, his head beginning to droop onto his chest.

Sally had watched with interest as the young man silently ate all she'd placed before him. Before he could fall asleep at the table, she pulled him to his feet. Taking a lighted candle stub in its holder, she opened a door that hid a flight of steep wooden stairs: beckoning him to follow, she climbed the stairs; standing aside as she reached the small landing, she indicated a room that was to be his.

It was difficult in the dim light to make out what was in the room, but Billy didn't care how big or small it was, he only knew he wanted to get into the bed facing him that, to his exhausted body, looked invitingly good.

In her motherly fashion, Sally helped him to remove his clothes. Within seconds, Billy was curled up on the bed and fast asleep, covered with a coarse linen cloth and a rough woollen blanket, as well as a handmade coverlet, fashioned out of small pieces of differently coloured materials.

Ever mindful of the night air, Sally then produced another blanket and, after carefully covering the sleeping young man, she smoothed her work-roughened hand over his fair hair, her heart full of compassion and achingly heavy with her longing for her own lost boy. Scalding tears, that Billy was unaware of, silently started to fall as Sally watched another woman's child sleep, in what had once been her own child's bed.

Watching the steady rise and fall of Billy's chest, Sally knew smuggling contraband goods into Cornwall was not the life for this young man; doing work that was not only illegal, but dangerous, nor was it her wish that he should be working alongside rough seamen who didn't know, or care, for a better way of life. She'd seen in him an educated young man, one who'd obviously grown up knowing a better life. In spite of the rough seaman's clothes that were a big part of his disguise, she could see his handsome looks, and his air of refinement in his actions, as well as his manners. It all betrayed his breeding; she could see that this young man had come from a different background to the one she'd always known. She also knew that she would have to be patient if she was to know his history, but patience was Sally's forte. She could wait!

Leaving Billy to his sleep, Sally wiped her eyes and took away the candle, before going to join her husband, her mind full of questions she wanted to ask; questions that might give her some of the answers she needed, and would explain the reasons as to why this young man had come to Cornwall and, more importantly, what was to become to him?

The next morning, Billy woke to sunlight streaming in through the small window of the room and the sounds of activity coming from the harbour down below. He climbed out of the bed and crossed the room to open the window, ready to breathe in the fresh Cornish air, the sky overhead full of gulls, screeching and wheeling as they raged at the fishermen unloading the day's catch from their boats berthed in the harbour. It was a familiar scene to him, one he'd witnessed many times before in the fishing villages near to his Breton home. It was a scene that, for a short while, brought back memories he found distressing, until he realised how lucky he was to have found such a safe haven as James and Sally's cottage home. Then, at last, he managed to shrug off his mournful thoughts.

Billy leant forward, the better to look at the carriers waiting on the quayside. He could see several wooden carts already waiting to move off, loaded as they were with woven baskets, lined with seaweed and full of freshly caught fish, prepared and ready to go to the market Billy could already hear in progress on the green; a parcel of land where the good people of Polperro enjoyed such things as markets and general get-togethers, events where, sometimes, dancing and music could be seen and heard. Billy watched for a while, intrigued by the Cornish scene, not unlike those he'd witnessed many times before in Brittany, but this time he was taking in the sights and sounds of Cornishmen as they worked, some of whom he recognised from the previous night's exodus from the shore, as they called out to each other as they lifted the baskets of fish onto the carts. Billy watched with a keen interest as the carts were soon manhandled away from the harbour, no doubt by those selfsame men that had trodden the cliff path with their horses the night before. They made their way through the narrow streets of the village, some with their wives accompanying them, calling out in a bid to attract customers, in their sing-song voices, that there was fish for sale.

Billy listened, intrigued by the Cornish way of speaking, aware he had much to learn if he were to remain safe from harm.

Reluctantly, he withdrew his eyes away from scene of boats and the activities taking place below his window, looking across instead for a while, at the rows of cottages ranged in tiers, all clinging tightly to the cliffs opposite.

He could see steps had been cut out of the steep granite, to enable people to climb to the top. Then he noticed the narrow lanes and the alleyways, all leading up and away from the village, to where he knew not, but knowing he would find out soon enough, when he went to explore them at the first opportunity.

It was a beautiful morning, his first in Cornwall. The sky was a cerulean blue, the same colour as the windflowers in the jug sitting on the table in the room downstairs which, apart from the meal, was the one thing he remembered from last night; the colour of the flowers reminding him of Marietta's eyes, causing him to wonder, for a moment or two, whether all was well with her and her family in Brittany. His other thought? Perhaps Sally had climbed the cliff path opposite and picked them?

He moved away from the window, turning to survey the room.

Apart from the bed, there was a wooden cupboard and the chest James had carried upstairs whilst he'd been asleep, otherwise there was very little in the way of furniture or ornaments in the room. The bed itself was a simple wooden affair, compact and practical, probably made by a ship's carpenter, for it was not unlike the bed in the captain's cabin aboard the *Mary Anne*. There was a plain wooden cross pinned to the wall and, for a few minutes, Billy wondered about the boy who had once slept there. What had he been like? Were they similar?

He opened the cupboard and found it to contain some clothes. They looked to be about his size, but he didn't touch them. Instead, he pulled on his old clothes; the seaman's trousers, found for him in a locker on board the *Mary Anne* by the Captain, and held secure about his waist by a leather belt the first mate had given him. Next, he put on the rough linen shirt, grubby and in need of a wash, a garment he'd been wearing for some time, and then finally, an old seaman's jumper, thick and warm, which the Captain had bought especially for him from an old woman at one of the ports. His own clothes discarded, as soon as he'd boarded the *Mary Anne*, as the

74

quality of them would have betrayed his heritage, even though they were old and had once belonged to his tutor.

He'd nothing to put on his feet except for his sea boots, again supplied by the captain, and, like his seaman's coat, drying out downstairs. The seaman's coat had been cut down to size by the first mate, the only person on board the *Mary Anne* to be entrusted with needles and thread from the Captain's cupboard and, like his boots that too was drying by the fire.

Once dressed, Billy went down the narrow stairs to where Sally was busy preparing food. She looked up and smiled as he opened the door and walked into the small room, telling him to sit at the table before producing a small bowl of buttermilk that she put before him and urged him to drink. Next came a chunk of bread, cut from the loaf he'd eaten from the night before. A dish of fresh churned butter came next and then another that held preserved fruits, cooked with wild honey, that Sally urged him to spread on the bread. Billy couldn't eat fast enough.

Sally smiled as she'd watched him eat. He'd looked half starved and impoverished the previous night, and in daylight he looked no better. Billy was, in her opinion, in need of mothering, something she was determined to do, once he'd been fed. She'd taken him, when he first arrived, to be about the same age as her boy Ben had been when he'd been lost at sea, but in daylight, with Billy sitting at her table, she could see he was no longer a boy, but a young man.

Suddenly, she turned away, her eyes filling with tears she had no desire for him to see, her heart aching with her longing for her own lost son.

Billy hadn't noticed much about the room when he'd first arrived except for the windflowers that had caught his eyes but this time, as he ate, he took his time to look around the room.

It was a homely and comfortable place; its furnishing simple, especially the wooden settle he was sitting on, and the scrubbed table, where his food was waiting; the two main items of furniture in the room and then suddenly he noticed a cupboard, fixed across one corner of the room.

From a closer inspection he could see it held small pieces of fancy china, very similar to the knickknacks and trinkets his mother had once loved. In front of the fire was an old wooden chair he thought James would use, as it looked well worn and comfortable, with a cushion on the seat that matched his bedcover; obviously another piece of Sally's handiwork and, next to James's chair, there was a much smaller wooden one that he assumed, quite rightly, to be Sally's.

Everywhere was spotlessly clean; from the freshly swept slate floor to the polished furniture. It was a simple home, one of many similar granite cottages in the small seaside village.

Hanging on the wall next to the inglenook fireplace was an oil painting, set in a simple oak frame. It was a fine portrait of an old man who looked familiar, the likeness of the sitter to that of James. It seemed at odds to Billy that a couple, who appeared to have very little, should have such an expensive-looking item on the wall of their cottage and, for the first time, Billy wondered if Sally and James had once been part of a much wealthier family.

At the other end of the room was another cabinet, this one much smaller and highly polished. A feminine piece of furniture, again so at odds with the rest of the room he thought it must belong to Sally, especially when compared with the scrubbed table and the rough-hewn settle where he sat. And that was the sum total of furniture.

The ashes from the previous night's fire had already been cleared away, and the makings of a new one had already been laid ready, waiting for a lighted spill to set it ablaze later, when the sea mist came rolling in to hang over the harbour, chilling the night air. The only other items in the room, as far as Billy could see, were a wooden candle box and a trug at the side of the fireplace, full of what he knew to be apple tree logs, for that had been the aroma he'd smelt when he first entered the cottage. It reminded him of when fires had been lit in his family home, now empty and abandoned. For a while, Billy felt sad, his mind filled with the memories of his home and his childhood, memories he never wanted to forget.

Of James, there was no sign.

'Where's James?' he asked Sally, who was busy tying the ribbons of a straw bonnet that hid her unruly reddish curls and shaded her eyes. She was dressed in a faded and well-worn blue cotton dress, ready to go down to the village.

She looked at him and smiled, placing a woollen shawl around her shoulders for there was a chill in the air. 'He's gone down to the harbour. If you've finished eating, we can go and find him.'

Billy washed his hands and face in the bowl of water Sally placed ready for him. With his fair hair slicked back, his seaman's jacket (which had dried overnight) donned and jauntily wearing a cap Sally had unearthed from a cupboard at the side of the door, he felt ready to face the good people of Polperro for the first time.

Once satisfied all was well, Sally ushered Billy out of the cottage and down the granite steps; swinging her basket and leading the way, she went down a narrow alleyway. Skipping in a lively manner between the rows of cottages, with Billy trying to keep pace with her, she made her way down to the harbour, where the local fishermen were working on their nets. Now the catch had been unloaded and was on its way to the market, the crews were busy getting their gear ready for the next day's fishing.

Of James there was no sign, until Sally clutched at Billy's arm and pointed towards a fishing boat, berthed at the far end of the harbour, where the man in question could be seen standing on its deck, paint brush in hand.

James saw them and waved and, as they drew closer, Billy could see he had been painting the name *Boy Ben* on the side of the boat.

Sally looked at the boat and then at James, unable to speak for the pain in her heart; tears were suddenly filling her eyes, tears she needed to release, that they might ease her pain. Seeing his wife's distress, James leapt off the boat and took her in his arms, her shoulders shaking as she tried to stifle her sobs against his chest.

James rocked her gently, shushing her, as one would a small child, at the same time holding her tight, kissing her cheek with such love, Billy had to turn away for a moment; the touching scene deeply affecting him, afraid that they would see his tears, unsure of what was expected of him, but instinctively knowing this scene didn't include him. It must be the name on the boat that meant something special to Sally.

Once her composure was restored, Sally moved out of James's arms and walked away from the boat.

Billy made to follow, but James called him back. 'Stay here with me boy, Sally needs a while to herself just now.'

'Who's Boy Ben?' Billy asked, once he was alone with James.

'Our son! He was about your age when he was lost at sea and not so long ago either. The fishing boat he was on got caught in an unexpected storm. Sadly, all the crew were drowned and the boat lost. His mother had begged him not to go to sea that day; she'd had a feeling something bad was about to happen but, like all youngsters, Ben wanted his own way and when his mother was out of sight, he left the cottage and boarded the boat, the rest you know.'

James sighed and looked out at the sea beyond the harbour, his thoughts obviously on what had happened.

'I'd refused to have him on my boat, as I wanted him to do something other than be a fisherman., It's a too hard and demanding life, but school and book learning wasn't for our boy. I should have known better and understood his need, for the sea was in his blood. There was nothing I could have said, or done that day, that would have stopped him. If he hadn't gone that day, he would have gone another.'

James, his eyes glittering with his unshed tears, turned and looked beyond Billy. 'Boats are lost every winter' he said quietly, 'no matter how good a sailor you are, or how good your boat. When the sea wants you, it takes you.'

James fell silent for a while, continuing to look out to sea. Grieving for one's lost child never got easier. Then he remembered the young man standing next to him and the conversation he'd had with the first mate of the *Mary Anne* the previous night, as they waited on the shingle as the cargo was being unloaded from the rowboat.

When James had been asked by Jed Pengelly if he would take care of the boy for Captain Sawyer, giving just scant details of the circumstances of Billy being in Cornwall, and of how the boy had cruelly lost both his parents and was in need of a home, James had felt a deep compassion for the young man. Now, he knew how Billy must have been feeling.

Martin Sawyer was James's older brother and, knowing his and Sally's grief at losing their only son, had thought Sally might find it in her caring heart to take Billy under her wing and give him a loving home. Looking at the boy standing beside him now, James knew they had to do the best they could to keep him safe, as Martin had asked, until he returned to the village from only God knew where, before any decision could be taken as to the boy's future. What James didn't know at the time was that Billy was more than capable of deciding his own future and destiny.

With Sally shopping in the village and no doubt gossiping with the other wives at the market in the square, James decided it was time to take Billy to meet some of the other village locals.

Some time later, after walking around the village, they just happened to end up at the fishermen's favourite inn, The Pilchards, where the smell of food cooking in the kitchen reached them as soon as they entered.

The ancient building, overlooking the harbour, was one of the oldest in the village (originally built a couple of centuries ago, to house the men employed in building the stone church that replaced the original wooden building). James pointed out the church to Billy, its square tower reminding him of the old church that stood in the square of the Breton village where he'd grown up.

Although not very tall, even Billy had to duck his head as he first entered in order to miss the smoke-darkened beams that stretched across the room.

A jugful of foaming ale was immediately placed in front of James, who reached out and poured a small amount of the golden liquid into a pewter tankard, before pushing it laughingly towards Billy.

'Here, boy, drink this. It will make a man of you!'

Billy drank some of the ale, unsure he wanted to be a man if this was what he would be expected to drink, having never drunk strong ale before. Walking across the room, he sat at a round table and looked at the other men in the room who, from their talk, all seemed to be local to the village and, from their apparel, fishermen. Sitting or standing in groups around the room, they were drinking and talking companionably together. Suddenly he felt conspicuous and foreign, beginning to wonder if his presence in the village would cause problems for James and his friends.

Billy had hardly spoken since arriving in Cornwall, except to acknowledge Sally or James, prudence keeping him quiet, even knowing he could speak English, for he knew his French accent would betray him and that he must learn to speak in the dialect of the local men as soon as possible. Otherwise, his presence would bring about problems, not only to himself, but to James and Sally, as well as to others in the village.

For the time being he thought it more prudent to remain silent, and let the fisherman think him stupid for his lack of conversation, rather than draw unwanted attention to himself, and the others.

After a while the men continued to talk as though Billy wasn't sitting amongst them, giving him the opportunity to listen and learn. The men were all confident the boy was indeed stupid and, with the strong ale making them rash, they were soon talking in hushed tones of matters that suddenly became of interest to Billy, but he had to strain to hear to what was being said. It appeared the men were looking for someone to finance another smuggling run from France!

Billy understood from the men's loose talk that an unknown person from another village had financed the last cargo and, from what he'd gathered, the village men were not altogether happy with this arrangement and wanted the next run to be solely for their benefit. Billy had nothing to contribute to the conversation, but continued to listen intently, hearing them say they had the use of a ship, and an experienced crew to sail it, their only problem, or so it seemed, was how to raise the amount of capital needed to purchase the cargo. Names of possible benefactors were bandied about, but of course they meant nothing to Billy. Presently, as the talk and the ale continued to flow, Billy, decided he'd heard enough and, after politely doffing his cap at the men – a gesture that caused a few raised eyebrows – he went outside to sit on the harbour wall, where he watched the hustle and bustle of men getting their boats ready to sail the next morning.

As he sat there, Billy's mind was racing, trying to digest all he'd seen and heard and, with the last of the sun's rays beating down on him, Billy not only watched, but also sat deep in thought, wishing there was some way he could help.

It was quite some time before he returned to the cottage, to where Sally was busy preparing the evening meal. As soon as he entered, he could smell a fish stew being cooked in the same black pot, suspended over the fire, as on the previous evening. Dishes were already set out on the scrubbed table, along with a new loaf of the coarse bread, waiting to be cut in the now familiar chunks, as well as a jug of buttermilk.

Sally motioned him to wash his hands and remove his coat, pouring a beaker of the milk and pointing to the settle for him to sit and drink.

'How was your day?' she asked, bending over to stir the contents simmering in the black pot.

'It was fine, thank you,' he replied. 'I walked around the village with James and then we went to the inn where we sat with the fishermen and I listened as they talked.'

Sally was frowning as she turned to look at the young man, his appearance at odds with his refined voice, his English spoken with a distinct accent that immediately pinpointed him as being from foreign parts.

'Billy, I think you'd better learn to speak as the villagers do, or we'll have the Excise Officer visiting us, demanding to know who you are and where you've come from, and, more important, why you're here in Cornwall!'

This was something Billy also wanted to know the answer to. Why *was* he here in Cornwall?

At that moment, the cottage door opened and in walked James, only slightly worse for drink, which Sally, by now busy dishing up the food, failed to notice, or chose not to, ignoring the slight slurring of his voice.

It wasn't until the meal was over and the bowls had been wiped clean with the bread, then stacked ready for washing, that Sally, a little exasperated at her husband, said her piece. 'We have to do something about Billy's speaking!'

'What's wrong with him?' James asked, looking askance at Billy.

'Nothing's wrong with him, it's just his speaking, he sounds foreign, and you know what will happen if the Excise men come across him. They'll take him away from us and he'll end up at the assizes before the magistrates, where they will surely try him as a spy and he'll be taken to Bodmin jail to be hanged! And I'm sure we don't want that, do we? What would Martin have to say, seeing as how we've been asked to look after him until he returns?'

James shook his head. 'Perhaps we should listen to what Billy has to say first, before we cause a stir about nothing? Come on then, young Billy, let's hear what you've got to say for yourself.'

Billy sat quietly for a little while, not knowing quite what he should say. Then he knew: he would tell them about his parents, and of his life before they'd been taken away and killed, and how he had been rescued from the same awful fate by Captain Sawyer, who'd taken him aboard the *Mary Anne,* and how his fancy clothes, once the latest fashion in France, had been exchanged for those of his tutor, and how the Captain and crew had dressed him afterwards in rough seamen's clothing, disguising him as a cabin boy, even cutting his hair into the fashion of a cabin boy, not tied back with a silken ribbon as in France, and how even his identity had been changed.

He then told them of his education with his tutor, Henri Masson, where he'd learnt Mathematics, as well as Greek and Latin, and how he'd learnt English, and of how his dream of following his father into the banking world, when he was old enough, had been dashed by events he had no control over. By the time he'd finished, Sally had tears in her eyes that, try as she might, she couldn't prevent from falling. Even James had had to swallow hard, for a lump in his throat was threatening to choke him.

By then the evening was getting late and it was dark outside. Sally had lit a candle while James put another log on the fire, where it had spluttered and flamed. Billy then continued speaking, until he'd told them the entire story of his life.

As he climbed the stairs later to his room, Billy's mind was full of his thoughts of his parents, and his old life, and the questions he had yet to find answers for.

His biggest question was how was he to live his life, now he was an orphan and living in a foreign land that was Cornwall? How best should he use his education and knowledge? Knowing full well he would never be a fisherman like James. The sea wasn't in his blood, unlike James and Sally's son, Ben. It was banking and commerce that flowed through his veins, and tomorrow he would have to think of how he was to make his fortune, since the wealth and properties he'd been born to, and should have inherited, had all but vanished the day the guillotine had fallen on his father and mother's heads, destroying centuries of prosperity for his family, as well as those who'd worked for them.

Billy knew it was up to him now to acquire his own fortune. He would never again be known as Willelm D'Anville, son and heir of the Marquis D'Anville, from now on he would be William Sawyer, known to all and sundry as Billy, but that was no reason for him to think he could no longer be successful! Success was not all in a name, but in effort and some luck, and he was determined he would make his own luck.

That night, he went to sleep to the sound of men and loaded pack-horses returning once more from yet another trek off the shingle beach at Talland Bay, promising himself he would do all he could to make his parents proud of him. But first of all, he would make his own fortune, in memory of them, and his lost heritage, and then one day he would return to his home in France and build a lasting memorial to his parents.

His last thought and solemn vow, as he closed his eyes and fell asleep, was that, one day, he would make the name 'Billy Sawyer' a name in Cornwall to be reckoned with.

Chapter 4
Life in Polperro

Billy awoke the next morning to the sun streaming through the small window of what he now considered to be his room, with the familiar sounds of activity coming from the harbour. He stretched his limbs, comfortable and at ease with his surroundings and, for the first time in weeks, he felt safe. He reached for his clothes, the cabin boy's clothes he'd lived in since joining the *Mary Anne* but they were gone! In their place was a pair of brown woollen knee breeches, and clean stockings; a freshly washed and pressed linen shirt, and a blue serge jacket, all items he'd seen in the bedroom cupboard the previous day.

Billy dressed quickly, his eyes suddenly caught by the oilskin packet the first mate had handed him on the beach, that he'd put into the pocket of his seaman's coat, and was now sitting on top of the wooden chest James had carried up the stairs on the night he'd first arrived. The selfsame chest that had come from off the *Mary Anne* and that he now assumed must belong to him, but how it had got aboard the *Mary Anne* in the first place was a mystery.

He opened the packet and found a key, immediately realising it was the one needed to open the chest. For a moment or two, he wondered what surprises it was about to reveal. With his curiosity getting the better of him, he inserted the key into the well-oiled lock, keen to know its contents. At the same time, he was dreading the moment, not quite sure if he was ready for what was in store for him and not a little anxious as to what the contents might reveal.

Turning the key, he heard the lock click open. He lifted the lid, his eyes widening in surprise at what he saw before him. He gasped and took a step backwards, to sit on the edge of the bed, astounded at what the chest held, momentarily stunned and amazed at its contents. He moved forward and lifted out a small pile of documents that lay on top, placing them on the narrow bed, their removal fully revealing the small fortune that lay before his eyes.

For a while, Billy was unable to comprehend his good fortune and closed the lid, sure he was dreaming, and that when he opened the chest again it would all have vanished!

His hands were shaking, and his body trembling as he picked up one of the documents from the bed, for he knew what they were, the top sheet in particular; a letter to himself, written in his father's own distinctive and flowery script on parchment. He took this one document and started to read.

Written were the words he knew his father had never thought that he would have to see until he was much older. His eyes filled with tears, knowing he would never see his father or mother again, but just holding his father's letter seemed to bring them closer and, for a while, he cried, until eventually his grief subsided enough for him to continue. After wiping his eyes, he looked through all the papers; his father's last will and testament that Billy read later, bequeathing Billy all that he possessed, as well as a collection of valuable documents that detailed his birthright, as well as the deeds to his family homes (the chateau in Brittany and the house in Paris where they had lived) and details of the bank, also owned by his family, and where his father had worked each day and where Billy had hoped to eventually join him when his studies were finished. And then he turned to some other documents that were the even older, historic sheets of yellowing parchment and old vellum, pieces that charted the purchase of another small chateau in the Breton countryside a couple of centuries ago by his ancestors, and where his grandparents had once lived and then, even more papers, most yellowing and fragile with age, listing land and properties belonging to the D'Anville family for centuries and inherited by his father, and now rightfully belonging to Billy, the new Marquis D'Anville, known now and forever more as William Sawyer, or by the nickname Billy, the name the Captain of the *Mary Anne* had christened him and which he was becoming to like.

Billy realised the documents and, quite possibly, the properties would have no value at all by now, as the properties were no doubt lost to him, since his father's untimely death, confiscated or, as he thought bitterly, stolen from him by those who thought it their right to deprive him of what was rightfully his.

Apart from the many gold ingots that three quarters filled the chest, there were gold coins by the score in linen bags, and boxes that held rings, bracelets and necklaces, all studded with diamonds and rubies, precious jewels that he remembered his mother wearing when she went to the court with his father., There seemed to be more than enough for his future needs.

The documents Billy knew would no longer have any intrinsic value, for the land and properties his ancestors had once owned would no doubt have already been allocated to a new occupier. Taken from his family in the name of the republic by the new regime. They now belonged to the citizens of France and Billy would no longer inherit what had once been one of the most profitable estates in all France, taken from him as ruthlessly as his father and mother had been taken. But thankfully he still had his life, even if theirs were gone, betrayed by someone they had once trusted, someone not satisfied with simply betraying them, but a person who must have known the extent of his father's worth, someone who had probably sat and watched as his parents had been killed, by a single cut of the blade belonging to 'Madam Guillotine', leaving Billy not only an orphan, but one who was bereft, his heart broken at the loss of his beloved parents, a loss that no amount of gold or jewels could ever replace.

Billy sat for a while longer in the small bedroom of this simple Cornish cottage, deep in thought as he pondered on how best he could use his inheritance. His immediate thought was that he should use the gold to fight in the courts for what was rightfully his, to restore his heritage, but this he had to dismiss, for he knew it would cost him dearly, probably more than the amount in the chest and then to no avail. So, if that was not a possibility, or even an option, maybe he should use it more wisely, and make the gold work for him, to give him a new life in Cornwall? But he needed to think carefully about his future plans before he started to use the gold. Billy's father had showed he had faith in him by the very existence of the chest and its contents, and now it was up to Billy to prove he had made the right decision.

Sally must have heard him moving about in the room, for he suddenly heard the door leading to the stairs opening and her calling out to him.

'Are you coming down, Billy? James will be waiting for you.'

'Yes, I'm coming,' Billy answered, placing the documents back into the chest and then locking it, but not before he'd removed a length of ribbon from one of the documents that he then used to thread through the key, putting it over his head and tucking the key under his shirt where it would be hidden from view. He would deal with his inheritance later.

As soon as he'd eaten the simple meal prepared by Sally – bread, and more of her fruit conserve, along with a beakerful of buttermilk – Billy made his way down to the harbour, where he could see James was already on the deck of the *Boy Ben*.

Billy could see some of the crew were already busy, unfurling the sails, and coiling the ropes, getting ready to sail.

James laughed as he saw Billy on the quayside. 'At last,' he said, 'the day's nearly over and you're just out of bed. For sure you are a slugabed!'

Billy laughed as well, bearing no malice as James reached across and gave him his hand to help him aboard. James had been startled for a few moments at his first sight of Billy. Dressed as he was in the boy's clothes, Billy had suddenly become the very image of Ben and, for a few moments, James had thought he was seeing a ghost!

'I see you're dressed to do some work?' James called out, with just a hint of sarcasm that made Billy laugh.

'Sally has taken my clothes and left me these to wear. Anyway, I'm not here to work, but to watch and learn, you said so yourself.'

'I'm glad she took your old clothes away, you were getting to be a bit smelly! You would have scared the fish!'

Billy felt embarrassed at his comment, until he saw the laughter in his eyes. Billy just shrugged his shoulders and laughed as well, for it was true that he did smell. It had been quite some time since he'd had the luxury of a bath or washed his clothes, as bathing hadn't been important whilst on board ship with Captain Sawyer, as everyone on the ship had baths only when threatened, or when they were in a place where water, hot or cold, was readily available, but Billy knew that he would have to rectify it soon, or who would take him, or his wealth, seriously? After all, he might look like a cabin boy, but he was still a gentleman and he needed to smell like one!

'Come along lad, I want to show you the coastline in daylight and now's as good a time as ever.'

'No fishing today then?' Billy asked.

'There are different types of fishing lad, and today we're going fishing for the human kind!'

Billy laughed, unsure of what to make of James's comment, but certain all would be revealed later.

Once the sails on the fishing boat were raised and it slowly began moving away from the dockside, James took hold of the wheel and steered the vessel out of the harbour and into the bay, with Billy at his side, watching closely his every movement.

Billy watched with a keen interest all the activities in the harbour as they sailed out past the breakwater, as well as those on board the *Boy Ben*, comparing the men with the crew on board the *Mary Anne*. But there was no comparison to be made, for Captain Sawyer's ship was much bigger, a different type of ship altogether, designed for long journeys, being a three-masted lugger, and armed with canons and swivel guns, ready to do battle; the *Boy Ben* was a much smaller boat, designed and made in Cornwall just for fishing. It held no guns that he could see, and that intrigued him, as he knew the Cornish coast was as dangerous a place as any other, and where trouble could be found just as easily. He would have thought it better to be armed and ready for such an event, but obviously not! To his mind, this was not a fighting vessel.

With one of his crew keeping a keen eye out for hidden rocks (it was many a boat's downfall when entering or leaving the small harbour), James skilfully sailed the boat into open water, avoiding the rocks that Billy could see quite easily through the clear water of the bay and, quite soon, they were heading along the coast, a following wind filling the sails as James expertly sailed the vessel.

As they sped along, James pointed out the coves and inlets, calling out the names of the secluded coves at either side of Polperro where, Billy was to later find out, contraband goods would be stashed if they couldn't be landed. Then they were passing Parson's Cove, just below Lansallos in Lantivet Bay, with James telling Billy the names of some of the other villages and hamlets on the coast as they sailed past.

They had been sailing for some time when, ahead, Billy saw the estuary that James had told him was the entrance to the small village of Fowey. As they got nearer, he could see from the amount of ships moored in the deep water that it was a busy port, where much trade was being done, despite the size of the village belying its capacity.

Suddenly, Billy was aware of a ship coming out of the harbour, heading in their direction. He called out to James, who said it was the cutter used by Customs and Excise. Instead of going into the harbour as he'd planned, James turned the wheel, shouting orders to his men to mind the sails, before steering the *Boy Ben* onto another course, this time heading for a port further along the coast, to where two villages (once called Meva and Gissey), were now one (the small fishing village of Mevagissey). Its numerous coves and caves upon either side were, James said, often used (like Polperro), by the smuggling fraternity as places to store and hide contraband goods until it was safe to remove them.

Once Billy had seen and admired the village and its new harbour, and then some of the other coves further along the coast, where smuggled goods would also be landed, James steered the *Boy Ben* into the open sea and then, turning the wheel and tacking into the prevailing wind, they were soon heading back in the direction whence they had come.

With its sails billowing from the stiff breeze that had blown up, James steered the *Boy Ben* back to the safety of the harbour in Polperro, sure that Billy had seen enough of the Cornish coast for the time being.

As the vessel made its way into the harbour, so it was faced with the Excise cutter that they had seen earlier in Fowey harbour. It was already moored and obviously waiting for the *Boy Ben* to appear.

'Billy, get below,' James called out. 'If the Excise men come near and want to board us, you're to act deaf and stupid, do you understand?'

Billy didn't, but being intelligent, he knew better than to disobey any order given by James. Like all young seamen, he had already learnt to instantly obey commands given by any captain, without question.

The *Boy Ben* gently made its way towards its mooring and, once safely home and docked, the crew dropped anchor. With the sails furled and stowed away, and all shipshape on board, the crew, along with Billy, and with James following, left the ship and made their way along the harbour to The Pilchards. There, they settled down to drink the frothing ale the landlord put before them, with Billy mimicking the crew's behaviour as though he'd done the same thing many times before.

They had been drinking for some time, when the outer door opened and in walked three hard-looking men. From their uniforms, Billy knew them to be seamen from off the cutter; an officer and two ratings, and, from the look of them, they were intent on trouble.

The officer walked across to where Billy was sitting, for he was the stranger in the room.

'Where have you come from?' he asked aggressively, obviously with the intention of scaring him.

Billy ignored him, although he felt more than a little nervous and anxious; his insides were shaking and his heart was beating furiously, but he had no intention of rising to the bait. Lowering his head and opening his mouth in a slack way, Billy let a dribble of saliva and ale spittle flow slowly from his mouth onto his chest. He could see out of the corner of his eye that James was about to say something, but after watching him closely, he decided against it.

The officer leant forward and poked Billy on the shoulder.

At this, Billy responded with a start. He lifted his head and looked over the man's shoulder, to a point just above one of the smoke-blackened beams, and crossed his eyes. This was a trick that had often amused my mother.

Billy could hear James and the other members of the crew coughing as they tried to stifle their gasps of astonishment and laughter.

Looking from Billy, then across to James, the officer asked, in a snooty tone of voice, 'Where does the lad live?'

'He lives with me,' James retorted, equally snooty. 'His parents are dead. You can see for yourself he's not quite right in the head and needed a home. He's not safe to be left. He's a little deaf as well,' he said, from behind his hand, as though imbibing a secret to the

95

officer, and, looking at Billy with an expression that even he could understand, he added, 'and he's definitely all wrong in his head.'

Billy very nearly laughed out loud at his words, but fortunately, he had the good sense and foresight to realise that this was indeed a serious moment in his life and that he should take care not to provoke the Excise men. Otherwise, he might indeed end up in Bodmin jail, as Sally had forecast.

James's pronouncement obviously displeased the officer enough for him to poke Billy yet again. 'You mind your ways, young man, or you'll be sent away!'

At this, James stood up and faced the officer, prepared to fight if need be and take the consequences afterwards.

'No one's going to send the lad anywhere,' he said, in a matter of fact tone that he only used when he was really angry. 'I've just told you he's deaf and not right in his head. You leave him alone or I'll have the magistrates on you.'

The officer said no more. With laughter following him and his men, they marched out of the inn, back to where the cutter was moored, leaving Billy, James, and the crew breathing big sighs of relief.

Sometime later, James looked out of a window overlooking the harbour and said, 'The cutter's just leaving; it's turning towards Talland. Perhaps it's on its way to Plymouth.'

'Aye,' said one of the men from James's crew. 'Hopefully it'll be out of the area fairly soon, for there's a ship due in at Talland tonight with another load for us, and in a few hours the men from the village will be down on the shore, ready to unload, and they won't want the cutter to suddenly appear from around the headland.'

'We've just got to hope the cutter does go to Plymouth then,' said another man, known as Davey. 'There's a rumour out that there's a ship due at Whitsand tonight, so they'll no doubt be wanting to be there as well.'

This act of sending the Revenue men out on wild goose chases appealed to all smugglers and even Billy was beginning to understand the humour of these simple men; not so simple when it suited them, as Billy was to find out many times whilst he strived to live and make his fortune in Cornwall.

At this exchange, James laughed and walked back to where Billy was sitting, quite relaxed now that the Excise men had left and drinking the ale that Billy too was beginning to get a taste for.

'Well done, Billy,' he said. 'Be careful, though, of those men. I'm not so sure they believed your act.'

Billy said nothing. He just raised his eyes and, looking directly at James, crossed them again. This time, the laughter from James and the crew rocked the room, the tension finally broken.

Like James, Billy wasn't so sure that the Excise men believed him to be half deaf and stupid, and he vowed to himself to take care lest his future life in Cornwall should be a short one; he still had plans to make for the dynasty that he was sure he would soon be creating.

Later that evening, after supper had been eaten and the table cleared, he went to his room and brought down some of the papers that he'd taken from the chest earlier, along with one of the gold bars, some coins, a ring that had been his mother's, and two small miniature pictures, putting them all on the table in front of Sally and James.

Sally gasped and went quite pale as she saw what lay before her. Her hands clutched her chest as she looked at Billy's treasures, unable to speak for a while.

James looked first at the gold bar (no doubt the only one he had ever seen), then at Billy. Leaning across the table, he picked it up and weighed it as he turned it over in his hand. 'Worth a small fortune,' he said, his eyes full of questions that he wanted to ask. 'Billy,' he said, his whole demeanour in shock at the sight of such wealth, 'where did this come from?'

'It belongs to me,' Billy said. 'It was in the chest you carried from the ship. My father, knowing his life was in great danger, gave the chest to Captain Sawyer some months ago, when the Captain last visited him in Paris. My father knew if he were betrayed and captured by the revolutionists, they would take everything he possessed and, if he didn't get the Captain to take it with him that day, he might not have a second chance. And of course he was proved right, but there must be much more than this hidden in the house in Paris, and possibly more hidden in the grounds of our country house in Brittany, as my father was a very wealthy man. The amount I have is, I believe, nothing to what there should be. Sadly though, I don't think I will ever be able to return to France and find what is rightly mine.'

Sally reached across the table to comfort him, holding his hand for a moment or two, until the lure of such treasures became too much and curiosity got the better of her. Releasing his hand, she picked up and closely examined the ring, trying it on for size, holding out her hand, so the light from the candle might reflect in the stones, sending prisms of light flashing before her astounded eyes.

The two miniatures were the next to be scrutinised. One, a small and exquisite painting of a lady, decked out in her finery, its golden frame surrounded by diamonds, the other, a painting on enamel of a distinguished-looking gentleman, both dressed in the court fashion of the day.

'Are these your parents?' she asked gently.

'Yes,' Billy answered, his voice full of emotion as his eyes filled with tears.

She patted his arm, unable to say the words in her heart; her heart aching for him, but he understood. However, not even her kindness was enough to ease his grief and, for a while, he sat quietly, trying to regain his composure.

James was still studying the gold, turning it over and over in his hands, weighing it up as to its value.

'What are you planning to do with this?' he asked at last, the glow of precious metal shining in the subdued light of the solitary candle and the soft glow of the fire. Gold, the one metal that is easy to distinguish, having a look that is eternal, and for which men have fought for generations to possess, though for Billy it was merely a means to an end and he had plenty more where that one piece came from. It was all his to do with as he wished.

'I don't know yet,' he answered truthfully. 'I have to think what would be the best way to use it, as I know it will be difficult for me to get back my houses, or the land that rightfully belong to me. I need to make the right decision as to how I might use this small fortune to make a life for myself in Cornwall.'

James sat deep in thought for a while, his mind no doubt full of his own ideas, for Billy could see, from the look on his face, he was thinking deeply.

He was a thoughtful man, one who considered carefully what he had to say before he spoke; this, Billy could see, was one of those occasions. To Billy's relief, James decided to stay silent a while longer, as it was not in his nature to make rash decisions and he knew enough to know that Billy might have some ideas of his own, and that smuggling contraband might not be one of them!

Once Sally and Billy had gone to bed, James put on his seaman's coat and a close fitting hat. After making sure the fire was safe, he extinguished the candle and quietly opened the cottage door, before silently making his way to join the other men and animals from the village, who were already making their way along the cliffs; they were heading towards the familiar shingle beach, ready to greet yet another boat loaded with goods that needed to be hidden in the village, away from prying eyes.

Billy spent the next few weeks working with James on the *Boy Ben*, fishing out in the Channel, often returning with a catch that was sometimes more than fish. Items, such as kegs and barrels, that had been dropped overboard when the Excise cutter had suddenly appeared and surprised the smugglers. Goods that had been left on markers, to be retrieved once the Excise cutter had gone from the area, chasing after another culprit, later, Billy would help to off-load the retrieved goods, heaving them off the *Boy Ben* onto wagons, ostensibly waiting on the quayside as though they were waiting for the day's catch of fish to be unloaded! It was a life a million miles away from the one that Billy should have been living in France, but, in a strange way, he had become content with his lot. For the time being, anyway!

Everyone in the village knew Billy by then, believing him to be a distant relative of James, a cousin from the north of England in need of care, which in some way excused his strange accent that, to Sally's delight, was gradually changing the longer that he lived and worked in Cornwall. Of course, James and the crew took great delight in making him repeat words and phrases that, at first, he found difficult, but soon even he could hear the change, which was all to the good.

His old clothes had been returned, washed and repaired, with the admonishment that 'Ben's clothes are to be used for best', or so Sally informed him. He had to ask what 'for best' meant. It was not a phrase with which he was familiar at the time. (Moreover, Billy *did* have a bath, in front of the fire. It was a luxury that, even as an aristocrat, he had never enjoyed. The used water was emptied out of the door to wash down the granite steps.)

'It's for when you go visiting, or go to church on Sundays,' Sally had replied, her eyes twinkling with humour at his naïve question.

'But I don't go to church, and as for visiting, who will I visit?'

'You'll soon find someone to visit and, as for going to church, we will go this Sunday.' She glared at James, just as he was about to interrupt her. 'It's time we went to give thanks for Billy's safe arrival from France, and for his good fortune!' she said, giving him no leeway to argue.

True to her word, the next Sunday, the three of them went to church, with Billy dressed in Ben's best clothes that were now his, and with James and Sally equally as finely dressed, thanks to the small amount of gold that Billy had persuaded Sally and James to use for new clothes for themselves. They walked together, as any family would, up the steep path to the Norman church, Billy's first experience of attending church in Cornwall and one that he quite enjoyed.

He thought the ancient building was simple yet beautiful, decked out as it was with spring flowers, the first of the season that Sally had told him the ladies of the village would have picked especially the day before.

The singing from the congregation was inspiring and, for the first time in many weeks, Billy felt a spiritual peace descend on him at the simplicity of the service. At times, he could feel tears welling up in his eyes, threatening at any minute to spill over, especially when the rector blessed the congregation and prayed for the lost souls of the parish. He thought of his parents at that moment and wished they were sitting in the pew next to him; instead, their bodies were languishing in a lime-covered pit, somewhere near to their Paris home.

He turned his head to look at the cross on the altar, to focus on his prayers, and, from the corner of his eye, he saw Sally watching, her eyes shining brightly with her own unshed tears; no doubt, her thoughts on her own lost soul, her dearest son, Ben, whose clothes Billy wore.

The rector was a short and very rotund man in his fiftieth year. With his silver hair and ruddy cheeks, he looked more like a farmer than a man of God. He gave a sermon that was meant to inspire the congregation to sin less and pray more but, from where Billy sat at the back of the church, the sermon did neither for many in the congregation, if the sounds of muted snoring were anything to go by. Most of the village men had been up the previous night, unloading goods from yet another rowboat, hiding them away before dawn broke and had yet to go to bed. This didn't prevent the rector from urging everyone in the church to pray for deliverance, which made Billy smile as he looked around the church at the village men, all fervently praying, not for the deliverance of their souls, but deliverance from the hands of the Excise men; those hated officers who patrolled the seas round Cornwall, keen to stop the activities that kept food on the village folk's tables and shoes on the feet of their children, as the menfolk tried to eke out a meagre existence for their families from fishing, which at times was very poor and dependent on the vagaries of the weather.

Billy believed, rather naively, that the rector was unaware of the activities his congregation got up to as he continued with his sermon, urging everyone to obey the Ten Commandments, and the catechisms they had all learnt when young. The commandment, '*thou shalt not steal*' raised an eyebrow or two, as most of the wealth in the village came from exactly that; not paying the taxes demanded by the government, by trading in contraband goods, therefore denying the Treasury of monies that should by rights have been paid in duty.

The village men shook their heads in agreement at the rector's words, but, to them, smuggling was merely work they needed to do to live. It was a way of life, as old as the granite on which the village was built, and it never crossed the minds of the village men they were being dishonest by stealing the unpaid taxes. It was just the way it had always been.

Billy enjoyed his first visit to the church and vowed that he would return one day soon and get to know the rector; he instinctively knew that the fellow, being a man of the cloth, would be educated and could well be of use in the future. Even at his tender young age, Billy knew the rules for success were always to cultivate those in a position of trust, for the authorities would never suspect a man doing God's work.

As they walked back to the cottage, Billy decided that he would visit the church again when services were not being taken. With that in mind, later that day, he asked James if he could have the following day ashore. James looked at him in an odd sort of way, but agreed to the request, doubtless wondering what scheme he had in mind.

The next morning, being a fine spring one, Billy set out to visit the church, climbing up the steep lane that took him onto the cliffs. He stopped to admire the view of the bay as he walked, looking over the cliffs for the beach where he had first landed, before he turned inland and found his way to the church by another path.

The church door was unlocked and, as he entered this hallowed place, the silence had such a profound effect on him that he knelt and prayed for a while, unaware that he was being watched.

Empty of its congregation, it was, as he had first thought, the most beautiful church he'd ever been in; not austere at all, especially the window over the altar where its coloured glass, portraying in pictures the stories in the Bible was illuminated by the spring sun streaming through, sending prisms of light directly onto the altar, as if positioned by the Lord God Himself.

After his prayers were done, Billy walked around the inside of the building, looking closely at the carved memorial stones laid against the walls, even getting on his hands and knees to read the inscriptions of those set in the chancel floor where ancient bodies had been buried. There was such an air of peace and tranquillity in the simple building that it reminded him of the church in the village near to his home, and where he had frequently worshipped with his parents.

As he walked around, looking and memorising all that he saw, he suddenly became aware of a young lady standing by the choir stalls. He immediately realised that he had seen her the previous Sunday and then he recognised her; Sally had pointed her out to him, with a glint in her eye, as she told him the young lady was the daughter of the rector.

Billy walked across to where she was standing. 'Good morning!' he said in his best English accent. 'I'm...' He was just about to introduce himself as Willelm, Marquis De Anville, when he realised his error and hastily substituted, with a slight stammer to hide his confusion, 'William Sawyer, better known as Billy to my friends!'

'Good morning,' she answered, in the prim and proper manner of a well-mannered and educated young lady. 'I'm Louise Spencer. My father is rector of this parish.'

Billy bowed low, as was the French custom when first meeting and making the acquaintance of any young lady. Taking the hand she offered, he kissed it, as he would have done had she been the daughter of one of his mother's friends, his French upbringing and aristocratic heritage coming to the fore, until he suddenly realised that, in Cornwall, he was no longer an aristocrat, but a common villager and one who now fished for his living!

Even so, she allowed him to kiss her hand and, at the same time, she bobbed a small curtsey and blushed in return, no doubt to the roots of the blonde curls that fell from under the straw bonnet she wore in such an enchanting manner.

'This is only my second visit to the church,' Billy said. 'Would you be so kind as to escort me around?' Forestalling her reply, he reached out and, taking hold of her hand and looping it through his arm, he walked her towards the altar. 'I understand this church has a long and interesting history?' he said.

'Yes, it has,' she said, quickly removing her hand, an act that amused Billy somewhat because he could tell that he had breached the good manners expected of an educated young man. He didn't care, for he wanted to get to know her.

Thankfully, Louise was not put off by his gaucheness as she answered him. 'I'm not completely sure of all the facts. Perhaps if I ask my father to tell me its history I can meet you again and tell you what I know, then we can walk round the church and investigate for ourselves?'

There was nothing at that moment that Billy wanted more in his life than to meet up again with the delightful creature that he had just met.

'Certainly,' he said, trying to dampen his excitement. 'I will meet you here next week, then?'

'Of course,' she said, bobbing another curtsey in his direction. 'That would be most pleasant.' With that, she smiled and walked away from him, out of the church and down the path.

He watched her go, his youthful emotions in some disarray, for he was beginning to know how it felt to be a man.

Later that evening, James sat in his chair, staring morosely into the fire, watching the logs burn anew before he kicked them into life.

'Billy,' he called, just as the young man was scraping the remains of a pudding from out of its dish, a sweet delight, called junket, that Sally had made especially for him. 'Do you remember saying you wanted to invest some of your wealth?'

Billy looked up from the dish. 'Yes,' he answered, unsure of where this conversation would lead.

'I have an idea for an investment you might like,' he said.

'Tell me what you have in mind and I will think about it,' Billy replied, wondering where this conversation was leading.

James smiled. Like Billy's father, he had proved to have an astute mind, having talked at length only a few days before as to how the young man should invest some of the gold from his fortune.

Billy had taken on board all that he had to say, but, after giving the matter some thought, he'd come back with a well-founded reason as to why he couldn't take such advice.

'Martin will be arriving here soon…' James began.

Before he could say any more, Billy interrupted him. 'Is he coming to take me back to France?' he asked.

'No. He's been in London on business and wants to see you as soon as he arrives.'

'And when will that be?'

'Maybe tomorrow, or even next week. It all depends on how long his business in London takes to complete.'

'What do you think he wants with me if not to take me back to France?'

'It's not so much what he wants with you, or what I want, but what you may want with him! He has need of gold, it's true, but if you invest some of your inheritance with him, you will quickly see a high return on your money, as your father did, and what then? With more capital you would soon be able to go into business for yourself.'

Billy sat for some time, silent and deep in thought, watching as the fire spluttered, its sparks flying up the chimney, like his thoughts. Perhaps this was what his father had meant for him to do, to go into business with the Captain, to continue with his business association.

At first, Billy had worried if he would be doing the right thing and that concerned him, but, the more he thought about it, the more confident he became. He knew that he was young, but he already had a little knowledge of finance and, with his education and upbringing, he knew that he should be able to hold his own in business. Perhaps, in time, he might even become the owner of a trading vessel.

He suddenly felt excited at the prospect of becoming a ship owner and couldn't wait for Captain Sawyer to appear; the Captain was a man accustomed to dealing with traders, and Billy was quite certain that he would be the man to advise him. All Billy had to do was to curb his impatience and wait for the day when the Captain arrived.

That particular night, Billy hardly slept at all for his excitement. He had too much thinking to do. He knew that he had to start and make decisions on what he should do with the gold and coins that languished in the wooden chest at the end of his bed, and then the jewels. Yet common sense told him that a young lady would one day come into his life who enamoured him, and who he would take as his wife, and then the jewels would adorn her neck and arms and ears as they had his mother's. It didn't help that he couldn't get the images of his parents from his mind whenever he touched the contents of the chest, wondering what action his father would have taken had he been in his shoes. It was as though his parents were with him. He even imagined that he could hear his father's voice talking to him as he had in the past. Serious as always, but there were no words of wisdom for him that night. Had his father still been alive, Billy was certain that he would have persuaded his son to follow the advice of James and use some of his inheritance to finance the smuggling activities of the village, but Billy had to be sure that this would be the proper use for his already considerable fortune. Did he really want to become richer than he was already? Maybe he did, but he was not necessarily certain of the reason why at that point. Neither did he want to be caught financing a smuggling run, for that would mean his fortune would be lost, along with his reputation, should the landing fail.

It was quite some time before he eventually fell asleep and, when he did, he slept fitfully, for he had yet to make up his mind what he was going to do. He did make one decision, however: he would do exactly as the Captain advised, with one or two suggestions of his own thrown in for good measure.

It was several days before Captain Sawyer finally came knocking on the door of the cottage one evening and walked in.

After Sally and James had made him welcome, he reached out and shook Billy's hand. The young man could see, from his face, that he was delighted to see him again.

'Billy, you're looking well,' he said. 'The Cornish way of life obviously suits you.'

'Yes, sir, it does,' Billy said, his thoughts more on learning what the Captain wanted from him.

But once supper was over, the four of them talked. There was much to say and discuss, so it was late before Captain Sawyer left to go to The Pilchards Inn, where he planned on spending the next few days.

By the time Billy went to his room, his head was spinning from all that had been said that evening. With still no firm idea as to what the Captain's plans were for his future, or whether he would be returning to France with him, he slept, dreaming of his past life until the face of Louise Spencer filled his thoughts and his dreams suddenly took another turn.

Chapter 5

Martin Sawyer. Captain of the *Mary Anne*

My first encounter with Willelm had been many years ago in Paris, at the home of his father, the Marquis D'Anville. I remember the boy had been quite young at the time, probably only seven or eight years of age, but it was a day I will never forget. I had been invited to meet Henri at his home by a mutual friend, who was someone I had done business with in London many times over the years, ever since I had acquired the Mary Anne. *Before I continue, I must explain I had spent several years in the British navy, after having had the good fortune to fall in love with Catherine, a young woman whose father thought I was unfit, morally and in every other way, to be his daughter's husband. (He was probably quite right in his assessment of me as a person, and of my character, but at the time thankfully, this had no bearing on Catherine, or her lasting affection for me.)*

Being a wealthy man and afraid of losing his only daughter to a man he considered unworthy of her affections, he decided to 'buy me off,' in an effort to get rid of me. Without my conscience troubling me one jot, I took the small fortune he offered and set about making myself even more desirable to his daughter! I must confess I had no battle twixt my head and heart, especially where my love for Catherine was concerned.

Being the rogue he thought me to be, it didn't take long for me to treble the amount he'd given me, for at the time I had a love of gambling. Within a short time, I had gambled his money for a stake in a game that thankfully I won, enabling me to buy a luggar from the Dutchman, Jaden Grist, but that is another story. Acquiring the luggar (which I swiftly renamed the Mary Anne, *after my mother) set me on my way to making a small fortune, and I was soon able to repay the money I'd taken from Catherine's father. It was only then, and with his blessing, that I married Catherine, the love of my life.*

Within a year, I had fathered my own daughter and was the happiest man alive, until, suddenly, tragedy struck; just a few months later, my beloved wife died of a fever and I was left to bring up my daughter on my own.

For a man who spends most of his life at sea, this was an impossible task. Believing my daughter, Eva, would be better off with her grandparents, I left her with them, to bring her up as a presentable young lady. I'm quite sure at the time they would have preferred it had I agreed not to see my daughter again, but this I refused to do and, although my time spent with her was but a few days each year, she was nevertheless my daughter, and I loved her, as I had loved her mother. As she grew up, she too came to realise and understand that although the sea ruled my head, my heart belonged solely to her, as no other woman had ever replaced her mother in my affections, and neither had another woman ever slept in my arms, nor would they.

Eva would have been much the same age as Willelm when I first became a friend of his parents. Had our children met as youngsters, I'm sure they would have liked each other, even though they were polar opposite in appearance: Eva was as dark haired as Willelm was fair. However, like Willelm, she was highly intelligent. She could

111

speak French, and had a smattering of Italian and Spanish, having grown up in a house with educated grandparents, who, thank goodness, had believed in giving her every opportunity to learn, even bringing in governesses from the three countries to teach her. By this time Willelm could also speak several languages, including English, which he told me some time later he'd learnt from when I talked with his father, which led us to enjoy many conversations as he got older. By then, he would tell me of his hopes and dreams, mostly of the time when he would be old enough to join his father at the bank the family owned. This was his main ambition. He longed to work with his father and I had smiled at the very precociousness of such a young man, for banking was indeed a serious business. At the same time I agreed with him that it was a necessary business and that maybe, one day, he would make his way in the world of finance, not realising how prophetic my words were at the time. As for my daughter, I only hoped she would make a good marriage to a man that her grandfather approved of. For the time being, however, that was in the future and at that moment, I had no need to worry on that score.

By this time, Willelm's father, the Marquis D'Anville and I, had become close friends as well as trusted business associates, an incredible occurrence considering the differences in our heritage and upbringing. He'd financed many of my ventures from his own pocket, especially those I first made to the Spice Islands. (Journeys that were to make us both exceedingly rich.)

Along the way, I somehow managed to get involved in smuggling contraband goods, bringing some of the goods I acquired into Cornwall at times, especially into Polperro, my home village, where my brother James and his family lived, and still do.

It was always my intention to retire from the sea one day, once I had made my fortune; to marry and live in Cornwall. However, France was in turmoil with its internal problems, in part due to the disastrous weather, which in turn led to a failure of the crops and widespread famine, and then its internal financial problems. It seemed my dreams of retirement might have to wait a while longer, for there is always wealth to be made from others' misfortunes, and I was not a man to step aside and ignore any chance that came my way.

The French people became angry at the indifference and the inability of the King, and his ministers, to solve the country's problems and, believing they would be better at solving the problems themselves, it was then they started to revolt. The revolutionists' intentions were to overrun the despicable regime of the monarchy, and for the populace to set up a new republic, which would be run by the people, for the people.

Suddenly, instead of me buying the luxury goods still available for those with gold to spare and trading with them, I was soon transporting Frenchmen and their families, those who wanted to escape this new regime, across the Channel, especially those who could afford to pay for the privilege and who had the foresight to see what lay ahead for France. I took them to safety in England, until France was settled and they could return home. The revolutionists were certain it was those with wealth and status, such as aristocrats, who were at the root of the country's problems and, with them disposed of by the guillotine, France would soon be the perfect country to live in. If only this had been true, as the country was soon embroiled in yet another war with England.

And so any plans for retirement I might have been considering, were of course put on hold. Without any serious problems, my fortune increased, as did that of my friend, and by now my business associate, Henri, Marquis D'Anville. Except that, as time moved on, he failed to understand his family's lives were in great danger.

He risked much by not taking advantage of our friendship and moving out of the country, even though I pleaded with him at every opportunity. I always knew he would be denounced as a traitor to France, simply because he refused to believe he was in mortal danger. Sadly, my fears were realised when I learnt later of his and his wife's deaths at the hands of the revolutionists, be-headed, as were many of their friends, by the infamous Madam Guillotine.

Over the years I had had much to do with the Marquis, both of us being sociable people who enjoyed each other's company in business and in pleasure, and soon we became trusted friends. At the same time, I watched as Willelm grew to become a handsome and intelligent young man. Private tutors were educating him, as in most aristocratic families. He was already fluent in several languages by the time he was thirteen. I think it was then I realised he would be a force to be reckoned with when he reached adulthood and entered the banking world, an ambition he had set his heart on. I must admit, I looked forward to seeing him prosper, as his father had before him. They were two of a kind, which made it even more poignant when the Marquis and his lovely wife were tragically arrested and executed for being nothing more than well bred.

But I am getting ahead of myself. There was even more unrest in France by the time Henri and Angeline were arrested. Rioting and plundering throughout the region became a daily occurrence, with

114

much talk of the people demanding that the country should become a republic. The King, and anyone with royal connections, became even more detested. These were sorry days for the monarch and his poor wife, with the country treating them with contempt and suspicion. Like even the poorest of the aristocrats, they were both despised.

I knew Henri and his wife, Angeline, to be upright citizens, genuine in their regard for those in their employ, treating them with care and consideration. As far as I knew, the thought never entered their heads that their way of life would ever change.

As an outsider, looking in on the country's dilemma, I could see France was faced with huge problems that at the time seemed insurmountable. The events that followed would be all the proof I needed to know that my instincts were right, as what I had long suspected turned out to be the truth. The riots and other events that followed, in and around Paris, as well as further afield in the country, proved my point, but by then it was too late to save my friend Henri and his beautiful wife, leaving me to worry for the safety of their son, Willelm.

Several months after returning from one such journey of taking aristocrats across the Channel to England, I received a message from Henri, requesting that I pay him a visit at his home in Paris. This I did, believing this visit would be like many others I had made in the past; a social occasion, as well as one where we would spend our time talking about the next voyage that I was intending to take. We would discuss the goods I would be bringing back, as well as the profits we would make.

As I have already said, Henri had funded many such trips in the past and, between us, we had made more money than I had ever envisaged possible. I was always careful not to expose him to scrutiny for his part in any of my plans. So far, this had been successful, but, on the day of my visit, I could see that he was greatly troubled. Angeline was present at the time and, while she was in the room, Henri denied my theories as being wrong; when she left the room, he finally admitted what I had feared for some time was right, telling me how he believed he might already have been denounced.

This was my worst fear. Much to my dismay, he confided that he believed that their lives were in great danger. Finally, he admitted he was afraid of the future, especially knowing he was under suspicion from the revolutionists and that it was probably only a matter of time before he would be arrested.

I asked after Willelm, but Henri assured me that he was safe, at least for the time being. He was staying with his tutor in the country, where he was finalizing his studies, before returning to Paris to work with his father in the family bank in a few months time, when he would be eighteen years of age. Once I heard Henri's suspicions, I feared for Willelm's young life as well.

My conversation with Henri that day had been a long one, most of the time taken by myself pleading with him to let me take them to England to safety, but my talk was to no avail. Even knowing his life was in danger, Henri still refused. His obligations were, he said, to his various employees, those at the bank, as well as his servants in his homes. They came first and were foremost in his life and therefore he would not countenance, at any time, or under any circumstances, leaving his home or his business to its fate, and neither would he agree to myself taking his wife and son to safety without him. He did have one request though: that I should take some personal items he had already packed for safekeeping with me. These would be for Willelm and, if I heard he and his wife had been arrested and their lives lost, then my undertaking was to take the items, as well as Willelm to England and keep him safe until the boy could claim his inheritance in France. He then asked that I become the boy's guardian until he was of age, an honour I accepted willingly, believing it would be a sorry day if and when I was called upon to carry out my obligation.

As his trusted friend, I assured Henri I would do everything in my power to keep Willelm safe. With a heavy heart, I shook his hand, knowing I could well be saying my final farewell to a brave and honourable man and his wife, none of us knowing if we would ever meet again.

More than a year has passed since that day in Paris, and Willelm is now safe in Polperro with my youngest brother, James and his wife Sally, living in the same Cornish village where I was born and grew up. He's growing into a fine young man from the snippets of news I have received, and has settled down well to life in the small village. He is, or so I understand, working hard with James, and is well respected in the village. I have made plans to visit Cornwall quite soon, but first of all I have my own business to attend to in London, and then I plan to lay up the Mary Anne *in Plymouth for a week or two for some minor repairs to be carried out and for more guns to be fitted. Armoury is something I need to enable me to continue combating piracy that is endemic in the West Indies, my plan being to travel there sometime in the near future. Once this is done, I intend to travel to Cornwall, to see my beloved daughter and to see for myself how Willelm is progressing, for the time is fast approaching when Willelm will soon become a man, and some thought must be made as to his future. Not that I can ever see him returning to France to claim his inheritance, as the troubles and wars there are not for the likes of him. I would rather he stay where he is safe. Until I've spoken to him, I will just have to wait and see, for he might well have other ideas as to how he wants to live his life, after living in the peace of Cornwall.*

As for my own life, I think of my daughter often and know, when I visit Cornwall, I will see her again. It is her future that also weighs heavy in my heart, the older I become. She is at an age when young men will soon be eying her up as a potential bride, and what if she should get involved with someone like myself, when I'd been younger? How would I feel, if she met and fell in love with such a ne'er-do-well as I'd once been? It's this realisation that makes me feel sorry now for the grief I caused my father-in-law when I fell in love with his daughter!

After sailing into the port of London and completing my business there, the crew and I sailed the Mary Anne *into Devon waters, anchoring at Plymouth where, as I have already said, the ship was to be put into the dockyard for some minor repairs (the result of a skirmish we'd had with pirates the last time we sailed in the waters of the Caribbean) and where new cannons are to be fitted, ready for the* Mary Anne*'s next journey back to the selfsame islands. I know those waters well and the dangers of sailing there; it is where piracy is rife and a plague rages in the area., Getting my ship well armed has to be my first consideration if we are to hold our own against those brigands of the sea. It is also vital to my business that I keep* my crew safe and the cargo of trade goods secure, so that I, and my associates, can continue to prosper.

Whilst the work was being carried out on the Mary Anne, some of the crew were 'stood down' to enjoy a rare few days with their families. Mostly, these were the men from the seafaring villages around Plymouth, as well as a few from Cornwall, as all my crew were West Country men, free both in mind and body. I never believed in having 'pressed men' on board my ship, a fact that has stood me in good stead in the past and one I intend to continue.

Leaving Jed Pengelly, my good man from Looe, who happened to be my first mate and second in command, in charge of the few men left on board to oversee the work. I took a ferry across the Tamar and hired a horse upon the other side of the river, before riding into Cornwall where I intended to see my brother James, his wife, Sally, and, of course, Willelm. After I had done that, I would then go to see my daughter, Eva, who lives with her grandfather near Fowey, but that was only a short ride on horseback from Polperro.

My journey into Cornwall was uneventful, as I avoided the places where I knew robbers were likely to be found, lurking, ready to waylay and rob any unsuspecting traveller. Knowing the countryside as well as I did, I avoided any trouble and reached the village well before dark, stabling my hired horse at the Crumplehorn, the local livery stables situated at the edge of the village, before walking down to the harbour.

I loved that walk! Perhaps it was the silence and peace that descends on the village when darkness begins to fall, or was it something else? I only know I loved the feeling as I stepped out of the livery stables, knowing I was nearly home, glad to once again call myself a Polperro man, a feeling many a Cornishman has shared when returning home from abroad.

As I reached the centre of the village, all that could be heard was the sound of the sea, lapping against the granite stones of the harbour, which was full of fishing boats, all waiting for the early morning tide.

I could see hazy tendrils of smoke pluming out of cottage chimneys. At the same time, I could smell the scent of the sea, mingling with that of the wood fires all filling the air, evoking memories of my youth. For a while, I was transported back to my younger days, when my parents would be waiting for us children to return home in time for supper.

The cottage door opened at my first knock. Immediately seeing and recognising me, James threw his arms around my shoulders and pulled me into the room. Sally was busy at the table, serving food from her cooking pot. Sitting at the table, waiting for the evening meal, was Billy, the person I'd come to see.

He'd grown taller and, if it were possible, was even more handsome than the last time I'd seen him, which would have been the night we had sailed into the bay, and he'd left the Mary Anne in a rowboat full of contraband, unaware he would not be returning to the ship, to go wherever the Mary Anne was next destined to sail. I never expected him to forgive me for what he must have thought as being his abandonment in a strange place, but from the look on his face, he had!

Like James and Sally, Billy had been expecting me. He rose from the settle and thrust out his hand in greeting and bowed, as I would have expected; his demeanour still that of an aristocrat, an *automatic action that no amount of working with rough seamen would ever obliterate.*

Smiling broadly, Sally reached up and kissed me on the cheek, after telling me to remove my outerwear, damp from the evening mist that was settling over the rooftops. She then placed a dish, filled with steaming fish stew in front of where she indicated I should sit. In only a few minutes, it was as if I'd never been away, the easy familiarity of family life taking over.

I needed to talk to Billy, to find out how he was faring in his new life. Once I'd satisfied my hunger, I asked him if he was happy and settled with James and Sally. That wasn't the only reason I needed to talk to him, as I wanted to ask him about his inheritance I had taken from his father's own hands. Not that I knew the contents in the chest, but I had guessed from its weight that it must contain a great amount of gold. If my thoughts were correct, I was more than a little interested in knowing how much. Also, if he'd given any thought as to how he had decided to invest it, but that would come later.

I could see for myself the lad had settled easily into living with James and Sally, and I wondered just how much he had told them of his previous life. Did they realise he was the son and heir of an aristocrat, more used to a life of wealth and privilege, with servants to do his every bidding and that now he really was the rightful Marquis D'Anville since his father was dead.

Billy was now an aristocrat, akin to royalty, with his former life completely different from the one he was now leading. If they did know his circumstances it certainly hadn't impressed them, and neither had it made any difference to how they behaved towards him. Poor and uneducated James and Sally might be, but that didn't mean

121

my brother and his wife had no manners or, for that matter, that they didn't know how to treat a stranger thrust into the heart of their family. As for Sally, I could see she'd grown to love the lad, as though he were her own flesh and blood. As I watched, she looked at him with such love and pride whenever he spoke it made me smile. Even James deferred to him, acknowledging the younger man's superior education and birth.

As for Billy, he sat and ate with great gusto, heaping praise on Sally's skills as a cook, with equally as much praise for James and his skills as a sailor, as well as that of a fisherman.

It was indeed fortuitous that Billy had gone to stay with them and I said as much, giving my own thanks for their hospitality on Billy's behalf, as well as my own, causing great embarrassment to my brother and his wife, as well as to Billy.

Later that evening, Billy brought down a little of his inheritance to show me, which, to my mind, seemed an enormous amount of wealth for someone so young. I didn't know then that Billy was more than capable of managing his own finances without any interference on my part, or on anyone else's for that matter.

The evening went well and it was late into the night before I left them to go to The Pilchards, where I knew a bed would be waiting for me. After wishing them all goodnight, I went on my way, promising to return the next day, as I wanted to speak further with Billy.

As I made my way to the inn, nothing stirred in the village. All was quiet that night; no sounds to be heard of horses with muffled hooves, or of men, puffing and panting, as they carried heavy loads from off the backs of their packhorses; neither were there any sounds *of doors being opened and shut quickly, as contraband goods were taken into the cottages to be hidden in cellars, or under nets in the sail lofts, and the many other places it would be imprudent of me to disclose. Thankfully, this was not a night when the women of Polperro would be worried sick over their husbands and sons, for they were all abed and sleeping, as good people should. It would be the morrow when another ship, laden with contraband goods, would come creeping silently into the bay. Then these same good folk would be fearful, as any smuggler or his wife would be, when danger is abroad and the Excise cutter is lingering just along the coast, waiting for the first sign of a ship in full sail making its way towards Cornwall, heading to one of the many bays or coves where smugglers, with their horses and carts, would be waiting to unload goods that would bring in a fine sum of money for those who had waited so patiently for the ship to arrive.*

The next morning, I rode across the cliffs towards Fowey, to where my daughter lived with her grandfather in a grand house that commanded the best views of the coastline and the sea. It was a journey I had made often. Not as often as I would have liked, but whenever possible, given my peripatetic way of life. It had been nearly two years since I had last seen Eva and I knew she would no longer be the little girl I remembered, but a young woman. As I rode up to the house, I remembered the first time I'd met my father-in-law, before I had even become a young seaman.

I was lucky enough to have gone to the village school, where my teacher saw beyond my callowness to the potential that lurked somewhere in my head. He saw and understood my intelligence, as well as the spirit in me that poverty would never tame. It was to this man I owed my later good fortune, for he spoke to my mother and father, convincing them I should attend classes after school had finished, instead of working on the fishing boats, cleaning them after the catch had been unloaded, as I was too young at the time to go to sea full-time. He thought I had the potential to make something of myself but, as I came from a poor family (as were most of the families in the village), the few pennies I earned from cleaning the boats were a vital part of my family's income. Mr Brewer, my aforementioned teacher, knew and understood this. He told my parents that, for every day I attended his class after school had closed for the day, he would give them what I would have earned (which was greatly generous for a man whose income was paltry, to say the least). This left my parents with no option but to agree to his proposition, and so it was through his generosity I became disciplined and educated, regardless of whether I wanted to be or not!

Once taken in hand by Mr Brewer, he educated me to such a standard I had no trouble convincing the Navy Board as to my suitability to train as a boy seaman.

On the day I left the village to start my training, I had walked along the cliffs to the grand house to say goodbye to Catherine, the love of my life, my childhood sweetheart.

She was a young girl I had known since we had both been small children, and my mother had been the sewing woman at her home. It was on that day I first met her father, the man I had now come to see and who, at that time, had detested me on sight. But that was many years ago and I knew on this day my arrival would get a different reception.

My father, a Polperro man, was born to be a fisherman. He scraped his living from the sea with my mother working at whatever she could in the village, and beyond, to help feed her husband and children. Once in the Navy, it would be my duty to see part of my wages, as little as they were, were sent home each week to my parents, as they had two other sons to feed and clothe, James and Simon, as well as my sister, Bethany, all much younger than I.

Several years later, both Simon and Bethany were dead, devastating my parents. Bethany was taken by a fever that was rife in the country at the time, a disease that had already taken many a life that year and then Simon died, tragically swept overboard from the fishing boat he worked on and presumed drowned during a fierce storm. This left James to carry the burden of looking after our parents until their deaths a few years later, by which time James had married Sally and had his own child; a son, Ben.

When Ben lost his life at sea, I feared for them both; the boy had meant the world to them, his loss as devastating as those of my siblings and so it had been good to see them both smiling again as Billy and I had talked. It was their good fortune he'd taken to them and I could see how much they already loved him, but now it was my turn to play the part of a devoted father. As I tied my horse to the iron ring set in the wall at the front entrance to the house, I wondered where Eva might be.

My thoughts, as always whenever I arrived at Cliff House, turned to her mother, Catherine. She had loved me deeply and waited for me, writing as often as she could whilst I did my training.

Whenever I had the chance to return home, she was the one person I wanted to see first, above all others. By this time, I had progressed in my naval career and my training to be an officer was nearly finished, all thanks to the influence of a friend of Catherine's, who had kindly spoken on my behalf when I applied to become an officer.

Catherine was twenty-five years of age by then, an age considered to be quite old for a woman to still be unmarried, and without a child. Her father was eager to see her married, preferably to one of the sons of the gentry that lived in the county, unaware she had promised herself to me. Had she mentioned this to him, he would have declared her to be mentally unstable and would have had her committed to an institution for the insane, such was his fondness for me.

He had thought I was a good-for-nothing young man the first time he set eyes on me, judging me only because of my poor background, mistakenly believing I had my eye on Catherine's future inheritance. He knew nothing of my character, only his suspicions that, as she was from a wealthy family, I had set out to seduce her with flattery, intending to marry her merely for my own financial gain. Nothing could have been further from the truth, for I loved her with every ounce of my being and would have died for her. Indeed, I often wished that I had, years later, when she passed away and I lost the love of my life.

Her father assumed, because I was a seaman, that I would have access to all the delights a naval man might be looking for in every seaport, quite sure my morals were low, that was if I had had any in the first place! He also thought it wouldn't take long for me to be well and truly corrupted by my naval life and therefore, under no circumstances, would I be permitted to court or marry his beautiful daughter, regardless of the fact that she loved me.

This state of affairs continued until I became a qualified officer with my master's ticket. I was then capable of owning my own ship, *if I could have afforded to buy one. And this is where fate stepped in, altering the status quo.*

Catherine told her father she wanted to visit friends who lived near Gunnislake. With his permission, for he knew the family well and believed them to be his equal, she travelled there, but it was me she was to meet and it was there that we sealed our love.

On her return home, she told her father we were to be married. Of course he was furious and determined I would not have his daughter's hand in marriage. It was then he 'bought me off', or so he thought.

With the money he gave me to disappear and leave his daughter alone, a small fortune in those times, I decided I would leave the navy and buy my first vessel, a three-masted lugger. This only came about because, at heart, I was an inherent gambler. Using the money her father had handed over, I gambled for a stake in a much bigger prize, which fortunately I won, taking over the ownership of a lugger from a Dutchman, Jaden Grist. Promptly taking on my present crew of West Country men,, within weeks we were sailing the ship into waters that were profitable, if you didn't mind where you went or with whom you did business.

It took very little time, from then on, to save the amount of money Catherine's father had given me and, on the day I repaid him in full, he grudgingly gave his consent to our marriage, still not convinced I was the best man for her. But she was certainly the best woman for me and I loved her dearly.

The following year, Eva our daughter was born and barely six months later Catherine was dead, taken from me by the same fever that years previously had taken the life of my young sister, Bethany.

And so it happened that Eva went to live with her grandparents, my own parents being long gone, and there she's been all these years, brought up by her elderly grandfather and, after her grandmother died, a succession of governesses.

The huge front door opened before I had chance to pull the bell cord and then suddenly, standing before me, there was a young replica of my beloved Catherine.

Eva ran into my arms and kissed me. My eyes filled with tears as I held her in my arms and clasped her tight to my chest, my face hidden in her dark curls as I drank in the sweet scent of her, letting it pervade my senses as I mentally gave thanks for her life.

'Papa, it's so good to see you!' she said, wriggling out of my arms and stepping back to take stock of me.

I felt in awe of this assured young woman who was no longer a child, but a young and beautiful woman. Everything about her reminded me of her mother, the way she tipped her head to one side as she scrutinised me, as if committing my face to her memory, and then the way her eyes crinkled as she smiled at me, a dimple appearing in her cheek, a sight I never failed to find enchanting.

'Come in quickly. Grandpa is waiting to see you,' she said, holding my hand and pulling me into the large hall that was much as I remembered. From there we walked into a room that overlooked the garden at the back of the house to where my father-in-law was sitting in a comfortable chair, his knees covered with a blanket.

I could see he had changed greatly since our last meeting, which must have been nearly two years ago; it was obvious he'd been ill, from the dullness in his eyes and the greyness of his skin. I was shocked at how much he had aged since I had last seen him.

He looked up as I walked towards him, his face lighting up as he recognised me. Holding out both hands to take hold of mine with his gnarled fingers feeling fleshless with age and infirmity, the blue veins stood out and distracted me for a moment or two.

'It's good to see you again, Martin,' he said, his voice no longer the strong voice I remembered, but weary now with age and infirmity. He held onto my large and calloused work hand, for even though I owned the Mary Anne *I still had to work as hard as my crew if I was to make a living from what we did. He looked into my eyes and smiled.*

'It's good to see you again, sir.' I said. And it was good to see him. We had learnt our mutual respect for each other the hard way, but I think on that day, he saw me more as a son in my own right, rather than the father of his beloved granddaughter.

I stayed for quite some time, talking with him, and then walking with Eva in the gardens of the grandest house I knew of in the area. We ate a midday meal together, just the three of us, and then, afterwards, my father-in-law and I sat and talked together some more in private. It was then I told him about Billy and his circumstances, and how the young man needed to find work, other than working as a fisherman.

My father-in-law listened intently, asking questions about Billy, and his family background; questions I thought at the time were just a part of his natural curiosity. I of course answered all his questions as truthfully as I could, wondering if he already had an idea for honest employment for the young man whom I had so timely rescued from persecution and possibly his death.

I rode back to the village later that afternoon and, as always, Eva was sad to see me go, clinging on to my arms and begging me not to leave, but I assured her I hoped to be back in Cornwall soon. Tearfully, she watched as I rode away from the house, down the lane to the cliff path that would take me back to the village.

Billy was working at the harbour as I walked back from the livery stables. He'd been doing errands for Sally and, in between times, he was helping James to prepare the Boy Ben *for the next day's fishing. He saw me before I saw him. Taking the opportunity, I asked him if he would like to walk with me a while, up to the cliff-top, before we had supper. On the way we talked, first of all about mundane things, and then to serious matters. I asked him outright if he'd decided what he was going to do with the contents of the chest.*

Giving a rueful laugh, he said, 'I've counted the coinage and stacked the gold, several times, and thought quite a lot!'

I could tell he was worried and concerned as to what he should do with his inheritance. 'I've even taken out the jewellery and looked at that closely. There's such an amount, I'm at a loss to know what to do with it all!'

'That's what I want to talk to you about. It's no good having wealth if you don't use it to your advantage. You must surely have some thoughts by now about how you can use it?'

'Yes, I have thought, but you may not approve.'

I laughed. It was not up to me to approve or disapprove, but I let the lad finish.

'First of all, I want to help Sally and James. They have so little, I would like to give them some of my wealth in gratitude for their love and care since I arrived in Cornwall. I had thought of buying some land for them, thinking it would be a good investment, and then

I thought perhaps buying them a home of their own would be even better. It would give them security. What do you think?'

'I think that would be a good plan to start with and it wouldn't take too much out of your chest to do just that. But how about making another investment first of all, that I can guarantee will bring in a large amount of money and within only a few months?'

It was at this point Billy put on his financier's hat and thought awhile. His father had trusted me, so why shouldn't he?

'How much would you need from my chest?' he asked, his guileless blue eyes staring steadily into my grey ones.

I told him the figure I had in mind. 'I need quite a large amount, as I have to go to France to secure the release of some people who need to be rescued. That takes a large amount of money; at present, I don't have the amount needed.'

Billy looked at me. His eyes widened.

'How much do you need?' he asked. 'I only need enough to help Sally and James, so I'm sure there is more than enough for you to use as well.'

I pulled him into my arms. 'Thank you, Billy, you are a true gentleman and you will be repaid a thousand fold for your goodness.'

The boy laughed, embarrassed at my show of affection.

We returned to the cottage later and while Sally cooked some food for us, I went to Billy's room where he showed me the chest and its contents.

There was more wealth before my eyes than even I had anticipated. Was it any wonder, I thought to myself, that the chest had been so heavy?

I looked at the piles of gold coins and bars of gold, stacked neatly on top of the chest, just a small amount Billy assured me of what was still inside the chest. He also said there was so much jewellery he had no idea as to what he could do with it, and then I saw a clutch of documents. From the way they were scattered on the bed I could see he'd started to study them.

'Help yourself!' he said casually, as only someone with an inordinate amount of wealth can do; pointing nonchalantly in the direction of the gold bars.

I took him at his word and set aside several gold bars, that I calculated would be as much as I needed for my present plans, smiling to myself as I looked at the amount left, realising there was more gold on top of Billy's cupboard than I would ever earn in my lifetime. The amount left on the chest appeared in no way to be fazing Billy, a certain sign of someone born to wealth.

Pointing to the ingots, I said. 'Billy, I want you to go and see my father-in-law and tell him how many more of these you have, and how much in the way of coins. He's a trustworthy man and will advise you the best way to keep them safe and, if you want to buy land and a cottage for Sally and James, he will tell you how to go about that as well.'

Being obedient and respectful to older and wiser people, as well as being educated and astute, Billy quickly agreed to my suggestion, promising he would go and see the old man as soon as he could.

Later, after we had eaten, I left him with a handshake and not without some misgivings, as I realised I was asking quite a lot from him, remembering he was still quite young. However, knowing his father, and the education Billy had received, I knew he would cope. He had a fine head on his young shoulders, one I hoped, along with his wealth, he would use for good. But I had no need on worry on that score, for Billy had many ideas (as I was to find out in future years)!

It was to be many months before our paths crossed again. Much was to happen in the intervening time, but that is in the future, of which, unfortunately, I have no insight.

Chapter 6

Meeting Eva

Over the next few days, Billy mulled over Captain's Sawyer's words and the request that he should visit the Captain's father-in-law. There was a problem: it was quite some way to walk to Fowey. Later that evening, he discussed the matter with Sally and James, who suggested that he could always hire a horse from the livery stables at Crumplehorn.

As Billy had been riding since he was a small child, this seemed to be a good idea to his mind. The next morning, having excused himself from going fishing with James, he made his way to the livery stables at the far end of the village, where he met for the first time with the owner, Daniel Parker, a Cornishman through and through. The fellow at first eyed Billy with suspicion when the young man entered the yard and asked him if could have the use of one of the animals, which was not surprising, considering that Billy was dressed in old seaman's clothes.

However, the Cornishman's attitude changed when he saw Billy's affinity with the horses that were being made ready for the day. Seeing that Daniel was none too keen to entrust any of the horses to him, Billy walked to where they were being groomed and volunteered his services. It was just as he had finished brushing the last one of the three animals, which he had been allotted to groom by an elderly man, whom Billy took to be the head groom, that in walked Daniel from across the yard to speak to him.

'You've done a good job there, lad,' he said, after a quick examination of the beasts, at the same time handing Billy a rake and a broom, 'but the stables need cleaning out and an extra pair of hands are always welcome.'

By the time Billy had finished, Daniel was ready to discuss business with him.

In his forthright way, Billy asked if he could buy one of the horses that he'd helped to groom.

Daniel looked at him with suspicion for a few moments, for the horses were not cheap hacks, but good horseflesh. He raised an eyebrow and an uncommitted smile, until Billy produced, from the inside pocket of his jacket, a leather pouch that held several gold coins which he shook out onto his hand. By this time, Daniel was definitely interested and, with Billy's refined speaking voice impressing him, he took the young man for someone better than the scruff that he had at first appeared to be. They haggled as to the price and, once they had agreed on one that was considered to be fair to both of them, Billy persuaded Daniel to throw in a saddle and reins as well.

The youngster had nowhere to keep the horse and Daniel agreed that Penhale, Billy's chosen name for his new steed, could be stabled and fed at the livery for a fixed amount, if it was paid in full, and in advance, for the next two years. Knowing that he would need a horse if he was to be able to work, Billy agreed and the pair of them shook hands. Billy felt that he had done well on his first business deal and, on top of that, he had also made a new friend in Daniel.

Once Penhale was saddled, Billy rode out of the village and made his way to the cliffs where he put the horse to gallop. Both of them enjoyed the fresh air and, for the first time since he had left his home in France, Billy found the freedom of being able to roam freely, with no thought that he was being hounded, exhilarating. At the same time, he attuned himself to the animal, sensing that it was enjoying the exercise equally as much as himself.

Billy rode hard, until he came near to the church where he dismounted, hooking the reins over the railings, and leaving the horse to catch his breath and to eat on the lush grass that surrounded the churchyard. The young man walked down the path to the church door, which, as usual, was unlocked. At the time, he though this to be rather odd but, when he mentioned it to James and Sally later, they had both laughed.

'It's normal practice hereabouts,' Sally said. 'It's so smugglers can use the church for stowing the goods sometimes, if the need arises!'

Billy wondered whether he would see the rector when he entered the church, but there was no sign of his presence. However, the church was not empty, as he had first thought, for he suddenly caught sight of the churchman's daughter, Louise, busily arranging freshly picked flowers on the altar.

Hearing footsteps walking down the aisle, she stopped and looked up from her task. When she saw who it was, she nodded in his direction and, after finishing her work came across, intending to speak to him.

'Billy, it's good to see you again,' she said, dropping him a small curtsey. This time, it was Billy's time to blush. 'I wasn't expecting to see you until Sunday.'

136

'I came on the spur of the moment,' he replied, watching as she too coloured at his direct scrutiny. She was beautiful, of that there could be no doubt. 'I have just bought myself a horse from the livery and I wanted to give him a ride and explore the countryside.'

She looked surprised and slightly incredulous at his words, raising delicate arched eyebrows over hazel eyes; her tone of voice told Billy that she disbelieved him, for he did not give the impression of being a man of means.

'You bought a horse? That must have cost you a fine sum!' She was obviously curious as to where he had found the money to pay for such a purchase, but she was too well-mannered to ask directly.

'Yes, it did, but my inheritance just about covered it,' he said. Even though he liked her well enough, he had no intention of telling her how much his inheritance was or, indeed, what he intended doing with it; perhaps he would later, but not right then. 'How did you get here?' he asked, having noticed that there was no carriage waiting outside the gates.

'My father brought me in the pony cart. He will be coming to collect me later, as we have a luncheon to attend at midday. Perhaps, now you have your own horse, you will come and visit us one day?'

'I would like that very much,' Billy said. 'I must be on my way too; I have an appointment but no idea which direction I should be taking.'

With that, he raised his hat and bowed, in his aristocratic French way, and, with a smile, she dropped him a curtsey in return, her cheeks colouring as she caught his eye.

Billy went to where Penhale was waiting; the horse's ears pricked up as he saw his master walking towards him and Billy knew then that this animal was going to be his dearest companion in the months to come. Penhale was as spirited and intelligent as any of his late father's highbred horses had been, which was exactly the way that he liked his horseflesh.

He mounted and, as he turned to heel the horse into a trot, he looked back and saw Louise waving. He waved back, knowing she too was someone that he would be getting to know better in the future, especially now that he had means of travelling.

For the first time since landing on the shingle at Talland Bay, Billy really began to like living in Cornwall. Perhaps the place had always been his destiny, rather than working in the stuffy premises of his family's bank in Paris.

Billy rode down to the harbour and left Penhale tied to some railings while he went to the cottage to speak to Sally. He wanted to tell her where he was going and to gain her approval of the horse, as well as get her directions as to where he might find Sir John Inney's house.

With the information that he needed, Billy wheeled the horse round and headed back up the lane to the cliffs (this time going in the opposite direction to the church), out along their heights, taking the route for Fowey.

He rode easily on his new horse, letting the animal have its head, until they came upon a turn where a signpost, with the name 'Cliff House' and an arrow burnt into its wood, pointed the direction that they needed to take.

As he rode up the carriageway, Billy was amazed at the size of the solidly built granite house, standing foursquare in grounds that were, he thought, nearly the equal to those of his family Chateau in Brittany (discounting the farmland).

The house itself was very grand, obviously belonging to a man of some distinction; at the same time, in spite of its grandeur, it still had the look of a much-loved home.

Polished granite pillars stood either side of a covered portico entrance, with an iron ring set in the wall at one side for his horse's reins, and on the other, a bell pull that he took hold of and rang after he had dismounted and tied his horse securely.

He could hear the bell ringing inside the house and, within minutes, the huge front door opened.

Billy was expecting to see a manservant in attendance but, to his astonishment, standing in front of him, and waiting for him to speak, was the most beautiful creature that he had ever seen, dressed in a fine blue silk gown, cut low to show off her young figure. She was about his height, slender of build, with dark hair that hung past her shoulders in ringlets, caught at the back with a blue velvet ribbon that matched the colour of her eyes which were the deepest of blue and fringed with black lashes. Those eyes, staring into his, had a guileless look and a candour that he found quite disconcerting, dressed as he was in his old seaman's clothes, but he knew, in an instant, that he was in love!

'Is Sir John expecting you?' she asked, rather imperiously, and her haughtiness amused him.

'No. He isn't, but I've been asked by Captain Sawyer to come and see him. If Sir John is at home, I would be obliged if he could spare me a few minutes of his time.' Billy could put on airs and graces as well, for he had grown up attending King Louis of France at his court.

At the mention of Captain Sawyer, Billy saw her start and wondered if she was Eva, the Captain's daughter.

'Please come in,' she replied. 'I will enquire if my grandfather will see you.'

Her reply answered Billy's question. She ushered him into a very grand entrance hall, where she motioned for him to take a seat before she headed off into a room that was presumably the old man's study.

Within a few minutes, she reappeared. She beckoned him to go across the hallway and, without formally introducing him, closed the door after he had entered the room, leaving him to face her grandfather, Sir John Inney, alone.

Billy was unable to tell which of them was the more surprised; Sir John or himself? He supposed that, in purely aristocratic terms, he outranked him. However, that was incidental now, since Billy was nothing more than a mere émigré.

Sir John was sitting down as Billy entered and, as the young man walked towards him, he tried to stand. Billy thought at first that he was crippled and begged him to sit, bending forward to take his proffered hand.

'It's good to meet you,' said Sir John, looking at him from under a thatch of silver hair; his rheumy eyes gave forth such a stare that, had Billy been one of the junior officers in his regiment, the young man would have quaked.

'Thank you! It's good to meet you too, Sir John. My friend, Captain Sawyer, has spoken highly of you and believes you might be able to help me.'

'I expect we will be able to help each other, if I am to believe my son-in-law. You must stay for lunch,' he said, quickly changing the subject and giving himself time to further assess his visitor. 'We're having some friends joining us for luncheon today and it would be good for you to get to know some of our local society.'

Billy looked at him in amazement. Did Sir John not see that he was wearing an old seaman's cast-off clothing? Obviously not, but it was clear that he wasn't dressed to meet company, especially if they were part of the higher echelons of Cornish society. He said as much to the old man, who just laughed, and rang the small bell that sat on the table at his side.

The door opened and in came the same young woman who had greeted Billy when he had arrived.

'Eva, this is Billy, a good friend of your father. Take him upstairs and see if you can find him something decent to wear. He's staying for lunch! There must be something suitable and remember, he is a gentleman!'

Billy followed Eva up the very grand dark oak staircase and then along a landing, until she stopped outside a room that she then entered. The young man followed her into a large room, with huge floor-to-ceiling cupboards ranged around the walls.

She opened the first cupboard door and looked inside, and then, with a sigh of disgust she closed it and moved onto the next.

'Nothing ever gets thrown away in Cornish houses,' she said in an offhand manner. 'There's more stuff here than enough, it's just a matter of opening the right cupboard until I find what I'm looking for!'

'And what exactly are you looking for?' Billy asked.

'I'm looking for clothes that will fit you, of course!' she said in the same imperious tone of voice she'd used earlier, the voice of someone who is used to dealing with truculent servants or those beneath her in society who had angered her.

She moved on, opening cupboard after cupboard, until she came to one where she obviously found what she was looking for.

'Right, this is what we need!' she said, reaching inside and withdrawing a pile of clothes that must have belonged to someone in the gentry, from the cut and quality of the items.

Billy felt indeed that this was his lucky day on two counts! First, new clothes, and second, meeting the most attractive young lady that he had ever had the good fortune to meet – apart, that is, from Marietta and Louise!

His heart, by now, was thumping in his chest, his emotions all awry with youthful lust for the lovely creature taking the time to see that he should be attired as a gentleman (something that she obviously thought he was not!).

First of all, she thrust into his waiting arms a pair of cream knee breeches, quickly followed by silk socks and a shirt of the finest linen. More items appeared; shirts with ruffles at the sleeve ends and at the neck; then cravats by the score, which she piled high on a table in the middle of the room. Holding up to the light each garment, piece by piece, she scrutinised them before selecting those she preferred, then passed them over for him to try on behind a screen that sat in a corner of the room.

Once he had donned the first outfit she had picked out for him, he began to feel like his old self again. It was a brown velvet jacket that fitted him as though it had been made just for him and was very similar in style to the one he had given to Henri Masson in exchange for his old jacket. Next, a pair of leather shoes with silver buckles that were exactly his size. As he donned each garment, he no longer felt like Billy Sawyer, cabin boy and trainee fisherman, but, once again, Willelm, the new Marquis D'Anville!

Eva meanwhile was on a mission; her intention was to make him into a gentleman. Suddenly, she stopped for a moment, her eyes

142

narrowing as she surveyed him, her lips pursed in thought, before turning away and rummaging in yet another wardrobe, finally coming up with yet another complete set of clothes, including a hat and polished boots, all eminently suitable for a country gentleman for when he went riding. These items, she told him, he was to change into before he went home and, to his surprise, he was to take the others with him as well!

It was a revelation to Billy that a complete stranger should care that he looked like a gentleman, when, from the clothes he'd been previously wearing, he appeared to be nothing of the kind; indeed, he had appeared more like a common seaman!

Now that he was properly dressed to appear in company, Eva led the way downstairs to a withdrawing room, where a servant had already helped Sir John to sit in a comfortable chair and await the arrival of their luncheon guests.

Sir John looked approvingly at Billy's outfit and smiled at him in a way that made him feel as if he had at last found another mentor, someone akin to his father.

For a few moments, Billy felt sad and depressed.

How my father would have liked this man! I know he would have approved; now all I have to do, to succeed in Cornwall, is to take Sir John's friendship and use every chance he can give me, as well as his experience, and use it to my advantage! Otherwise, I am nothing short of a fool!

A glass of fine sherry was pressed into his hand (he wondered if it had come in by the back door, a euphemism for having been smuggled into the county) and soon he was talking to Sir John of inconsequential matters; the serious talk would take place later. It was a surreal moment for Billy, for it was as though he was back in his parents' house in Paris, helping his mother and father to entertain their guests. It struck him that life in a Cornish home of quality was very much like that of an aristocrat's home in France, except that, in Cornwall, he was free to walk and to talk, with no one about to denounce him as a candidate for the guillotine, a spectre which, had he been in France, would still have been hanging over him. He mentally crossed himself, thanking God that He had thought to save him, but was it for a special reason or purpose that Billy had yet to know?

The young man could hear Eva in the adjoining room, no doubt the room that they were to dine in, where she was busying herself as the hostess, making sure the table was prepared as she wished, with a side table loaded with extra glasses and several carafes of wine and brandy.

Billy wanted to talk to Sir John, as Captain Sawyer had asked, but the old man patted him on the arm and said, 'Hush now, Billy, we will talk later, after my guests have gone.'

And so with that, Billy had to have patience, sipping at the fine wine, the likes of which he hadn't tasted for a long time, but which he appreciated all the more for that.

It wasn't long before there was the sound of visitors arriving and, to Billy's surprise, moments later, in walked Louise with her father. The rector appeared equally as surprised at his presence, although at first neither of them recognised him until he spoke.

Louise looked at him, her eyes taking in his new clothes and the difference they made to his bearing and manner. As for her father, he made no comment as to Billy's new mode of dress, as he had never seen him wearing his old seaman's clothes, only Ben's cast off's, which were marginally better than the old ones Billy was used to wearing.

Sir John introduced the young man formally. 'Rector, I would like you to meet William Sawyer. I'm hoping he will agree to come and work for me, but as yet I haven't asked him. So, until I have, and we have discussed his prospects, he can't tell you anything!'

The rector looked hard at Billy but said nothing. Sir John continued, with a laugh, 'For the time being, we will have to let the young ladies entertain him!'

Billy laughed as well, to be polite, as did the rector, although not quite as enthusiastically as the young man would have liked. Perhaps the churchman thought him to be from a questionable background.

Eva placed Billy between herself and Louise at the table, with her grandfather and the rector opposite. It was a pleasant enough luncheon and the food was delicious, as one would expect in a grand house. It reminded Billy of his mother's fashionable luncheons, at which he had always been expected to attend when he was free from his studies. Therefore, he had grown up learning to talk to her lady friends and their husbands, and, at that lunch, all his past training came to the fore. Instinctively, he knew that he had passed whatever first test Sir John had set for him, knowing that his heritage and upbringing was to his advantage.

He might have grown up attending royal events, but it was evident to Sir John that high company didn't impress Billy at all and why should it? The young man had been born into such a life; even though he was no longer going to be known as the Marquis D'Anville, he could still behave as though he was!

Later in the afternoon, after the rector and Louise had left, Billy went into Sir John's study with him and, once his manservant had settled him into his comfortable chair, they began to talk about the young man's future.

It was late by the time Billy rode back to Polperro and stabled Penhale. He walked back to the cottage, there to be greeted by James and Sally, eager to know what had happened to him, especially as they saw him wearing his new riding clothes and carrying the parcel of clothes that he'd been given at Sir John's.

Sally clucked with delight as she felt the silk and then the linen, brushing the nap on the velvet jacket with hands that were gentle, the fabric no doubt reminding her of other days in the past, her eyes shining with awe at the quality of the fabrics. Seeing her fascination with my new clothes, Billy couldn't resist asking her where Sir John would have found all the items that he was now wearing,

'He has always had nephews and apprentices staying, so it's quite natural he should clothe them. I used to make some of their clothes as well, when I worked at the house. Just look at the shirt you're wearing! I can see that's one I made years ago. Miss Eva must take good care of them!'

Billy said nothing more, just grateful for Sir John's gift, for fine clothes had always made him feel good and it was then that he decided, before he did anything else, that he would use some of his gold to make Sally and James's lives better. They were to have the best of everything that his gold could supply and the very first thing he intended buying was an outfit for Sally, as Billy intended to take her and James to visit Sir John Inney at 'Cliff House' just as soon as he could; for they too had to hear what Sir John proposed for him. However, all that could wait until the next day, as he was exhausted and, within minutes of getting into Ben's bed, he was sound asleep.

Therefore, he heard nothing of the horses, hooves muffled, as they returned to the village.

He had decided, on his way back that evening, that in the future it would be his goods that were brought in, and that he would be the one waiting anxiously for a rowboat to land on the shingle and disgorge its cargo. It would then be his responsibility to see the cargo was unloaded and taken to its various hideouts, before being dispersed to wherever it was finally bound. That night's cargo, however, wasn't his responsibility and, once again, he slept soundly in Ben's old bed.

Chapter 7

Sir John Inney

My life has been one of adventure and service ever since I can remember. I grew up in Cornwall as the only son of loving parents who had spent their lives working hard to improve the wealth of the family, so that, when I inherited my title, and lands on the death of my father, there was a significant increase in my heritance, By this time, I was nearly thirty years old and had been married to my childhood sweetheart for several years. We had been blessed with a daughter we named Catherine, after my paternal grandmother, an indomitable woman who was feisty as well as charming! In my younger days, I had been an officer in the Devon and Cornwall Light Infantry regiment, serving wherever there was trouble, as soldiers do, until the untimely death of my father and I had to return to civilian life to take on the responsibilities that came with my title and inheritance; the family wealth having being accumulated by the sheer diligence of my father and his father before him, who had had the foresight to see that Cornwall was a county where wealth could be taken from the land. It was through their foresight and intuition, and, to some extent, their bravery, for they went into uncharted areas of the world, to where the family became involved in mining ores and minerals from the ground, something that had been started centuries earlier, as can be seen in the many excavations in the county, starting in the Bronze Age, and possibly even earlier, for Cornwall is an

148

ancient land, inhabited at first by tribes that came from places far, far away, peopled by those who had brought with them ideas that were to infiltrate to other parts of Britain. By the time I was grown up, Cornwall was experiencing a time of prosperity that would change and violate its landscape forever.

During my younger days, I had journeyed to the Americas many times, travelling to South America and Mexico, staying with friends of my family at the hacienda, San Miguel near Huasca, where my father had made huge investments in the silver mines. It was there I came to have many adventures, on occasions escaping with my life, and being saved from certain death only by sheer good luck and the goodwill of those natives, who worked in the areas where I travelled. But these stories have no bearing on my present life, except to say they reinforced my desire to help another young man, one who I have come to know and to like and, more importantly, a young man I believe I can trust and have faith in.

My wife reared our daughter on her own whilst I was abroad with the army and also later, when I was travelling abroad on my family business, all of which she did with great fortitude and patience. Thankfully, Catherine grew to young womanhood without any problems, causing us no angst, until the day she fell in love with a young man that I failed at the time to have any faith in as a prospective husband. Perhaps it was because I knew Martin Sawyer came from a poor family. At the time, I thought him to be a waster, unaware I was going to have to change my mind when he turned out to be someone quite different.

But what can a father do when a daughter, such as Catherine, should fall deeply in love with a young man you believe to be a waster? You can do as I did, and try to pay him off, but by then he'd been mentored and educated by the local schoolmaster, who had encouraged him to better himself, knowing the young man to be highly intelligent, even though he came from a family of poor fishing folk; simple people who had had no benefit of an education. (This I found out later is no yardstick for whether someone is intelligent, or not.) His mother I knew quite well. She'd been a sewing woman at my home, and sometimes our cook, should our regular woman be away from the house. She was a kindly woman who, over the years, spent many days helping my wife to keep our home running smoothly. She also had a fine skill in the kitchen that I never saw bettered, even in the grand houses I visited, where fine food was cooked and served. As for the young man's father, I only knew him in passing, but he seemed to be a hardworking fellow, as well as being truthful and honest, or so I believed, not knowing at the time of his smuggling activities, illegal activities I only knew about later. I was shocked at first to learn that everyone in the village was involved, as were most of the people in the other coastline villages in the county, until I suddenly became involved... but that also is another story. Of course, I benefited from these activities, but that is not to be disclosed to the Excise men either, or they will come running to me for the duties unpaid to the Revenue!

I was glad when I heard the young man was about to enter the navy, believing his absence from the village would deter my daughter from wanting to marry him. Yet there is no fool like an old fool and these two young people managed, quite ably, to dupe me into me paying him off with what seemed at the time to be an enormous sum of money to stay away from Catherine! Of course this pay-off didn't work out quite as I had imagined! Backfiring on me in a way I could never have imagined. When Catherine assured me her affair with the young man was over, I, stupidly presumed that was the end of the matter, and again, like a fool, I believed her, never thinking for one moment she could tell me a lie. Meanwhile the young man had bought his own ship, using my money, of course, to buy a stake in a gambling session with a Dutchman. I myself did not believe in gambling, knowing it was a foolish way of losing all that one possessed, but, luckily, Martin Sawyer won, taking full control of the Mary Anne *and quickly amassing a small fortune on his first two trips to the Caribbean. This enabled him to repay the money I had given him to stay away from my daughter! Little did I know then that Martin Sawyer was not only the master of his own ship, but a master smuggler as well!*

It had never been my intention to sanction a marriage between them, but as soon as Martin Sawyer's circumstances changed, and I could see Catherine's devotion to him hadn't altered one jot over the years, I had in the end to give my blessing for their union and finally, I capitulated, and agreed they could marry.

I must say he turned out to be a loving husband to Catherine, and a good father to Eva, my granddaughter. It was just unfortunate that my beloved daughter should have died of a terrible fever within the first year of Eva's life and, of course, Martin was distraught, as were my wife and I.

He had to go back to sea, as it was his living, and he knew of no other that would be as profitable. From then on, we took care of Eva, bringing her up as though she was our own child. She's sixteen years old now, and beginning to show an interest in young men, and I dread to think what I would do if she were to take up with some young rogue, but what am I to do? I cannot lock her up and keep her away from the opposite sex. What sort of man would I be to do that?

I tried once before to prevent true love from being fulfilled, intervening between two young lovers, when I should have left well alone.

To my cost, I found out that interfering doesn't work, so, this time, I knew I would have to use a different method, but I also knew true love will always find a way of succeeding, no matter what! I'm pleased to say I had no worries on that score, once Billy Sawyer came into our lives.

Martin comes to see us whenever he's in Cornwall. He keeps his family ties close to his heart, and I know he loves his daughter more than his own life: also, he has made no plans to bring another woman into his life, which I believe to be a shame, for he is a good and loving man and it doesn't seem right that he should live the rest of his life without the love of a good woman beside him.

On his last visit, he told me about a young man he'd brought back from France. I had heard of this boy's family previously, from my business contacts in London. To hear they had been so cruelly killed was a terrible shock but, thankfully, Martin rescued the boy, who is now lodged with his brother, James, and his wife, Sally, which must be good for the boy, as I know them both well and would trust them with Eva's life, if need be.

Martin told me Willelm, whom he calls Billy, is well educated. He speaks several languages fluently, including English, albeit with a flourishing Cornish accent, and that he needs to work, doing something that will use his brains and his intellect. He has had a try at fishing with James, but Martin would rather he did something more befitting his station in life, the young man being the Marquis D'Anville, not that his name or title will carry any weight in Cornwall. But Martin has named him William Sawyer, falsely claiming him to be his son, in an effort to keep him safe.

I have been semi-retired for many years now, but I still have many interests that I think I could use the young man for, and I have asked Martin to send him to see me as soon as possible and I will take it from there.

And so it was, the day following Martin's visit, that the young man appeared at my door, where he caught not only my eye but if I am to believe the evidence of my own eyes, those of my granddaughter as well!

He impressed me straightaway; his looks and bearing were perfect, a credit to his upbringing, and he certainly looked like an aristocrat, even in his old clothes. As it was the day we were expecting the rector and his daughter for luncheon, I had Eva fit him out with some clothes that befitted his station in life, for it would be unseemly for him to look less than what he is. Also, it is my belief that it always pays to dress well if you wish to influence those with whom you want to do business. A lesson the young man had already learnt, or so I gathered, from my conversation later with him. It is also my intention that Eva shall play a part in his education on how to behave while doing business with the Cornish – and the English – although I'm sure he is well versed in the niceties of good behaviour. Being naturally well-mannered, and well-educated, he will take little training in the ways of the county's gentry that he will, if I have my way, soon encounter.

I have asked that he come and stay with us for a few days, that I might assess him, and for me to discuss with him how he can not only help me, but how I can help him. And so now I must wait and see how my prospective protégée develops… I have a feeling he will do me some good, as I must admit to being a little bored with retirement!

Chapter 8

Moving On

Billy came to look upon Sir John Inney in the same way as he did Martin Sawyer: part saviour and part father figure. They were the two people who had had the most influence on his life since the loss of his parents and the leaving behind in France of his good friend and tutor, Henri Masson.

First of all, after truthfully discussing his inheritance with Sir John, he took the old man's advice and arranged to bank most of his gold at the bank in Bodmin, the county town that was highly recommended, using some to purchase a house in the village for Sally and James. The house had to be one Sally liked, rather than one James would have chosen. Once Sally was satisfied with the purchase, and he had lodged money for them in gratitude for their hospitality, to ensure they would be able to live in some style, he then funded a couple of smuggling trips to the Channel Islands (a short distance away from Cornwall) for James and the crew of the *Boy Ben*. Only then, did Billy ride out to Cliff House, with his clothes packed in a new portmanteau (made to his design at the saddlers in Bodmin), to take up residence with Sir John and his granddaughter Eva.

Originally, Billy believed this was to be for only a few days, to see if he came up to the standard Sir John envisaged for his apprentice, but, once he had settled into the routine of the household,

Sir John managed to persuade him to stay permanently. The only sorrow he felt was leaving Sally and James, but, after explaining his reasons for leaving, Sally had reached out and held him in her arms for a while and it was clear that she understood.

Billy borrowed a cart from Sir John's stock of vehicles to carry the now much depleted sea chest back to Cliff House with what was left of its considerable contents, intent on using the remaining amount of his inheritance as frugally as possible; he knew that he would need a tidy sum of capital in the future if he was to achieve his aims of going into business for himself. The only problem was that, as yet, he had no idea what this business is to be,

Sir John and Eva were delighted to have him in the house; Eva especially, who, at the time, had already taken him completely to her heart. It was only a couple of years later that he learnt that she had imagined them to be a couple from the first day that she had met him, believing at the time that he had other things on his mind, rather than romance.

If only I had known!

Martin Sawyer made another visit to Cliff House before he sailed on his next voyage to the Spice Islands. He told them that he would be away for at least a year, which left Eva in tears, and Billy to comfort her as best he could, once her father had left. At the time, the young man wished that he could have gone with him, but he also knew that travelling to foreign climes would have to wait a while as he had work to do for his mentor, Sir John.

Unknown to him, Sir John had taken an instant liking to him. He learnt later that the old man admired his intellect, as well as his personality, even acknowledging his superior education and upbringing. Sir John had decided, at their first meeting, that Billy would be the ideal person to inherit his wealth and businesses; if the young man should fall in love with Eva and marry her, then, in time, he would have the great-grandchildren every man needed if his family dynasty was to continue.

To this end, Sir John made his own plans over the next few months, plans he intended carrying out. His first was to take Billy to see all the interests he'd inherited or acquired over the years; he wanted the young man to learn all there was to know of his businesses, as well as to meet the most influential families of the time in the county (mostly his business partners), and then others added to his list, those with similar interests in mining and fishing. The pair of them stayed at their grand houses in Cornwall and Devon, and even further afield, meeting their sons, as well as their daughters who, Sir John hoped, wouldn't captivate Billy before the young man had had the chance to get to know and fall in love with his beloved Eva. Of course, he wasn't to know that Billy was already in love with the young lady in question!

It was Sir John's plan for them to make a grand tour of the county, to see all his acquisitions, and all to be done by travelling on horseback, which he knew that Billy would enjoy. But when he discussed his plans with the young man, and then showed him the maps of where he intended for them to travel, Billy began to worry for the old man's health, knowing this would probably make his plan unfeasible. Sir John, however, didn't seem to think it would be a problem at all. He intended to take the journey slowly, staying, en route, with as many of his friends and acquaintances as possible and taking several months to complete his mission.

They discussed his plans and the places he wanted to stay at, none of which Billy knew. Of course, the young Frenchman was assured, they would be made more than welcome wherever they stayed. Being able to rest for a few days between visits would enable Sir John to recover before moving on, as he intended Billy to get a full picture of what was expected of him in the future, as well as to get to know the county.

Eva was the one person who worried the most about her grandfather's intention of travelling the length and breadth of Cornwall. Her main concern was whether he would survive the journey; she even enquired from his doctor as to how safe it was for him to travel such long distances, over rough terrain in some places, and all on horseback. Sir John had discounted taking a carriage as being inconvenient on some of the country roads and byways, and neither did he wish to inconvenience his hosts by bringing along a large entourage of servants, other than his valet, who had been with him since his days in the army.

Sir John didn't care a jot what anyone thought of his health, least of all his doctor, for Billy's arrival had injected him with a new zest for life and once again he was feeling in high spirits. For the first time in years, he was full of enthusiasm and keen to get started, especially when, almost daily, replies started to arrive from his friends and business acquaintances, saying that he and his young companion and valet/servant/groomsman or whoever he wished to accompany us, would be more than welcome to stay, as long as they wished, and that parties and dinners were already being arranged in their honour!

With his plans at last made for Billy's apprenticeship to commence, Sir John Inney was a happy and contented old man, one who couldn't wait for the day to arrive when they would leave Cliff

House and seek out the hidden parts of Cornwall where he had placed much of his wealth.

Eva was allowed to have her friend, Louise Spencer, the rector's daughter and her lady companion, to stay during their absence, in order to keep her company. Once they were installed and comfortable, Sir John and Billy, with Johnson, his valet cum everything else, mounted their horses and rode away; the young Frenchman was about to properly begin his apprenticeship.

They rode away from Polperro, heading across the county towards St.Austell, calling in first of all at the Stannary town of Lostwithiel, where Sir John had recently acquired a new mining interest, which he was keen for Billy to see. He also wanted his protégé to view the ancient castle, which, at the time of the Black Prince, had held a commanding position over the town and the river but was now derelict. They then rode onwards to St Austell, or rather into the lush countryside just outside the town, where the mining of kaolin was progressing quite nicely.

Onwards from there, they rode to Pentewan, again to view one of Sir John's many interests; this one, a newly built pilchard-packing shed. Then, on to Mevagissey, a small seaside village Billy had already seen, where smuggling was rife (and, as the young man knew, was one of the favourite places for the Revenue Cutter to lie in wait) and where Sir John wanted to view the new harbour he had invested in, as well as to assess the pilchard industry that was proving to be a thriving and profitable business.

Whilst there, they stayed with a family at Heligan, the first of the large country houses that they were to stay in. There, they could walk through the grounds down to the quay at Mevagissey to see the newly built sheds and watch as the fish were being salted, before they were packed into barrels and sent off to Portugal in one of the many ships that could now be found anchored outside the small village.

Heligan was a lovely house and one that Billy particularly enjoyed staying in as a guest, it being modern for its time, and where the daughters of the house were excellent company. Nothing was too much trouble for them, least of all their enthusiasm for teaching him the latest dances from London.

The family even held a grand ball in their honour, not that Sir John danced. Instead, he played cards that night with the master of the house, thankful that Captain Sawyer didn't attend, him being a master gambler, as his ownership of the *Mary Anne* attested.

After a few days rest at Heligan, for Sir John to recover, they then set off down the coast to Falmouth, where he had insisted, when they were first planning our tour, that they were to stay for some time.

It's a deep-water port that takes the largest ships afloat and, because of this, it was where the packet ships set sail for the colonies. Billy knew most of the routes, as Martin Sawyer had often talked of them whilst he had been aboard the *Mary Anne*. Billy also knew it was the Captain's intention to follow those same routes sometime in the future, journeys which, at the time, the young man had romantically thought might have included him!

As it happened, they ended up staying in Falmouth for over a week, as Sir John had much to do in the way of business as well as many discussions with his partners and other associates… including Billy, of course. All this fired the young man's imagination at the mention of buying spices and exotic items rarely seen in Cornwall, especially when their conversations were about places where the sun always seemed to shine.

After their prolonged rest at Falmouth, Sir John had recovered sufficiently for them to travel down the coast to The Lizard, the most southerly part of the county, to where serpentine stone was being mined and where that too was being exported.

Their hosts were some old friends of Sir John from his schooldays. This was a much more sedate visit, as his friends too were elderly and not capable of dancing the night away; at least their stay gave Sir John another chance to rest and enjoy their company.

Billy took the opportunity of enjoying their extended stay by taking long bracing walks along the coast, enjoying the sea air and the scenery, the coastline reminding him of the Breton coast in parts. Sometimes, as he looked out at sea, his eyes would well up with tears, his heart aching for his beloved home in Brittany, for this was a bleak and barren area in comparison with other parts of Cornwall that they'd so far travelled through; it was an area that he failed to like as much as other parts of the county, for he much preferred the more wooded areas around Lostwithiel and Mevagissey, but he could well understand Sir John's liking for the place, especially the superb accommodation and the wonderful food and drink his host and hostess provided for them. It was here that he had his first romantic encounter with a young woman, the granddaughter of the owners, also staying for a short visit, a young lady who made it quite clear that he was welcome into her bed at any time, should he so wish. However, being young and innocent, and in love with Eva, he had blushed furiously and politely declined her invitation.

From the Lizard, they then travelled down the coast, stopping to look at the tin mines en route, as well as making short flurries onto the moors at Helston, before going back to those on the coast, where some of the mines, to Billy's horror, went under the sea.

One day, it was proposed by a mine captain that Billy ahoiuld go down and see for himself the conditions that the men worked in. The very thought filled him with dread but, if he was going to invest some of his gold in mines in the future, then it was up to him to have a look. Out of curiosity, he went, and found them to be appalling, as well as very dangerous. It was then that he made up his mind to discuss the lack of safety in some aspects of mining with Sir John, just as soon as they arrived back at Cliff House; Billy believed that Sir John had a duty of care to those he employed, a fact that the old man agreed on after their discussion and one which he acted on as well, one of the first mine owners to do so.

Billy spent a great deal of what little amount of spare time he had by writing copious notes in his journal at the end of each day, wherever they were. This led him to ask questions at every opportunity of their hosts who, without exception, were all men who had business interests in either mining or fishing. They were all quite happy to oblige him, telling him facts and figures at the time that made little or no sense to him. However, he was about to learn what it was to be an investor and, in the future, he appreciated all the knowledge they passed on to him.

At Godolphin, they enjoyed several days visiting with one of Sir John's partners, who had arranged a gathering of several other families from the county to join them. This is where Billy enjoyed himself the most; hunting and fishing with the men during the day and then, in the evenings, dancing with the ladies. Once again, the latest dances were tried out and Billy found himself talking during the many intervals with several other young men and their sisters, who all seemed to be intrigued by his relationship with Sir John, believing him to be his grandson until he informed them that he was in fact his apprentice. This caused great amusement amongst Sir John's friends, and their wives and daughters, for they believed that only mines and engineering had such young men. Billy heard many months later that some of Sir John's acquaintances had followed his example after meeting him and had taken on young men to train in the running of their companies, all of which the young man thought to be an excellent idea.

They arrived at Marazion a few days later than planned, due to adverse weather conditions that had disrupted their travel arrangements. Once at the house, Sir John was taken ill, and they had to stay for a while for him to rest while he recovered. This illness worried Billy greatly at the time, but the old man quickly recovered and was soon clearly itching to be on his way again, just as soon as his host's doctor had given him the all-clear after warning him not to overdo the riding.

The doctor could have saved his breath, as Sir John insisted on crossing over the water to St Michael's Mount, to stay with the family who lived there and who were Sir John's greatest friends, before going on to Penzance.

This was the most interesting town of all those that Billy visited (at least, to his eyes), with its wide-ranging views across Mount's Bay from the house where they were staying. He thought the fanciful buildings made it the most elegant of all the towns in the county. It was, so their host informed him, a haunt for smugglers and for the navy men, who liked to press gang men from the town into the service of the King. This fact made him keep a low profile whenever he ventured anywhere without Sir John, or Johnson, at his side.

Then it was on to Land's End and St Just; mining areas, where Sir John also had interests. Then they were riding along the narrow coast road that overlooked the rocky coast; a graveyard for the many ships, or so Johnson informed Billy, ships whose lives had come to an abrupt end during one of the many storms that raged along this stretch of water in the winter months.

And then they were heading along the coast again, to the farthest west of the county, to St Ives; to where Sir John had even more mining interests he wanted Billy to see and become familiar with, each new mine different from the last.

From St Ives, they travelled the few miles inland to Hayle, there to inspect an engineering company Sir John had a new financial interest in. He spoke at length with the engineers of their new invention, a steam vehicle, and of how he could contribute financially (for he was always keen to add to his investments), before they rode to the north coast of the county, criss-crossing the moors. They then returned to the coast road once more, stopping off at all the other places where Sir John had interests, continually being entertained by the Cornish gentry at each of their stately homes, at the same time teaching Billy as much as possible, in as short a time as possible, about his businesses and his other interests, as if his time was running out and he had to tell his protégé everything that he had to learn in as short a time as possible.

They had been away from Cliff House for several months, and it was nearly two years since Billy had left the home of Henri Masson. He was beginning to feel tired himself, young as he was.

Surely, he thought, it was time for them to return home?

Even if Sir John wanted to carry on with his journey, Billy needed to give his head a rest, for it was filled with questions for which he needed to know the answers. Also, he needed to relax, to let all the knowledge that he had gained sink into his head, before any more was expected of him. Last of all, he wanted to see Eva!

And so it was, on a fine Cornish afternoon, with a clear view of the sea looking out towards Talland Bay and beyond, they rode towards Cliff House.

By then, Sir John was beginning to look like a tired old man. Together with his valet, Johnson, and Billy, his companion and apprentice, they rode up the drive to Cliff House, to where Eva was eagerly waiting to greet them. The granite house sparkled in the sunlight and looked wonderful, as did Eva, with her dark hair blowing in the breeze; she had already been forewarned by letter that they would be arriving that day.

Billy couldn't wait to tell her of their adventures and the places that they had visited, or of the people that they had met on their travels. There was so much for him to relate, especially the antics of the young men and their sisters and cousins (the nouveau riche of the county) that he had met at the dances held in the ballrooms of the grand houses in their honour. He told of how elegant the older ladies and their husbands had looked, dressed as they were in the latest fashions. No doubt, these had only recently arrived from London or Bath, a town that, to Billy's surprise, was a place where fashionable men and women had started to prefer to live, rather than in London, which was his own much-preferred place, being the more cosmopolitan from all that he had heard.

But Eva didn't want to hear any of this; she thought them to be mundane details and was completely unimpressed, having grown up with gentry and with the grandeur they enjoyed. She only wanted to know if he had missed her, but of course she couldn't ask that! It would have been deemed too unseemly and too forward, but that was all she really wanted to know.

Billy put his arms around her shoulders and kissed her on both cheeks once he had dismounted from his horse, exactly as he would have done had they been in France. Holding her tight, his heart skipped a beat as he realised that his feelings for her were deeper than before, or perhaps it was merely that his absence from her had made him realise just how much he loved her.

Sally and James were the first people that Billy wanted to see the next day, and then, of course, there was Louise, the rector's daughter, who had returned to her own home the week before the men's arrival and whom he already considered to be one of his dearest friends (after Eva, of course). He had corresponded with her whilst he had been on his travels with Sir John.

Sally and James had already moved into their new home; 'Hope House', in the centre of the village, a house built on the site of a previous medieval hostelry.

Sally intended to re-open the house and run it as a hotel. They seemed to be quite comfortable there, even though Sally told him that she missed her small cottage, as well as him.

Billy had missed them too, preferring their simple way of life, if the truth were told, to the one of excess and pomp that he had experienced on his travels with Sir John. Even though he had grown up in luxury and privilege in his own homes in France, he was amazed at how his taste for luxury living had changed, especially since his travels with Sir John, leaving him preferring the simplicity of his past life with Sally and James. There was something honest about their lives that appealed to Billy and which he tried to emulate at Sir John's; he was fully aware that this might seem strange to some, especially when most people were striving for luxury and possessions.

Billy took his time as he told them of his travels and of the many extraordinary homes that he had visited, giving them the gossip of the gentry, which he knew would amuse them, especially Sally, who always wanted to know the ins and outs of fashion and style, and of how the gentry lived.

Whilst Billy had been away with Sir John, James had been fortunate with the contraband runs and it was obvious that they were better off for having had his money to fund the expeditions. After several lengthy and sometimes heated conversations with James, it was decided that Billy would fund yet another run and then they would stop for a while, mainly because the Revenue men were getting too nosy for his liking. Also, it might have been just a coincidence, but every time *Boy Ben* left the harbour, the Revenue cutter seemed to be waiting for them out in the bay.

For a time, James wondered whether someone in the village was actually feeding the Excise men information as to their destination. But who would do such a thing? All the crew and their families were benefiting, as all profits from the runs were divided equally, so why would any one of them want to sabotage their own plans? It was a conundrum that James intended to solve until, one morning, fate solved it for him by an unfortunate accident occurring in the harbour.

Two boats, jostling for moorings, crashed into each other, holing the *Boy Ben*, which promptly sank. Scuppered accidentally, was the general consensus of opinion by those who had seen what had happened, but it left James and his crew with no apparent means of a livelihood until, fortunately, Billy stepped in once more and commissioned a new boat from the boatyard in Polruan.

In the meantime, the young man was studying hard at Cliff House. Every day, immediately after breakfast, he could be found in Sir John's study, sitting at the desk that he had been given for his sole use; this bureau was soon covered in ledgers and documents, all relating to the many businesses that Sir John had interests in. Billy was expected to study these and comment upon them later, after Eva had served afternoon tea with small fancy cakes she'd made personally, hoping to snare him with her prowess as a cook. Little did she know that he was already snared; he was just afraid to voice his feelings, believing that they were both far too young for such a serious matter as marriage. It was a frustrating time for them both, but Billy had no intention of compromising her virginity until she was his wife.

Billy would sometimes think about his past life in France, especially when the figures in the ledgers started to blur, and he would start to daydream, wondering about Marietta and how she and her family were faring. There were other questions that he would have liked answers for; such as, had her family managed to avoid begin arrested by the Revolutionary Government?

As for her father, was he still involved with the militia? And had she married Jean-Luc? He hoped not! A vain hope, for, to his mind, Jean-Luc had seemed determined to marry her, regardless of whether she loved him or not!

Billy would have liked to write and let her know that he was safe, but then the thought struck him that this might not be a good idea for two reasons: one, it might implicate her in his escape, and that would have serious consequences for her should the powers that be get to know, and second, it would let the authorities know of his present whereabouts, which was something that he didn't want to happen, as it was part of his future plans that he should return to France quite soon and find the rest of his inheritance. Also, it was quite feasible that spies from France, perhaps knowing where he was, could well be amongst those émigrés arriving in great numbers in England, and might even travel to Cornwall to find him, when he would be in great danger from being assassinated.

As yet, there had been no sign of such people, but he was always wary when he ventured away from Cliff House.

It is not yet the right time for him to return to France, especially after he heard of the massacres and the reign of terror ruling all daily life in the country. He heard news with monotonous regularity from the émigrés landing in other ports along the coast; people seeking a safe haven in England, away from the turmoil; those escaping from their own kind, as well as the war France had declared yet again on England. As much as Billy wanted to return and find what was rightfully his, it was better that he remain in Cornwall for the time being, where he was safe and occupied, until Captain Sawyer returned from his latest voyage and he could discuss the matter with him.

And so his current way of life became the regular pattern of his existence and would continue to do so for at least the next few months as he worked diligently at his apprenticeship with Sir John, becoming his trusted assistant as well as taking on the role of a much loved grandson which the old man had never enjoyed before.

Finally, news arrived from James that the new boat, *Boy Ben II*, was ready and waiting to be launched at Polruan.

The day arrived for the naming and launching ceremony; Billy accompanied Sally and Eva to Polruan (both ladies looking equally enticing and captivating in their new gowns and bonnets, bought especially for the occasion,) all of them arriving in one of Sir John's carriages.

There were many tears cried that day, mostly by Sally, and not all of them at the sadness of losing her only son; some were as a blessing for the day that Billy had arrived in Cornwall, as well as for his inheritance, something that had proven to be a godsend for James and his crew, especially now that the means of their livelihoods had at last been restored.

There was much cheering after Sally named the boat and it had been launched into the Fowey River, where it now sat, bobbing on the incoming tide, waiting for the rest of the crew to get on board for its first voyage.

Like James, Billy couldn't wait to go out on the new boat, to see how it performed, and, with James at the wheel and all the old crew on board, manning the rigging and the sails, the newly named *Boy Ben II*, sailed gracefully down the river, away from the boatyard where it had been designed and built. Even though it was only going down the coast as far as Mevagissey for its maiden sail, it was nevertheless an historic occasion and Billy, for one, wouldn't have missed that day for half the gold that remained in his chest.

The look on James's face, as he caressed the wheel, showed how he felt as he ordered the crew to put the boat under full sail, wanting to see how his new boat handled and how many knots he thought she would be able to attain.

Thankfully, *Boy Ben II* had a fine turn of speed, which would prove to be invaluable in the future when she was pursued by the Revenue Cutter whilst on its way home from a smuggling run to Guernsey, but on that day, there was no need to make a hasty escape from trouble; there was not a single sighting of the Excise men for the whole time that they were at sea.

From then onwards, the weeks flew by, quickly turning into months, and then into another year, and soon it was three years since Billy had first landed on the shingle at Talland Bay, where he found himself beginning a new life in Cornwall.

Eva, meanwhile, had grown into a beautiful young woman and Billy had fallen even more deeply in love with her, spending whatever time he could with her when released from his studies and his work for Sir John (he often travelled across to Bodmin Moor, and down to St Austell, to carry out the old man's bidding, as well as further afield, so that his time was precious when he was back at Cliff House and free from his duties).

They could often be found walking along the cliffs, hand in hand, or sitting in the heather as they studied the coastline, wondering how many caves held smuggled goods and where he would steal a kiss or two, with only the gulls watching as they circled overhead.

It was on one such outing that Eva reminded him of the date and that her father would soon be returning home from the Caribbean. Since then, every time Billy went down to the village to visit James and Sally, he hoped to hear of the Captain's impending arrival, or even to find him sitting in Sally's kitchen, drinking fine tea, or rum, or perhaps even brandy that had recently come their way from the latest smuggling run.

On Billy's last visit, they had started discussing what would happen when the *Mary Anne* did arrive. Would the Captain stay in Cornwall and give up the sea, as he had often said was his ambition? Or would he return to the sea and continue to sail to far-off countries, such as the Caribbean, to continue trading? It was a difficult question to answer, for both Sally and James knew that he had seawater running through his veins, as had their dearest son, Ben, a condition from which many a seafaring man suffers.

Billy wanted him to return so that he could ask him to take him back to France, for the young man wanted to seek out the rest of his inheritance, being quite sure in his own mind that his father had hidden more of his fortune in the grounds of the chateau. The one big question was: would the Captain be willing to take him?

It was only a few days later that a rider came to Sir John's house with a message, telling everyone there that the *Mary Anne* had been sighted leaving the Sound at Plymouth and was sailing towards the Cornish coast, where it would soon be weighing anchor at Talland Bay. Eva and Billy were to go there straightaway to greet it, which, of course, is exactly what they did!

Chapter 9

The *Mary Anne* returns

Martin Sawyer and his brother James, as well as Sally and her family, had all grown up in the same quaint little fishing village of Polperro on the east coast of Cornwall. We already know a little of Martin's story, and of how he became the master and captain of the *Mary Anne* and a little of James, with whom Billy lived when he first arrived in Cornwall. But we know very a little about Sally, except she was the eldest of several children born to Martha and John Richards, a long-standing Polperro family of simple Cornish fisherfolk, one of many generations coming from the same village and had been married to Martin Sawyer's brother, James, for many years.

Like most of the children born and raised in the village at the time, Sally had only enjoyed a skimpy education, unlike her brother-in-law who'd been blessed with a healthy and enquiring mind, as well as the good fortune to be mentored by his schoolmaster, Mr Brewer, a man originally from Plymouth and himself an educated man, with an altruistic purpose in life, to educate those less fortunate than himself. He also had a private income from an inheritance, without which he would have been unable to live and work as he did.

Sally was herself intelligent, though in a different way to James, soon educating herself in the ways needed by a young and attractive woman once she'd fallen in love with James.

It was not expected at that time for any woman to be educated beyond the basics of learning to read and to write, as well as to know the basics of simple mathematics that was at least sufficient for her needs, except perhaps for those born to wealth and high position and who had large homes to run.

It was more important for the likes of Sally to have the know-how of how to rear children, and be able to make a decent home for themselves and a husband, rather than to bother about too much book learning and, neither was it expected for a simple woman to become a businesswomen. In fact, in some cases this was actively forbidden by their menfolk, believing at the time women were not as clever as their husbands, who should be allowed to make all the decisions with no interference.

It was also expected for women to marry young and to waste no time before raising a family, so when Sally and James met and they fell in love, they followed tradition by getting married at the same church their parents had worshipped in for years, the selfsame church high on the cliffs, just up the lane from the village green, where Billy had first met Louise, the rector's daughter.

Coming from a family with many children, it was a surprise to Sally when she realised she was only going to be the mother of one child, her dearest boy, Ben, with no more following and then losing him so tragically, just after his fifteenth birthday. This had devastated her and James beyond belief, but Billy's unexpected arrival from France, only a few months later, had helped a little to assuage her grief and, within a few short weeks, he'd put a solid hold on her heart, replacing in some little way the ache losing her beloved son had left.

Seeing Billy dressed in Ben's old clothes for the first time had been a heart-wrenching experience for Sally, but it was the least she could do, to provide him with clothes, especially when he'd arrived looking so disreputable in the old clothes Martin had found for him to wear, when Billy had first boarded the *Mary Anne* in France.

Sally soon grew used to seeing him dressed in Ben's clothes and, after a while, it somehow comforted her, even though she had difficulty at times in remembering he was called 'Billy' and not Ben!

Since then, Billy had grown both in stature and confidence and the young man she had first met gradually changed. Now she watched with interest as he grew to manhood, dressed in the fashion of the day for a young gentleman of means. Her pride in him was immense when she saw him mounted on his horse, riding through the village, en route to his latest meeting on behalf of Sir John, thankful that at last he had finally taken on the mantel of a country gentleman, which of course he really was.

To Sally though, it was a pity he couldn't use his own name. 'Willelm D'Anville' was so much grander than 'Billy Sawyer' but perhaps that would change in the future? She knew, for the time being, if he wanted to keep safe, he had to behave as though he was a Cornishman and no longer a French aristocrat of some wealth, especially one who had had his home and his heritage taken away from him by a rioting rabble of French men, and women.

Hope House, which Billy had insisted on purchasing for them in the village in return for their care and kindness since his arrival from France, was quite large, having some years earlier been run as a lodging house for travellers. Its then owners had eventually grown too old to run it as such and the house had reverted back into being a family home. Sally had chosen the house even though most of it was shut off and unused. After she had talked over her ideas with

James and Billy, she convinced them both that she could make a business out of such a large property. The house was big enough for her ambitions, and with no work needing to be done either.

James tried to talk Sally out of it, believing it would be too much work for her, but she had merely scoffed at his way of thinking, having decided she was going to re-open the house especially for those who visited the area for work, and were in need a bed for the night.

For a woman with little or no education, Sally was equipped with a fine business brain. She could see for herself that Cornwall and the village were entering into a prosperous age what with new mining ventures taking place in and around the village and in Cornwall generally. She was certain there were many people, such as the likes of merchants and engineers, who would want to stay overnight, rather than make the long and arduous journey over what were then just simple tracks across the moors, to the growing towns of Bodmin and St Austell, merely for a night's stay, and to any other traveller who ventured along the cliffs, looking for a place to stay while they enjoyed the scenery and the ambience of the quaint fishing villages.

As it happened, Sally was proved right and, within a few months, Hope House was a flourishing concern, employing several women from the village to help.

She made one of the downstairs rooms into a dining room and it was there, at midday, and again in the evening, where she would serve meals to those who had the good sense to follow their noses to where the aroma of good food was cooking.

Billy was greatly impressed; his admiration for Sally's enterprising ways increased every time he visited, pleased his fortune was making life good for those he now called his family, for that was what he truly thought them to be.

It was to Sally he talked about his blossoming romance with Eva, trusting her instincts, knowing any advice she gave him would be right and that, if he was at all sensible, he should follow it.

James was quite different. He was a solid and reliable man, as honest as any smuggler could be. But first and foremost he was a fisherman, and an able captain of his new sailing vessel. He was also a man who cared for his crew, young and old alike, all who shared his love of life and his passion for the sea and fishing. He was also a devoted husband to Sally and to the memory of his young son, as well as to Billy, now grown into a young man, the young Frenchman entrusted to his care. His other care was for his brother Martin who was much older and wiser and due in any day soon from his latest voyage, when no doubt he would regale them with exciting stories of places James and Sally could never hope to see.

Eva and Billy were on their way from Cliff House to meet the *Mary Anne*, when they first saw the ship sailing into the bay, looking as majestic as ever, with her sails full. Even as they watched, they saw them gradually being lowered and furled, so that by the time they reached the shingle beach, ready to wait for the rowboat that would deliver the Captain, the ship was already safely anchored in the bay.

The Captain saw them whilst he'd been standing on the deck, waiting for his turn to join his passengers in the rowboat. He waved to them in greeting, the last to leave the ship except for the standby crew, who would be staying aboard.

Billy and Eva watched as the passengers disembarked onto the shingle. It was obvious from their dress that these were more émigrés escaping from the tyranny of their own country.

Seeing some to be elderly ladies, Billy ran to assist them as soon as the rowboat skittered onto the shingle beach and, for the first time in three years, he heard his mother tongue being spoken. It brought such a pang of sorrow to his heart that for a few moments he felt near to tears, something he hadn't bargained for, as well as a feeling of homesickness for his own country and a terrible longing to see his parents, a feeling of loss that was never to leave him.

These were the first émigrés he'd met since he'd arrived in Cornwall and his heart ached for them.

They looked so bedraggled and sickly from the voyage it was quite clear they all wished for nothing more than to be on dry land, preferably not in England, especially knowing their mother country was at war with the English and afraid of the reception that awaited them. The sensible ones, knowing it was far better to be in a foreign country such as Cornwall, rather than in France, where the danger of betrayal to the revolutionists was more likely to come from a friend or neighbour and, once in Cornwall, that would not happen.

Once the émigrés were all standing on the shingle, with their luggage piled nearby, Billy had already spoken kindly to most of them. He asked them, from whence they had come. Did they come from near his old home, was his first enquiry. Their talk became voluble at times, so much so that even he had difficulty in understanding their garbled explanations as to why and where they had come from. It was obvious Hope House would soon be full and, with the boxes and bags quickly loaded onto a small cart that had suddenly appeared on the shingle. (An enterprising fisherman, seeing the *Mary Anne* approaching the bay and realising there might well be passengers landing, had taken it upon himself to bring his cart down to the shingle; any opportunity to make a few shillings.)

Following the cart, the visitors started to walk back to the village, glad at last to be on solid earth after their sea journey. Billy was leading the way, talking to one visitor in particular. An elderly man, who held tightly onto Billy's arm as they walked up the steep and rocky path from the shingle beach, and then along the cliff-top being the only way into the village. He told Billy his name was Marcel Dupris and that he was a widower. Sadly, his wife had died while the group were waiting for the *Mary Anne* to collect them from the same port Billy had escaped from. While they walked, Billy asked if the old man knew Marietta's family.

'Of course!' Monsieur Dupris said, happy to talk. 'Her father was responsible for my arrest!'

Billy was shocked. 'Are you certain?' he asked. 'Are you sure it was the captain of the Militia who arrested you?'

'If not him personally, it was definitely one of his men who forced his way into my house, of that I am certain. They came in a group, the one leading them was as well known to me and my family as any man who comes from a family that have lived in the same village for more than sixty years!' At this, the old man spat on the ground. 'Had I thought he was about to turn us in, I would have killed him myself.'

Billy understood how the old man felt. 'Do you know if the captain of the militia's daughter, Marietta, is still living at her home?'

Monsieur Dupris looked at Billy, wondering why this young man should be so interested in the whereabouts of a young Frenchwoman.

And then he knew. He suddenly recognised him. This was no ordinary young man whose arm he was holding, this was the son of Henri, the Marquis D'Anville, but what was he doing in Cornwall? Discretion stopped him from asking more questions; it was not his business but, if the young man wanted to confide in him, then that would be a different matter altogether.

'Marietta was married a few months ago I believe, to one of the scum that paraded themselves as saviours of the country and, as far as I know, she has moved into a new home with new husband.'

After further questions, the man then proceeded to tell Billy where he thought Marietta had gone to live, which was only a couple of miles from the port. Information Billy needed to know if he were to save her.

Billy nodded and said no more, afraid to tell the old man that he also came from the same village and was the son of the Marquis D'Anville, believing what the old man didn't know was safer for them both and unaware that the old man had recognised him. It was better, or so Billy thought, if everyone believed him to be a North Countryman and a relative of James and Martin.

How much easier it would have been had they been honest with each other, but it was a sign of the times that no one in France trusted anyone else, not even blood relatives, especially with the spectre of the guillotine hanging over everyone's head and a false word, spoken out of turn, could easily result in the loss of another life.

Even in Polperro and amongst those he thought of as his friends, there were times when even Billy didn't feel entirely safe.

So, Marietta had married Jean-Luc Dupont after all! Well, there was nothing he could do to change that, but in his heart Billy felt sad. She'd been his friend for many years and now he worried even more for her safety, as Jean-Luc Dupont was not the type of man he would have wished for her to marry, especially as he had a reputation for being a bully.

It was at the thought, that Marietta might be in more danger from her new husband than the terrorists, that Billy's heart ached. If only he could rescue her and bring her to Cornwall!

Eva, meanwhile, had run into her father's arms as soon as he'd stepped onto the shingle and, like Billy, was now helping some of the others who were capable of walking to gather their belongings. The rest she helped to load into another cart that had joined them, before helping one young woman, holding a small child in her arms, to make her way up the path. Within an hour, everyone was walking or stumbling into the village, being guided to Hope House, the most obvious place for them all to be lodged until it could be decided what was to happen to them.

Sally, of course, went straight into her role as hostess, and soon the émigrés were all eating with gusto the simple meal she'd placed before them. They were all starving, having seen very little in the way of food, good or bad, during the weeks they'd stayed in hiding as they waited for the *Mary Anne* to come into port.

Sally's simple fare, cooked fresh each day, along with fresh baked bread, soon found willing mouths and never was there such a crowd of satisfied customers as those émigrés on that day. It did Billy's heart good to see them eating with such relish and enjoyment, their ordeal in France put temporarily to one side now they were in the relative safety of Cornwall.

Captain Sawyer joined the visitors in the dining room, also more than happy to be eating Sally's good food after months of eating ship's fare. When he too had finished eating, he took Billy to one side.

'Billy, I feel the time has come for you to spend some more of your gold.'

'Another smuggling run?' Billy asked.

'No, not a smuggling run, but a trading voyage to the Caribbean!'

'You know you can have whatever you need of my gold, but on one proviso, that I come with you before you go. I need to go back to France to save a friend, and then you can go to the Caribbean.'

Martin Sawyer looked steadily at Billy. He then turned to look where Eva was sitting, deep in conversation with the young Frenchwoman of a similar age, the one with the young child on her lap.

'What about Eva?' the Captain asked. 'Are you prepared to leave Cornwall and her, with the possibility you might not return? What if, when you get to France, you are arrested and imprisoned? You know what will happen to you. The revolutionists will have your head for sure!'

Billy thought for a few moments. The Captain was right. He hadn't given any thought as to how Eva might feel. His mind was too much on Marietta and his desire to rescue her from her ill-fated marriage, to someone he hated with a passion! But surely, Eva would understand that?

It was late in the evening before they returned to Cliff House. On their way home, Billy and Eva had spoken of the émigrés and what was to happen to them once they'd recovered from their journey. Would they stay in Polperro?

Eva thought not. Other émigrés had arrived before Billy's arrival and had quickly dispersed to other parts of not only Cornwall, but into Devon, and thence on to London, where there was already a considerable enclave of French men and women living and working in the city. Her grandfather was the man to ask, she suggested, giving Billy something to think about.

The following morning, before Billy had even opened the ledgers and started on his work for the day, Sir John Inney came into the room and sat down opposite him, his mind obviously on the same matter.

In a concerned manner he said, 'I understand a crowd of French émigrés are newly arrived in the village?'

'Yes, Sir John! The *Mary Anne* arrived yesterday in Talland Bay. Eva and I went to meet them and took them to Hope House.'

'Capital! The best place for them! I had quite a few staying here some time ago, but it was a great strain on my good wife. It's so much better if they stay together, especially as none of those could speak English.'

He pursed his lips and steepled his hands under his chin, a sure sign he was thinking.

'We must make arrangements for them to travel onwards. I will go down to the village later, and you must come along as well. Your French is necessary if we are to converse, as I well remember how difficult it was the last time!'

As promised, Sir John rode down to the village with Billy after they'd eaten luncheon, where they met with the émigrés who appeared to have settled quite happily into life at Hope House. After a number of conversations with them, that Billy had to translate, it was decided the visitors would stay with Sally and get their strengths back before travelling onwards. In the meantime, Sir John would make arrangements for them to procure accommodation in London, which was where they mostly wanted to go. It was fortunate his contacts in London could find temporary homes for them and, with their futures satisfactorily organised, Billy and Sir John left and returned home.

It was during their ride back to Cliff House that Billy told Sir John about his friend Marietta, and her fate, and of his wish to rescue her.

'I would like to return to France with Captain Sawyer when he leaves in a few days' time, but I still have a lot of work to do for you, so it will be impossible for me to leave just yet. I will have to wait until the next time he comes home. I just hope it will not be too late by then to save her!'

'No, Billy! You will go with my son-in-law when he leaves this time. From what you've told me, you have no time to waste! In any case, my work will still be here when you return.'

With that, Billy went to speak with Eva. He had to tell her that his dearest friend was in great danger and that he needed to find her and bring her back to Cornwall.

Eva could feel tears welling up in her eyes, but she too knew there was no way she would ever be able to persuade Billy not to go. He was too honourable a young man to leave someone he cared for in need of help.

It was then Billy finally became a man. With his mind made up, he decided he would propose marriage to Eva, just as soon as he returned to Cornwall.

Chapter 10

Billy returns to Brittany

Once Billy had decided he was going to return to France, and Sir John had agreed, it was then up to Billy to persuade Captain Sawyer to take him, which was going to be no mean feat.

With Sally busy with Hope House, now it was full of émigrés, and James fully taken with his new boat, both were too occupied with their own affairs to take any notice of Billy, or even to enquire as to his dour expression when he visited Hope House the next day.

At least the émigrés were no bother as their days were already filled with getting to know the area: learning the byways of the village, walking round the village lanes and up the paths, going out onto the cliffs, enjoying their newfound freedom after their escape from France and the guillotine, and taking every opportunity to look wistfully at the sea in the direction of Plymouth, hoping they would soon be on their way to London.

As for the women, they were kept busy helping Sally to cook and prepare their meals, as well as showing her the French ways of preparing and cooking food. All of this pleased her, for, as always, she was keen to learn and to improve her knowledge, as well as picking up their language, especially the language of cooking!

For the French women, cooking with Sally was a welcome distraction; anything to pass the time as they waited for Sir John

Inney's connections to arrive to take them away from Cornwall, that they may join their compatriots in London.

James had equally as much to worry about, with the Revenue Cutter often moored in the harbour and making life difficult for any possible smuggling runs. It did not help his mood either that the French émigrés were taking up too much of Sally's time. The only good thing, their lives were so busy, they had no time to worry, or to discuss, whether Billy was making a mistake in deciding to go back to France, regardless as to the validity of his reason.

The next evening, after supper at Cliff House, Billy sat down with Eva and discussed his concerns for Marietta. He told her how he believed his friend's life was in great danger and, being the generous and kind-hearted person she was, her advice that he should do as his conscious deemed to be right made him realise just how fortunate he was to have fallen in love with her.

'Billy, all I ask is that you take care. I want you to be safe. You might be walking into a trap if you start to ask questions as to where Marietta is when you land.'

'You must not worry on that score. Monsieur Dupris has already told me where she was staying and, unless she's moved to somewhere else, that's where I will look first.'

Eva's comment was foremost in his mind when, later, he'd sat and had a discussion with Martin Sawyer about his reasons for wanting to return to France when the *Mary Anne* set sail within the next few days.

The Captain tried to persuade Billy not to return, but his reasoning fell on deaf ears; he soon realised his concerns were to no avail, that the young man was determined he was going to France to rescue his friend and, if need be, her mother as well.

Finally, it was decided, Billy would return, but this time, at the Captain's insistence, he was to go in disguise; dressed as a French sailor, as Captain Sawyer believed travelling in disguise from Roscoff to the house where Marietta was thought to be living in the next village, would be safer. It was too near the port for him to be dressed as an English sailor and to this end the Captain rode into Plymouth the next day where he purchased a couple of outfits, for he'd decided Billy would not be going alone to save his friend. He wanted him to blend in with the local population of seamen when the ship docked at the port. Travelling with a companion dressed the same would be infinitely safer than travelling alone.

Fortunately, the Captain was well acquainted with the owner of a chandlers shop in the Barbican, which is where he purchased two French sailors' uniforms. Being worse for wear and not used to the strong ale pressed on them in the hostelries in Plymouth, the pair had lost their clothes playing a game of chance with a couple of English sailors, who were used to cheating to get their way and who knew that the clothes would be a welcome addition to the chandler's stock. The money paid by the chandler would be a welcome addition to their pockets for buying more ale.

The French sailors were lucky, for they were found, naked and lying in a gutter, by a Good Samaritan. Once they'd sobered up, he kindly kitted them out in some old clothes before taking them to their ship, where they were deposited on the side of the dock.

There was no doubt that they would face an inquisition for being out of their uniforms. The charge: being improperly dressed! This meant a whipping for them both. (This was just before the French declared war on England' otherwise, Billy's story might have had a far different outcome).

Captain Sawyer knew it would be hazardous time for Billy once he'd landed at Roscoff, as the roads around the port were sure to be patrolled by troops and because of the internal war raging in France, cover would be sparse. How Billy would manage to get to his destination would take some ingenuity but, knowing that he had already walked and ridden through the area during his own escape, the Captain had to admit the young man's chances would be much improved by going in disguise. The only downside to that course of action would be if he were unfortunate enough to be caught, he would then be quickly tried and guillotined, not as an aristocrat, but as a spy!

A few days later, Captain Sawyer and Billy boarded the *Mary Anne* with Billy kitted out as a French sailor, prepared to work his passage alongside the usual crew. They were a disparate lot, but a group of men Billy knew well. He also knew any one of the crew would kill for him, at least for a piece of gold, and without a second's hesitation or a qualm as to whether they were doing right or wrong, especially if he or the Captain asked.

The Captain decided, well beforehand, that he would send one of his crew with Billy to act as his escort when they pulled into port, regardless of whether Billy wanted one or not. He owed it to the young man's mother and father to care for him. Also, he was concerned for Billy's safety, a responsibility he would never relinquish, not until he was dead himself, which he hoped would be later rather than sooner. To this end, he'd chosen Jonas Matthews, a young seaman from Polperro and one of his crewmen, to take on the role.

The *Mary Anne* finally sailed out of Talland Bay on a fine afternoon, heading along the coast to Plymouth where Ned Pengelly, the first mate, as well as being the quartermaster of the *Mary Anne* provisioned the ship, filling the hold and every available space in the galley with enough provisions to last for several months as the Captain intended sailing to warmer waters once Billy had rescued his friend, taking them along with him. Not that he'd told Billy of his plans, feeling sure the young man would protest and demand the *Mary Anne* return to Cornwall straightaway!

The *Mary Anne* was soon sailing out of Plymouth Sound, leaving Devon and the Hoe behind, taking the same course as the *Mayflower* had once taken as it had made its way to the Americas.

The sails were soon filled with a fresh wind. From the colour of the overhead clouds, a force ten would shortly be blowing up and would no doubt turn into a fierce storm, something no one on board wanted to think about, especially as they would be sailing through the night when darkness seemed to highlight the danger in every wave.

The crew, along with Billy, worked hard to make the vessel shipshape for the journey to the port of Roscoff, tying down anything likely to be a danger during the storm. Soon, the *Mary Anne* was making its way to France through huge troughs and lows, with the rain lashing fiercely down once the storm broke for real.

To Billy, the day he'd been found by the crew in the tavern at Roscoff now seemed a lifetime away as so much had happened since, especially his falling in love with Eva.

Meanwhile, back at Cliff House, Sir John Inney was doing his best to console Eva, his granddaughter, who was still distraught, and had been ever since Billy had boarded the row boat that had come from the *Mary Anne* to collect him and her father from off the shingle.

She'd watched as her beloved menfolk where rowed to where the lugger was anchored, surreptitiously wiping away her tears, determined to show how brave she could be, unsure whether Billy knew how she felt about him.

She'd wanted to go with them, but her father and grandfather wouldn't hear of it. It was a preposterous idea, they had told her, Billy was a young man who needed to do what he felt was right for his friends, without being emotionally blackmailed by a young woman who didn't understand that Marietta, Billy's friend, and her family, were as important in his life as she was. Even this didn't do anything to console her, in fact it only made it worse, because now she had started to imagine Billy had fallen in love with his so-called best and dearest friend and perhaps that was the reason for his concern, and the real reason for him being hell-bent on saving her!

Nothing could have been further from the truth as far as Billy was concerned. His heart belonged solely to Eva and, being a true gentleman, he knew he would never do anything to destroy how he felt about her, but there were times when he wished he had proposed marriage to her before he'd left. That was in hindsight, something we are all guilty of being blessed with!

It was fortunate for Billy the men of the crew knew and admired him and, once the captain had explained where the *Mary Anne* was heading and why, they had all rallied round, especially Jonas, who'd been chosen by the Captain to go with Billy when they landed.

Jonas was a little older than Billy and not only was he a skilful sailor, but one also trained in hand-to-hand fighting, and even handier with a pistol, or whatever weapon was to hand. The Captain had particularly chosen him because he looked similar to Billy, which was handy, as with their blond hair and deep blue eyes they could quite easily have been mistaken for brothers. A fact that would make it easier for Billy to blend in when they landed, as being on his own would prove difficult, considering he still looked like an aristocrat even though he was dressed as a French sailor. With Jonas at his side, and both young men dressed the same, it was hoped they would look like two sailors merely on leave from their ship. A disguise the Captain and Billy hoped would work – if not, and they were caught, they would certainly be tried as spies and guillotined. Therefore, it was imperative they should not attract attention from anyone, especially someone with a suspicious mind.

The storm had abated somewhat as they neared the port and the ship had hoved to, ready to anchor. The Captain took Billy and Jonas to one side, making it plain the *Mary Anne* would only be able to wait two or three days at the most before it set sail again, giving them in reality one clear day in which to find Marietta and her mother and bring them back to the safety of the ship. The ship's manifest claimed it would be staying in the port only long enough for unloading the goods the harbourmaster had previously ordered, and then the ship would have to make its way out of the area. The war started between England and France didn't permit English boats to stay in port any longer than necessary, but, being a Cornish vessel and flying the black and white Cornish flag, the Captain knew he could forestall the departure for a day or so longer, simply by saying there was disease on board and that a sick sailor needed to be treated.

Once the *Mary Anne* was safely berthed in the small harbour, Billy and Jonas walked quickly down the gangplank before ambling across the hard in a nonchalant manner, as though they had all the time in the world and with permission to go wherever they pleased.

Billy set off, with Jonas following hard on his heels, confident from his talk with Monsieur Dupris that he knew which way to head in order to find Marietta. According to the aged émigrés' information, it was barely two miles from the harbour and should take very little time to make their way there, until, to Billy's dismay, they suddenly came across a group of men heading down the road towards them, all wearing the uniform of the revolutionists' army, with the distinctive tricolour cockade pinned on the left-hand side of their red headgear.

Seeing these men at close quarters alarmed Billy for a few moments, unsure of their motives. He whispered to Jonas to keep quiet should they be accosted, but they were simply waved on by the group, who were obviously not looking for a couple of sailors making their way home. Nevertheless, Billy and Jonas still felt afraid.

Good fortune must have been smiling on them, for the revolutionists, seeing the two young sailors had no means of transporting smuggled goods, chose to ignore them, dispersing in the opposite direction with no questions or comment asked as to the two young men's intentions, obviously believing them to be on legitimate business in the area, it being a place where seamen would be expected to live. Therefore, within a few minutes and trouble free Billy and Jonas had reached the entrance to the house where Marietta was supposed to be living.

The gates were wide open; without a care in the world, the two young sailors strolled casually down the tree-lined, but deeply pitted carriageway as if they had every right to be there, halting only when they reached the outside environs of a large stone-built house.

From the state of the exterior, and the general air of neglect and dejection about the house, it looked as though no maintenance had been done for quite some time.

As there was no response to his rap on the door, Billy was beginning to assume it to be the wrong place; he knocked again, with still no response, although he was quite sure they were being watched from one of the windows on the upper floor. Suddenly he heard a woman's voice calling out for help, a voice he knew immediately, recognising it as Marietta's!

He tried the door handle but the door was securely locked and couldn't be opened. Understanding what was happening, Jonas meanwhile had skirted the house, examining the ways he could find that would give them a means of entry.

Billy called out Marietta's name, hoping it was her he could hear, but, at the same time, afraid someone from one of the houses nearby would hear him calling and come to investigate. Thankfully, no one appeared.

Shocked that she'd recognised Billy's voice outside, Marietta suddenly knew help was at hand. More than that, she knew her rescuer. With her heart swelling with hope and gratitude, she called out his name. 'Willelm, help me! Please help me!'

Billy could tell she was distraught and that he needed to get her out of what was obviously her prison, but how was he to get inside the house?

The next moment, the problem was solved by Jonas running to where Billy was standing.

'Did you hear that?' he asked, with a look of puzzlement on his face. 'Whoever's inside is calling for someone called William!'

'Don't worry Jonas; it's Marietta, calling me! Willelm is really my name, all we have to do is to find a way to get in!'

'Come with me, I've found a way!' said Jonas, sounding a little puzzled, but he was quick witted enough not to argue or ask questions. 'There's a small window at the back I can break and get through and, I am sure, once inside, I'll be able to unlock the door.'

'Right, let's go!'

Within a few moments they were at the back of the house, where Jonas quickly smashed the window with a stone he'd found nearby. The sound of breaking glass and wood seemed terrifyingly loud and, for a while, Billy was quite sure they would be discovered.

Jonas knocked out the jagged glass as best he could and climbed through the narrow window, with Billy following.

Within seconds, they were soon quickly walking through the house, to find Marietta standing in the hallway, waiting for them to appear.

Jonas stood aside for Billy to enter first, watching, open-mouthed, as the most beautiful creature he had ever seen ran sobbing with relief straight into Billy's arms.

'Willelm, I cannot believe you've come to save me! How did you know where to find me?'

Billy held her tight for a few minutes, giving her a chance to calm down.

'From Monsieur Dupris! He managed to escape from France and is now in Cornwall with his family. He told me where you were!'

Billy knew they had no time to talk, as they had to leave straightaway if they were to get back to the *Mary Anne* before Jean-Luc should return home and demand to know what was going on.

'I've come to take you to Cornwall. Can you be ready to leave in a few minutes? Your mother as well, if she wishes to come, as I understand she lives with you?'

'Willelm, I can be ready in minutes, but my mother isn't with me anymore!' Marietta's eyes filled with tears. 'Sadly, she died a few weeks ago, but I do have someone else I want you to save!'

Billy waited for her to say who that was, but she was in too much of a hurry to get away from her prison and had raced off, heading up the stairs to an upstairs room with Jonas following, prepared to carry her baggage, leaving Billy to wait downstairs and keep watch, anxiously pacing through the rooms, looking out of the windows in each room, sure that Jean-Luc must soon be on his way home.

With no sound of Jonas and Marietta coming down the stairs, Billy was afraid time was running out for them, until he heard the sounds of a small child crying, and then the realisation hit him that Marietta must have a child.

Billy could feel his heart rate increasing with his anxiety. They must be on their way, for Jean-Luc would be really angry when he arrived back to find not only that his wife had vanished, but also so had his child! Billy knew there was no time to waste. They had to hurry!

The next minute, Marietta came down the stairs. In her arms, he could see she was holding a small child wrapped in a blanket, with Jonas following close behind, carrying an assortment of bags and packages that he dropped at Billy's feet, claiming there were no more and that they should make haste and leave before Marietta's husband returned and they were found.

Billy laughed ruefully. 'I know Jonas, let's go!'

This time, they left the house in the conventional way but, this time, through a door at the rear of the house, knowing no one would have known anything untoward had happened unless they went to the back of the house and saw one of the windows devoid of glass, which Jonas had prudently cleared away as best he could.

Billy took the child from Marietta's arms, leaving Jonas to carry the baggage, and, with Marietta hanging onto his arm, the three of them anxiously walked down the driveway, keeping well into the trees in an effort to conceal themselves from the prying eyes of anyone in the next house, or in the nearby hamlet; at the same time they were all silently wondering what would happen if Jean-Luc should suddenly appear. What they would do then?

It seemed to Billy to take an inordinate amount of time to reach the port, hampered as they were by Marietta, who found walking on the dusty and rutted road to be a painful experience. Jonas would willingly have carried her as well as the baggage, had he spare arms, having already decided she was the loveliest woman he had ever seen. He knew then that he would have died for her had the occasion arisen!

It was fortunate no one was about until they reached the harbour; by that time, it was dusk and those men left were going about their business, giving them no thought at all.

By the time they eventually made it back to where the *Mary Anne* was berthed, the light was fading fast. The threesome and the child, well-hidden under Marietta's shawl, finally made their way onto the ship to be greeted by Captain Sawyer, already alerted to their arrival by one of the crew he'd sent to wait by the tavern, with instructions to keep a watch out for them walking down the road to the harbour.

Once they were all safely on board, he summoned the crew to get the ship ready to sail immediately. His intention was to get out of the harbour before any hue and cry occurred, should Marietta's husband arrive home earlier than usual to find his house empty and his wife and child gone!

Captain Sawyer had had many strange items on board his ship over the years, but none so strange as a mother and her baby. It wasn't that babies are strange; it's just that working vessels were not known to be places where mothers usually bring their infants. But this child was destined to be a traveller; its berth on board the *Mary Anne*, a drawer, cleared of the Captain's belongings and set up by Ned Pengelly as a bed for the child. Ned was himself the father of four, all grown up now, so was well used to small children. With Marietta comfortably ensconced in the Captain's cabin, along with her son, named Nathaniel, the *Mary Anne,* unbeknown to Billy and Marietta, set sail for the Caribbean.

Billy had stayed at Marietta's side while the crew were busy, concerned for her well-being, but now his mission to rescue her from her ill-fated marriage had been satisfactorily accomplished, he was ready to return to Cornwall.

Unfortunately for Billy and his plans, the *Mary Anne* sailed out of the port and, instead of heading towards Plymouth, the Captain had silently turned the wheel to give them a left-handed bearing, heading the ship towards the Bay of Biscay.

By this time it was dark and Billy was unaware they were heading to a part of the world he'd only read of in books, or heard talk of by the crew when he'd been previously on board the ship.

The crew had no cares for where they travelled, the Caribbean was as good a place as any for them, all being seasoned travellers. It was only Billy and Marietta who were ignorant of sailing in the waters of the Caribbean and the fact that pirates roamed the area.

After several hours' sailing and no with sign of England's coast on the horizon, Billy felt duty bound to ask Captain Sawyer just exactly where the *Mary Anne* was heading.

'Well, 'tis like this young Billy,' the Captain said, his face taking on a serious look Billy had rarely seen before. 'We're bound for the West Indies. There's a cargo out there waiting for us and I thought the sea air would do you good.'

'But what about Marietta and the baby?' piped Billy. 'They were supposed to be safe and sound in Cornwall by now!'

'Yes, I know that's what you thought, but unfortunately that isn't what's going to happen. I have to meet a man on one of the islands and there wasn't time to go to Cornwall and then come all the way back again. So, I'm afraid, young Billy, a sea voyage is what you're in for. I'm sure your lady friend won't be minding at all, it will be a rest for her, and the babe won't care where it's at, as long as it's fed and watered.'

And so it came about that Billy, Marietta and Nathaniel found themselves on an unexpected sea voyage, to a land where the sun always seemed to shine and where the sea was turquoise blue, a colour Billy had never seen before. It was, so he understood from Jonas, who'd been on a previous voyage with the *Mary Anne*, a place where the sands were golden and hot on the soles of the feet, and where exotic fruits and spices grew in profusion; all items the English had suddenly acquired a newfound taste for, and where dark-haired beauties walked proudly, their breasts bare, wearing skirts fashioned from the grasses that grew in profusion on the islands.

Chapter 11
Marietta

Billy and Marietta's parents had been acquaintances for many years, often to be found socialising at events held in the village, hence the friendship between their children. Being neighbours in such a small area of France, it was quite natural they should wish their children to have friendships with others of a similar age. And so it was that Marietta and Billy had quickly established a friendship that endured, even though their lives had taken different directions over the ensuing years Once Billy reached an age where his education became of greater importance, he began travelling abroad with his tutors. Betwixt times, he would return to the family house in Paris until he went to stay with Henri Masson, his last tutor in the Normandy countryside, to complete his formal education; only occasionally did he spend holidays at the family chateau in Brittany, which, of course, was near to where Marietta and her family lived.

Marietta had grown into a beautiful young woman with her dark brown hair falling in waves onto her shoulders. Her eyes, a beguiling shade of blue, mirrored the sky on a summer's day with an innocent expression to them that had led many a male, young or old, to want to know her better. Sometimes, they became a shade of grey, with a pensive expression in them that made her look thoughtful, as if her thoughts were far away from the mundane happenings around her.

Marietta was intelligent and capable, a young woman with a brain to match any educated young man, but she was also vulnerable; innocent, without any of the wiles and ways of a much older woman. Had she perhaps lived in the city at that time, she would probably have had more experience of men than she did, but then that may well have detracted from her natural innocence and charm.

Like Billy, Marietta had also been educated at home by a succession of virginal and prim governesses, as convention and her parents' social standing demanded. Once she reached sixteen years of age, as was usual in France, she would then have a female companion; a refined young woman, who would have been expected to instruct her in the niceties of the French way of life when she left the confines of her upper class home. This was something that would only happen on the occasion of her marriage, which would have been arranged by her parents.

Apart from the few male children she'd known from the village, including Billy, the only other males she knew of were her much older male cousins, who all lived in the north of France, so Marietta's knowledge of men was scant. Consequently, she was unable to distinguish between a young man, with a dishonourable intent on her person, from another who wanted only to cherish her.

It was about this time that Jean-Luc Dupont, a young man who lived in the nearby village and who had known Marietta from her much younger days, had actively started to pursue her. He had based his interest on his much earlier childhood friendship with her and, being attracted to her and very desirous of her bodily charms as she reached maturity, he made his intention to marry her quite clear to his parents, hoping that they would act as go-betweens, before any other young man could lay claim to her.

Marietta was not particularly enamoured by Jean-Luc nor of his desire to court her, especially when her father and mother had told her of his interest; she remembered his behaviour as a young boy and abhorred both his gaucheness and arrogant manner.

He was quite handsome, in a dark-eyed way, but without the refined behaviour she desired in a suitor. Marietta instinctively knew he was not the man for her. Jean-Luc, even knowing how Marietta felt, refused to stop his pursuit of her with no intention of being swayed from his ambition to have her as his wife. Marietta was the one prize he wanted above all others, so he took every opportunity to ingratiate himself into the family, flattering her mother when he called on Marietta, even persuading her father to enrol him into the local militia he commanded.

It took quite an amount of manipulative behaviour on Jean-Luc's behalf in the militia before he was given permission to visit the object of his affections and that was only because Marietta's father had seen another side to the young man; a side he thought to be desirable in a future son-in-law, having found him to be an able soldier, swayed by the young man's ability with a firearm.

Regardless of Marietta's protestations that she was not prepared to be wooed or courted by him, her father simply overruled her, and, therefore, much to Marietta's disgust, Jean-Luc was allowed to visit whenever his militia duties permitted.

Jean-Luc's parents were of course delighted that their only son was being allowed to court the daughter of a family of some esteem, who, as well as being wealthy, were descended from minor royalty, although by then, in France, being connected in any way to royalty was a sure way of making a short visit to the Palais De Justice, and then to having one's head speedily removed by the blade of the detested guillotine.

Had Marietta's father known then that Jean-Luc Dupont was an aggressive bully, he would not have acquiesced quite so easily as he did to the young man's first approach for permission to marry his daughter. He would rather have sold her into slavery!

Unfortunately, Marietta's father had been well and truly taken in by Jean-Luc's military prowess, not realising this was a side to the young man's character that showed him for what he was, a man capable of inflicting harm on Marietta's person.

Parents in the country at that time held the whip hand when it came to choosing marriage partners for their daughters and Marietta's were no exception, even though she was quite capable of choosing her own husband. So it was a sorry day for all concerned when Jean-Luc made his first, fully approved visit, where he openly stated his intention to Marietta they would marry, regardless as to whether she wanted to or not.

This first formal visit had happened only a few days after Billy had called to see Marietta, as he was en route to meet Captain Sawyer in Roscoff, when Jean-Luc had apparently arrived at the house, demanding Marietta should marry him as soon as could be arranged, citing unrest in the country as a reason for his haste. He even stated that he was in a position to safeguard Marietta's life if she was married to him. If only this had been true!

Marietta had at first vehemently refused Jean-Luc's request for her hand in marriage, crying bitterly to her mother and father that she didn't love him; even refusing to see him when he called again a few days later to renew his request. Refusing to even consider the matter, she claimed that she would rather enter a nunnery than marry him until her mother told her that, should she continue to refuse to marry him, the family might possibly be arrested as enemies of the new regime. They would then all be incarcerated in a prison, where, quite possibly, they could end up losing their lives. All these threats were designed to frighten her into agreeing to the marriage. It was, of course, emotional blackmail on a grand scale by her parents but, being a loving daughter and not too keen on losing her own head, Marietta finally gave in and agreed, knowing this was not going to be a marriage made in heaven.

Therefore, what should have been the union of two young people in love and a joyous family occasion, was, for many reasons, anything but!

The groom was worse for wear when he arrived for the ceremony, smelling highly of wine and brandy and slightly dishevelled from too much merrymaking the night before with his militia comrades.

Marietta knew she should have turned and fled from the church, leaving him standing alone in front of the priest, but her father held onto her so tight she could hardly move, let alone escape.

Her voice was hardly discernible when it came to repeating the marriage vows; so quiet in fact she later swore she had not answered the priest's questions. Then later, at her home, where a great deal of wine had been drunk, it became obvious to those few friends and family who'd been hurriedly invited, that Jean-Luc was an uncouth young man, his language being coarse and crude, altogether confirming his lack of manners to all and sundry, especially when he was heard laughing, as he told some of those assembled, of his intention to bed Marietta as quickly as possible, and have his wicked way with her.

To those present, most thought his spirits were high because he was happy to have Marietta as his bride and that he was merely fooling around; or perhaps it was the wine taking control of his tongue? What no one knew was his possession of Marietta later that evening was done in such a manner as to be nothing short of rape, his abuse so cruel Marietta never got over it. Her virginity was taken with such force she was injured. It can only be imagined how she felt as the man, whom she was supposed to love and honour for the rest of her life, was one she already hated with a passion, a feeling that would never diminish as he demanded she give her body to him.

Jean-Luc was the cock of the militia the next day. In his eyes, he'd possessed the most beautiful woman in France and, hopefully, he would sire a child with her before the first year of their marriage was over.

Marietta was so traumatised by the whole event she could only fervently wish never to have a child with the despicable man she'd been blackmailed into marrying. Unfortunately for her, she became pregnant within a week or so of committing herself to him in marriage. It was to be another violent episode, several months later, that would put an end to her pregnancy but, within weeks, she was pregnant again; this time, she bore the child Billy had carried so tenderly in his arms, after her rescue, as she'd been taken aboard the *Mary Anne* to safety.

How Marietta came to be incarcerated and left alone in the house was explained to Billy and Jonas once they were on board the lugger and making their way to the West Indies. It was a story that failed to improve with its telling; only proving to Billy that Jean-Luc needed to come to a humiliating end and, if he had anything to do with the matter, he hoped it would be at his hand.

After their marriage, Jean-Luc had immediately moved Marietta into the home of his elderly mother and father. Thankfully, and much to Marietta's delight, they were a kindly old pair, unlike Jean-Luc, who seemed impervious to her growing hatred of him.

They went out of their way to make her welcome and treated her as a much loved daughter, not that this went any way to making her marriage any the happier, on the contrary, it only served to make her more determined to escape her husband's clutches just as soon as she could. Her only problem was how to organise this event so that it didn't cause her new in-laws and her own parents any problems.

For herself, she would gladly have died trying to rid herself of the man she was tied to for the foreseeable future. It must have been fate, or perhaps it was her destiny, that soon after her baby son was born, Jean-Luc was promoted and given a house in the country, a short distance away from his parents' home, the house having been requisitioned by the local revolutionists after the deaths, at the hands of the guillotine, of its owners. Given no other option, Marietta had no choice but to leave the relative safety of her parents-in-law's home and move into what had once been someone else's home. It was a place where she was surrounded by the mementoes of what must have been a previously happy home, all of which led her to becoming increasingly more depressed, especially knowing she couldn't alter in any way the fact she was living in a house brutally taken away from its rightful owners by the so-called newly formed Revolutionary Force.

Once installed in the house, Jean-Luc forbade his young wife to leave it at any time unless he accompanied her, afraid she would take flight and he would lose her and his child. He even made provision for a woman from the village to come in each day to clean and bring food, telling the woman his wife was unwell and needed to rest, giving Marietta with no excuse to leave the house.

It was imprisonment, not just of her body, but of her mind and soul, done in such a way that meant Marietta couldn't fully describe her emotions at her imprisonment to Billy and Jonas, who by then had fallen deeply in love with her. It was an attraction she reciprocated, drawn to him by his kindness and obvious adoration, although, at the time, her thoughts were mainly on the welfare of her child and the fact she was still legally married to Jean-Luc. Also, she could speak no English and Jonas could speak no French. But true love has a funny way of overcoming such obstacles, as they were to find out.

Jonas could often be found, when released from his watch duties, dangling the baby on his knee, gurgling at the child and making him laugh, a sight that amused the crew and especially Billy, who could see that Jonas and Marietta had indeed fallen in love.

The voyage across the Atlantic to the West Indies proceeded well, once they were out of the Bay of Biscay, an area of water notorious for its storms.

Captain Sawyer stood at the wheel, steering the *Mary Anne* with a prowess that was wonderful to see. He occasionally discarded his Captain's coat once the temperature rose as they sailed ever nearer to the West Indies, showing his strong and powerful bare arms, his veins standing out like ropes as he steered his ship with just the lightest of touches on the wheel. He was an instinctive sailor, caressing the wheel as a lover would caress the breasts of the woman in his life.

With fair winds filling its sails, the *Mary Anne* responded like a greyhound released from its trap at his touch, the lugger travelling at such a speed across the Atlantic towards the Caribbean islands it surprised Billy, this being his first long sea voyage. His only thoughts, now Marietta was safe on board with him, were for Eva, and how she would cope when she finally realised he wouldn't be returning to Cornwall quite as soon as she'd hoped. Would she be harbouring jealous thoughts of him and Marietta? If only he could let her know she had no need to concern herself on that score, for it was apparent to all on board that Marietta had eyes only for Jonas and, of course, her young son, Nathaniel.

So far, the voyage had taken over a month since leaving France with the air becoming ever more fragrant with the aromas of exotic fruits and flowers the nearer they sailed to the islands, where the Captain and crew were to collect their cargo that was destined for London.

The nearer they sailed towards their destination, the higher the sun rose in a cloudless sky and, with very little wind to fill the sails, the young sailor, who should have been acting as lookout on top of the mainsail spar, had climbed down and was sitting on the deck, taking a break from his duties. He was relaxing with the rest of the crew who, all fed and feeling somnolent, had been lulled into a state of false security by the fact there had been nothing to see on the ocean for days on end.

Along with the mind numbing heat pervading their senses in the midday heat, all of them wished for nothing other than to be in their hammocks. With never a sign of any other vessel on the horizon, they had all consequently become complacent and idle until, suddenly, their rest was rudely shattered as a small boat, obviously an ancillary vessel belonging to a brigantine, had sailed silently up to the *Mary Anne*, its sails filled with a breeze that had suddenly sprung up. The intention of its crew was to board the ship and make mischief for the crew of the *Mary Anne* as they took the ship for their own use.

One minute, there was silence on board, except for the occasional sound of snoring. Then the next, there was a great a commotion to be heard as the invaders, yelling blood-curdling screams, suddenly appeared on deck, some of them wielding cutlasses as well as pistols, having used a huge net thrown over the side of the ship as a scrambling device. This all happened to the surprise of the crew of the *Mary Anne*, who were all lolling about the deck in a state of complete disarray and laziness, contrary to ship's orders. Taken completely unawares by their unwelcome visitors, they paid the price.

As the racket finally registered with the crew, they suddenly woke up to the fact they'd been boarded by pirates – a dozen, or maybe more, evil men – whose sole intent was on capturing the ship and claiming it as their own.

From the amount of weapons the pirates were brandishing with great displays of dexterity, it was obvious they were prepared to fight to get what they wanted, but surprise had been their greatest weapon. It was also quite obvious to the Cornish and Devon men of the *Mary Anne* that the intruders were quite prepared to murder them all if necessary to achieve their aim. They had really been hoping to capture the vessel with no shots fired, but they hadn't reckoned on the likes of the first mate, Ned Pengelly, who until then had not been on deck, lazing like the others, but in another part of the ship, peacefully unaware of what was happening on deck until he heard the commotion. Within seconds, Jed knew pirates, those desperados of the oceans, who should be avoided at all costs, had boarded them!

Like the crew, Captain Sawyer had also been sleeping. Having given up his cabin to Marietta and her baby he'd been catching up with his rest in a hammock, set up by Ned Pengelly in the crew's quarters. He needed to rest after the boredom of several uneventful watches and, therefore, had been sound asleep, until the shouting of the crew suddenly woke him.

It had been the noise of the shouting, along with the sound of gunfire, as one or two of the pirates had fired their weapons to round up the crew of the *Mary Anne* before any indiscriminate firing occurred, and the pirates were themselves injured. Unfortunately, the invaders hadn't reckoned on Captain Sawyer's crew, who had at last started to put up a fight. Thankfully, they'd all been wearing their pistols, which boded well for them. The pirates, on the other hand, were all experienced in the art of piracy and very keen to take the ship without any harm coming to themselves, but they hadn't reckoned on the crew of the *Mary Anne*, who were equally determined the varmints would not be taking the vessel from them by any means, fair or foul.

By now, Captain Sawyer had realised and understood what was happening. Starting to get his brains into some sort of order, befuddled as he was by sleep, he knew he had to take on the pirates at their own game.

But it was Ned Pengelly, that good man of Looe, and second in command of the ship, who proved to be the man of the moment. He too had been below decks, in the main hold, checking on the state of the food supplies, when he'd been alerted to the events happening on the main deck; events that caused him to believe strangers with evil intent were aboard and that trouble was not just brewing, but was actually happening.

Ned stood stock still for a moment or two and listened, realising it was no good getting into a panic as the crew would be looking for him, in the absence of the Captain, to take charge.

Knowing he needed to keep a clear head, Jed struck lucky. He started to move stealthily through the hold, making his way through the ship, his loaded pistol in his hand by the time he reached the far end. Listening all the while, he mounted a small narrow ladder that led to the aft deck keeping his head down in case he should be seen, deciding to mount a counter attack from the rear without the pirates being aware of his presence.

Billy had also been resting in his hammock. Upon hearing the noise on deck, he too had come from his quarters. Quickly rousing himself, he reached for his jacket. He removed his loaded pistol and placed it in his waistband before making his way quickly and as quietly to the foredeck; keeping out of sight as well as he could from the pirates, who were busy rounding up the crew. By then, most of the crew were standing in a group on the main deck, with two of the pirates about to tie them together and lash them to one of the masts, having already made the crew discard their weapons.

A minute or so later, Billy heard the sounds of yelling and the noise of gunshots being fired. To a man, the brigands looked around, unable to tell where the ambush was coming from, unaware there were other members of the crew below decks.

The next minute, Ned Pengelly appeared on the aft deck, his pistol raised as he went to take aim at the first pirate. Then Billy appeared, along with Captain Sawyer, who had jumped out of his hammock and raced up the ladder onto the main deck in a flash, arriving just as Billy and Ned were about to start firing at the brigands. At the same time, Ned was calling for the crew of the *Mary Anne* to stand fast.

Suddenly, and in unison, the Captain, Billy and Jed each gave out a blood-curdling yell and, without any thought to their own safety, started firing their pistols with the sole intention of killing any one of the pirates who just happened to be within range. One by one, the invaders began to fall, many fatally injured, onto the deck. It was the surprise attack made by Ned, along with the back-up by Billy and the Captain, that had been the winning stroke of luck for the crew of the *Mary Anne*.

It took only a few minutes before they managed to unravel themselves and then, having picked up their weapons, the crew were soon getting stuck in, starting to shoot at the invaders until they were nearly all slain and lying on the deck in pools of blood and gore.

Billy managed to kill one pirate, a man he took to be the leader of the landing party. He'd had a clear view and, without any thought for his own safety, had fearlessly aimed and fired, shooting the man through the heart without hesitation. The next shots came from the Captain, who was carrying two guns. He had quickly aimed and fired off one shot directly at the pirate who'd had the misfortune to have taken over the ship's wheel, obviously intent on steering the ship off its course until he suddenly realised the futility of his position. Without a thought to his colleagues, he dived into the sea, even though he was badly injured. The Captain's next shot was at a pirate heading towards Billy with the intention of killing him but, after seeing what had happened to his crewmate, he made good his escape before he too found himself injured, the captain's shot narrowly missing him as he plunged overboard into the ocean.

Without a doubt, the *Mary Anne* and its crew had had a narrow escape. The pirates that were uninjured had already made their escape by jumping overboard, gone before Ned Pengelly and the crew could detain them and swimming towards their own mother ship which had suddenly drawn near. It was blatantly flying the 'Jolly Roger,' a flag depicting it to be a ship fully intent on plundering any other vessel that happened to be in the area; the sight of it intended to scare weaker ships into submission, but this time the pirates were unlucky, for the crew of the *Mary Anne* were not as feeble-minded as many others had been. Once they knew what was happening, the crew had fought heroically for their own lives and for the sake of their ship. Captain Sawyer was proud of them all, his gallant crew of West Country men, who asked for no more in life than the chance to sail on the *Mary Anne* with him, as the ship sailed the seven seas.

Captain Sawyer stood on the deck and took stock of what had happened, viewing the bodies lying on the deck in front of him with disgust. Seeing they were beyond help, he asked his men to tip them overboard, at which the crew cheered, although a few kind Christian words were said by the Captain as each body was sent down to Davy Jones's locker, via a door, hastily removed for the occasion and used as a chute.

Meanwhile, the pirates' brigantine, with its crew picked out of the sea, had raised its sails and was soon no more than a speck on the horizon, too far away for the guns on board the *Mary Anne* to be put to any use. By this time, the crew had cleaned the decks of the blood and guts from the dead pirates, just as the ship's carpenter and his mate had finished putting to rights the damage the ship had incurred in the fracas.

To say the least, by the time the ship was clean and tidy Captain Sawyer had become angry, not only with the crew for allowing their senses to be addled by the sun, but also with himself for not being more vigilant, especially knowing full well the seas of the Caribbean were infested with pirates, and where a plague of lawlessness reigned supreme. Pirates were a pest to all those who dared to sail in the warm waters of the West Indies and especially to those hoping to trade goods, desired by people who had no idea of the dangers involved in getting such exotic items, that the likes of Captain Sawyer and his crew travelled so far to purchase.

The islanders, of course, detested pirates for they kept honest traders away. They were those evil men that plundered the islands of items, other than spices, even taking some of the island women and men to use as slaves, a practice that had caused the islanders to be on their guard, even when honest strangers sailed into the waters wanting to trade with them.

With the *Mary Anne* shipshape and tidy once more, Captain Sawyer called for the crew to join him on the main deck, where he then proceeded to tear a strip off each and every man on board for failing in their duty to keep a watchful eye out for pirates. He was sure in his own mind that it wouldn't be the last visit the *Mary Anne* would have from such rogues and varmints that roamed the high seas, from those looking for easy pickings, or an income, dishonestly earned.

Captain Sawyer told them they would soon be in the area where such varmints dallied most of the time, waiting for the unwary sailor, and where a ship, such as the *Mary Anne* would be highly prized by any pirate wanting a vessel that was well built and speedy. It was imperative, he told them, that each man in the crew should keep his wits about him, that they should keep a wary eye open at all times for anything unusual happening in the area.

As for Ned Pengelly, he too was told, in no uncertain terms, that a member of the crew was at all times to climb the rigging to the top of the mainmast and keep a watch out, that the ship's crew might be aware of other craft in the area, at least until it reached port and was safely anchored. Even then, someone was to be on guard at all times.

Marietta and her young son, astonishingly, had slept through most of the action, only being roused when she had heard Billy and Ned's antics as they dressed and prepared their weapons. After a while, and hearing no sound of fighting, she'd climbed warily onto the deck to act as nurse if necessary to the crew, once the pirates had departed.

Jonas had been on deck at the time of the invasion, one of the crew to have been tied to the mast and, once released, had been responsible for the death of one of the brigands, a fact that displeased him; him being a Christian man who preferred to live a quiet life, rather than one filled with fear and terror and gunfighting. He'd suffered a nick on his left arm from the stray use of a cutlass, which Marietta happily bandaged and cooed over for days, happy to be of use to the one man she'd finally found to be to her likening, other than Billy, whom she adored but knew wasn't the man for her.

And so the *Mary Anne* continued on her way to the Caribbean islands, with the crew much more wary this time and with the temperature rising each day as they drew ever nearer to the island where they were to drop anchor, ready to load their cargo.

It was less than a week later when the sailor on lookout duty shouted down from the top of the mainsail mast that land was ahoy, and then it was only a short time before the ship was sailing into the bay that was its destination.

The island was perfect; a beautiful jewel set in a verdant setting. Even from a distance, the crew could make out the palms and coconut trees, and the thatched simple huts belonging to the residents. The nearer the ship sailed to the island, the easier it was to see the islanders waiting on its golden sands, waving excitedly as the ship sailed into the bay, ready to drop anchor.

Some of the island menfolk even sailed out to greet the ship in their dugouts, their faces covered with beaming smiles as they welcomed the crew of the *Mary Anne* like long lost brothers, for this was not the first time the *Mary Anne* had sailed to this island and, hopefully, not the last.

Only when the sails had been lowered and furled did Marietta, holding Nathaniel in her arms, come on deck to watch in fascination as the Captain began manoeuvring the ship to its resting position in the bay; the crew standing to attention, and lining the deck, until the shout came to lower the anchor. Then the rattle of chains could be heard above the sound of the natives singing their song of welcome.

The island was a veritable haven to the sea-weary crew, with its hot and golden sands and its palm trees waving in the light breeze that fanned the island. The sea looked wonderful, a turquoise blue, its waters so clear and clean the fish that swam there were clearly visible; their colours were vibrant and enticing for the fishermen in the crew, all of them used to the dull colours of the fish that they caught in Cornwall. There were even sea turtles to be seen swimming in the clear water, huge lumbering creatures when on land but seemingly weightless when in the sea.

The crew couldn't wait to disrobe and dive in to refresh their travel-weary bodies, but not before the Captain had given the order for some of the crew to stand by for unloading the goods they'd brought from England, goods that had never been seen before in the islands. The others, however, were allowed to rest easy and do as they desired, which, to most of them, meant time to bathe in the warm waters of the Caribbean Sea that surrounded the island.

Billy waited until the crew had refreshed themselves before he too dived into the water, along with Jonas, leaving Marietta sitting on deck under a parasol the Captain had found for her in one of the holds. Nathaniel was lying on a blanket on the fore deck, buck naked, his chubby legs kicking in the air.

Marietta and the child posed such a pretty picture it brought a tear to the eyes of most of the married men of the crew, men who sorely missed their own wives and children. Marietta, however, was never left alone for very long, as Billy, or Jonas, were never far from her side when not on duty.

It was plain for all to see that Marietta had indeed fallen in love with Jonas, but what of her husband? He was the only stumbling block to them being happy together. Seeing them so much in love made Billy decide he had to find a way to dispose of Jean-Luc. It wouldn't be easy, he knew, and neither did he know that these thoughts would occupy his mind for several years to come before the problem could finally be solved.

It was not Captain Sawyer's plan to stay on the island any longer than was necessary but, seeing his men enjoying its delights, and with everyone enjoying the hospitality of the islanders, he delayed sailing for a few days. However, once more of the cargo for England had been delivered from other islands and was loaded, there was no longer any excuse to remain; the next day, the crew were summoned on deck and told to get the ship ready to sail.

When the sails were finally unfurled and hoisted, and the anchor lifted, the crew waved goodbye to the islanders as the ship sailed out of the bay to the strains of the islanders singing a farewell song, waving palm fronds as their farewells, sad to see the *Mary Anne* slowly making her way out of the bay, as it headed towards the Atlantic ocean and home.

The lugger made good progress on her journey homeward, encountering the usual tropical storms but without experiencing any untoward damage, or meeting any more pirates, before heading into the cold waters of the Atlantic as it made its way to England where the lugger's first port of call was to be London, where Captain Sawyer was due to unload the ship's exotic cargo. Once this had been done it was his intention to sail his ship to the West Country, and in particular to Cornwall and to Talland Bay, where he intended to stay for a few days with Eva and Sir John at Cliff House. As for Marietta, Billy had decided she was to stay with James and Sally. Jonas would be staying with his mother and continue to work on the *Boy Ben II* until he could persuade Marietta to live with him.

Once the *Mary Anne* had berthed in the pool of London, and while the ship's cargo was being unloaded, Billy left Marietta in the capable and loving hands of Jonas and made his way through the docks. He took a carriage into the city, to the Bank of England in Threadneedle Street, where he intended discussing his finances and his future plans for his inheritance with a man he was sure he could trust, Sir Walter Lumley, a friend of not only his late father but also of his Cornish mentor, Sir John Inney.

Chapter 12

London

London was a bustling and slightly daunting place to many young men, but not to Billy. Because he was well travelled he knew how to survive when in a strange place, ever since he'd been on his grand tour of the continent with his tutor, Henri Masson. He'd seen the evil side of life in many of these places, as Henri Masson believed his students should not be immune to the bad side of humanity. Billy was looking forward to seeing London, having never spent time in such a place before. He had lived in Paris for many years, but London was a different matter altogether. It is a city with many faces.

It was its elegant face that charmed and pleased him greatly as he rode through the streets in his hired carriage, giving him the opportunity to admire the newly built houses. He was riding through the area where the Great Fire had done the most damage, as it had raged and burnt everything in its path. To Billy, these newly built houses were reminiscent of those near to his Paris home; grand residences, houses designed for the gentry, while others were not quite so grand, reminding him of the simple townhouses in the villages near to the family chateau in Brittany. There was yet another face of the city, a place where thuggery and vice of every sort abounded, where no one would wander the back streets unaccompanied – not if they had any sense – for rogues and varmints dwelt in these dirty backstreets where evil deals could be made if one didn't mind with whom one did business. This wasn't the sort of business Billy had in mind that day, his was legitimate, with a man who had been well-known to his late father.

As he made his way, he could smell the river before he saw it. It was a stinking waterway, full of filth from the sewage and rubbish the inhabitants threw in on a daily basis and where, once upon a time, copious amounts of fish would once have swum. Even so, it was this waterway that brought the trade into the capital and, when the tide turned, it would make its way out to the sea, going past Gravesend, where many ships, all recently arrived from foreign climes would be waiting to proceed to the docks, their flags showing whence they had come, dropping anchors at the wharves. There, dockers would be waiting to unload the cargoes onto carts (vehicles not unlike the tumbrils in Paris that had carried the aristocrats to their fates) before being trundled through the cobbled streets to one of the many warehouses lining the banks of the Thames, and where the goods would be stored, before being transported onward by carriers to their final destination.

From what Billy could see, as he dismounted from the carriage he had hired to transport him to the Bank of England, it was apparent there were extremes of wealth and poverty in London, just as there had been in Paris, except that in France it was mostly the poor peasants filling the streets these days, distinguished by their red caps, showing them to be revolutionists, and all looking for blood.

London, poor as some areas might have been, seemed to be a much more cheerful place, but maybe Billy would change his mind when his eyes have been fully opened, and he has come to know it better…

He smoothed down his wayward hair and walked into the imposing building that housed the Bank of England, eager to meet Sir Walter Lumley, the man whose name his father had written down on one of the many documents in the chest, with instructions that Billy should contact him if he ever arrived in London.

Sir Walter was a man that his father had wanted him to get to know, his name just one of many names on the documents Billy had found in the sea chest, along with his gold.

The concierge, a small man dressed in the flamboyant uniform of a lackey at the bank, was standing behind a desk in the foyer, his face portraying an instant dislike of the young man who stood before him. He took Billy's details and promised he would send a servant to find the notable man Billy wanted to see. He gave Billy a somewhat strange look that might have been because of the young man's attire.

Billy was clean, but not dressed as one would expect of someone calling to do business with one of the most influential men in the capital. He was dressed as he was in his everyday clothes, the clothes of a French sailor having long been discarded and packed away by the Captain, perhaps to be used at another time when a disguise was needed again.

Once he'd made an appointment to see the great man later that afternoon, Billy excused himself and made his way to the nearest gentleman's tailor in Savile Row. There, he purchased a new outfit that was much more in keeping with his rank. However, even that purchase was fraught, as the owner debated whether he should do business with Billy or not. It wasn't until several gold pieces had been placed into the tailor's hands that a suit of clothes, promised to another client, miraculously appeared and became Billy's. Next, a shave and a haircut, before he presented himself once again to the concierge, who by this time had begun to wonder where the unkempt young man had suddenly disappeared to. This time, noting the change in Billy's appearance, the concierge told him politely, but with a certain amount of diffidence, to take a seat, one of many around the reception room, and wait until he was sent for.

Billy sat and waited, keenly alert to the people who entered the hallowed portals, wondering what their business was about. It was an hour or so later when Sir Walter Lumley finally sent word that he would see him.

There can be no doubt that Billy's education and upbringing was his greatest asset. His refined speaking voice, even with the slight Cornish accent he'd tried so hard to attain, and his handsome appearance, were his best attributes. (His French accent had almost vanished, after the time he'd spent with Sally and James, and then latterly while working with Sir John Inney.) He'd even learnt the language of the sailors he sailed with on James's boat, sometimes using words Sally had teased him not to use in refined company. Occasionally, Billy succumbed and used words and expressions that gave him away as not being a true English gentleman, even if, as now, he was dressed as one.

Presently, a uniformed lackey arrived in the foyer and escorted him to the room Sir Walter Lumley obviously used as his office.

It was an elegantly panelled room, enlightened by a large sash window that overlooked Threadneedle Street, where Billy could hear the sounds of sellers peddling their wares in the street below.

Sir Walter Lumley stood up from his desk as Billy entered the room, appraising the fair-haired handsome young man walking across the room, shaking him by the hand once Billy had introduced himself as Willelm, the Marquis D'Anville.

Sir Walter looked puzzled, having expected a Billy Sawyer to be his visitor. He looked even more so when he realised Billy was the son of his old friend. Shock and horror crossed his plump face when he learnt the details of the deaths of the young man's mother and father. He briefly took Billy into his arms, embracing him in a fatherly way, unable to say what was in his heart at the young man's loss.

Once the proprieties of their formal introduction were done with, Sir Walter asked Billy to sit down opposite him at the rather grand mahogany table that doubled as his desk, prepared to listen to what his young visitor had to say.

They talked for some time, of matters relating to France and its troubles since the terrors had begun, and to how Billy had escaped, and what he'd been doing in Cornwall ever since. Suddenly, realising Billy had probably not eaten for some time, for by then it was getting late in the afternoon and Sir Walter was in need of sustenance himself, he took a small bell from off the table, which he rang and, when a servant entered in response, he asked that they should be served refreshments; all of which, minutes later, Billy devoured hungrily once the food was set before them.

Billy was quite taken with Sir Walter: he found him to be an uncomplicated man, quite the opposite from Billy's late father. Sir Walter being a short and portly man, in his late fifties or so Billy assessed, with a ruddy complexion that led Billy to believe, quite rightly, that his host enjoyed his food and drink, having watched the older man drink most of the carafe of wine, which was included in the repast, of which Billy drank only the one small glass, wanting to keep a clear head for the business he intended doing. His thoughts were completely validated when Sir Walter rang the bell for the manservant to replenish, for a second time, the carafe of wine which, when finished, seemed to have had no effect on Sir Walter at all.

It had taken only a few minutes and several probing questions, before Sir Walter realised he could speak to Billy as an equal and especially when he realised he was indeed the new Marquis D'Anville, although Billy was quick to point out this was no longer a name he used, as his influence as an aristocrat was virtually non-existent.

Knowing the young man's ancestry as well as his late father's business acumen, a door was opened in Sir Walter's mind and, suddenly, he became much more deferential. Now that Billy's financial heritage had been established, he decided that the young man's education would have given him at least a reasonable working knowledge of finance, enough, at any rate, for him to comprehend the simplest of financial documents. Sir Walter visibly relaxed. He spoke to Billy in a manner that was slightly different from their first encounter, when he had at first appeared to be imperious and stand-offish.

Billy related the details of his parent's deaths, as well as a few scant details of his rescue by Captain Sawyer from Roscoff, a man also familiar to Sir Walter, as he too had done business with the Captain in the past, and fully intended to continue his association in the future.

Billy then told him of his present circumstances, and how he was now living and working with Sir John Inney at Cliff House near Fowey, as well as how he was being mentored by the great man himself. To Billy's surprise, he turned out to be an old adversary of

Sir Walter's from their younger days, when they'd both been desirous of the same woman, but where Sir John had won the woman in question.

They had much to talk about, with Billy speaking of his work with Sir John Inney as his apprentice, at which Sir Walter raised his eyes in surprise. And then of his recent voyage to the West Indies, from which Billy had just returned, finally imparting the knowledge to the older man that a small part of his inheritance was lodged in Cornwall and that he was looking for some form of business he could invest in; a place that would prove to be a gilt-edged investment for some of his gold.

Sir Walter Lumley's eyes nearly popped out of his head at the mention of gold, wanting to know the ins and outs of how Billy came about his inheritance. And when Billy informed him of how he came about his good fortune, Sir Walter's eyes nearly popped right out of his head, especially when Billy told him how much he wanted to invest. The older man stuttered and stammered as he tried hard to elicit how much Billy had in his possession. Billy was not prepared to tell him the full amount, having been well advised by Sir John that the less said about one's wealth the better, being aware that there were many rogues in the business world who would like nothing better than to remove all the gold from Billy's control faster than a ball could leave a musket, if given the opportunity.

Billy did make the comment that he had homes in France he could no longer lay claim to, an aside that seemed to impress Sir Walter even more, even though Billy told him the new Revolutionary regime would, in all probability, have already appropriated the properties, and the chances of him ever living in them again were very remote. (He made no mention of his belief that more of his

225

inheritance was hidden somewhere in the grounds of the Paris house, or at the chateau in Brittany, or that he intended to visit France again before another year was out to try and find it).

Sir Walter then proceeded to give Billy a short history of the Bank of England, all of which Billy found to be quite interesting, but he wasn't about to deposit his gold in the 'Old Lady of Threadneedle Street', as the bank was affectionately known in the City, for the bank to use in bankrolling the navy, as had happened when the bank had first been founded. He wanted his wealth to be more secure than that, with no strings attached that would tie it up for an inordinate amount of time. He wanted to invest in short-term projects to start with, investments that would bring him in a large amount of interest as quickly as possible, as he had much he wanted to do with his fortune in the future. What those future plans were to be, Billy, for the moment, wisely kept to himself.

It was planned that Billy would return to the bank on the morrow, giving Sir Walter time to decide what would be the most suitable investments for his inheritance. In the meantime, Sir Walter invited Billy to join him and his family at the Drury Lane Theatre that evening, and for dinner afterwards, where he hoped Billy's youthful good looks and his aristocratic manners would impress his daughters, who were both in need of a husband, thinking to himself that a young man, such as Billy, would be more than welcome as a son-in-law! Especially if he was as rich as Billy seemed to be, but little did he know that Billy's heart was already spoken for…

Chapter 13
Cornwall

Billy returned to the Bank the following morning, leaving Captain Sawyer and his crew to finalise the unloading of the ship's cargo. He intended joining the ship later that day after he had spent more time with Sir Walter, who by then had listened to his wife and daughters extolling Billy's virtues until he was sick of hearing them. It was obvious the previous evening had been a success for Billy, as had his effect on the Lumley family for, within an hour, Sir Walter had given him a list of all the investments he thought suitable for him to consider. With a firm handshake, Sir Walter had then said his farewells, sending Billy back to the *Mary Anne* with his wishes that they meet again quite soon, that they might do business together.

By the time Billy's carriage stopped at the gangplank of the *Mary Anne,* the ship was already loaded with the goods needing to go to the West Country and was ready to sail.

Captain Sawyer, Marietta and Jonas, with Nathaniel in his arms, were eagerly awaiting his return, keen to know how his meeting with Sir Walter had fared, but this had to wait until the Captain had given his orders for the sails to be raised.

Within a short while, they were making their way down the Thames, heading for the open sea and thence onwards to Plymouth.

Once out at sea, Billy spent time on deck talking with Martin Sawyer, telling him of his visit to the theatre and dining afterwards with Sir Walter Lumley and his family, and especially of Sir Walter's daughters, both of whom the Captain was familiar with, and then what the great man had advised him to do with his inheritance.

This interested Martin Sawyer, especially hearing Sir Walter's recommendations, making little comment when it came to giving Billy his own advice, except to warn him that he should never be swayed by anyone else's advice, to heed it certainly, but to be wary of telling anyone your business, and especially Sir Walter Lumley, who had a reputation in the city for lining his own pockets when it came to stocks and shares.

Martin Sawyer told Billy that he must use his own judgement before committing any amount of gold to the older man's schemes, unless he was absolutely sure it would be to his advantage. The Captain made no mention of his own dealings with Sir Walter, mainly because he too had been swayed sometimes to invest in schemes that had yet to yield Sir Walter's predicted results...

Only time will tell who's advice was right, as Billy knew the Captain to be a gambler by inclination, but mostly only when the odds were stacked in his favour, as when he'd gambled and won his lugger from the Dutchman, Jaden Grist.

The journey back to the West Country was uneventful, with ne'er a sign of pirates in the grey waters of the Channel and certainly no sign either of the Excise cutter signalling for the ship to heave to, to be inspected as they neared the Cornish coast, having sailed from Plymouth in the early hours of the morning after unloading the rest of the cargo from the West Indies. And so, at last, the *Mary Anne* finally sailed into Talland Bay, this time bringing two new émigrés, Marietta and her young son, who were themselves to experience and fall in love with Cornwall, God's wonderful county, the place where Billy too had fallen in love, with Eva!

The small procession made its way up the steep cliff, then along the familiar, but uneven, path on top of the cliffs. The path now edged with gorse in full flower, giving Marietta her first true sight of the Cornish countryside as they headed towards the village, where Billy intended to leave her and Nathaniel in the capable hands of Sally, whom he knew would love having them to stay.

It took only a few minutes for Sally to understand, from Marietta's broken English, that the baby needed feeding. With the baby fed and put to sleep in one of the many bedrooms in Hope House, Marietta found her way down to Sally's kitchen where, before Sally could stop her, she was helping to prepare the evening meal for the other travellers, who were all waiting to be fed. At last, Sally had found herself the daughter she'd always wanted!

The next morning, Billy brought Eva down to the village to meet Marietta and, as soon as the two young women met there was an instant friendship and then another, once Jonas put in an appearance as well.

Eva could see how much in love they were, finally banishing any previous doubts she might have had as to Billy's love for Marietta to the back of her mind, for it was obvious he loved Marietta, but only as a dear friend. As for Marietta, she only had eyes for Jonas!

Jonas wanted Marietta and the baby to be with him all the time, but he knew he would have to bide his time before he asked her to marry him, knowing she still had a legal husband. Within a few weeks, they'd decided to throw convention to the winds, deciding they would live together. As Sally's old cottage was available to rent, they moved in together, giving Marietta a home of her own, with a man who truly loved and respected her, and her child, unconditionally. Of course the villagers were unaware of her circumstances and at first disapproved of her unconventional life, living with a man who was neither her husband nor the father of her child. After a while, however, they all came to accept that was how it was to be, and nothing was ever said against the beautiful young French woman and her handsome child, who, thankfully, looked exactly like its mother.

It wasn't many months before Marietta could be seen to be expecting another child. Beaming with delight, Jonas held her hand when, a few months later, Marietta was safely delivered of a daughter, the first of many children she was to have with him over the years.

But more of that later…

Meanwhile, Billy had returned to his life with Eva and Sir John Inney, who was in good health and spirits, as well as eager to know how Billy's journey to find his friend had gone. He laughed delightedly as he'd listened to Billy's account of his rescue of Marietta, and then of his adventure with the pirates as they'd sailed in the Caribbean, and then finally, his visit to Sir Walter Lumley, in London, and Billy's first visit to the theatre and his consequent meeting with Sir Walter's family.

Billy told Sir John of the advice he'd been given by Sir Walter, and his talk afterwards with Martin At all of which, Sir John had merely nodded his head, keeping his own counsel for the time being.

The next morning, sitting with Sir John in his familiar study, discussing the pros and cons of his financial affairs, and how best he should use his inheritance, was not unlike the times when Billy would have sat with his father as he discussed the finances relating to the family bank. Like Martin Sawyer, Sir John advised him to rely on his own judgement and certainly not to discount any advice he might have been given. Telling him it was always wise to try and look at any advice from two angles, the one for and the one against! He was to think quite carefully before investing a large amount of his fortune in stocks and shares that were as yet unproved, as it was a brave man who speculated with a fortune, believing another would be quite as easily made, when in fact it often turned out to be the opposite, an easy way in which to lose one.

Billy couldn't help but think that Sir John, like the Captain, might well have invested in stock and shares that were still to come up trumps. Well, he didn't intend to do the same, he only intended to place his inheritance into investments that were safe, although in the future that wasn't always the case when he began to speculate, believing as he got older that one had to speculate to accumulate!

Billy then told his mentor of how Sir Walter had been very complimentary about him, which made Sir John laugh.

'He wasn't very complimentary when I stole my wife from under his very nose! He was furious, the devil even challenged me to a duel!'

Billy laughed. 'He obviously didn't win!'

'Of course not! I was not so stupid as to accept such a wager. My wife was worth a lot to me but, as she said herself, she was not worth dying for, and she certainly didn't plan on marrying him in any case, had I lost the wager!'

'What did you do to get out of having to fight him?'

'I asked him to be my groomsman at our wedding!'

'And that was sufficiently good enough for him to call off the duel?'

'Of course it was. He loved my wife very much, but even he realised he would have been on a hiding to nothing had he killed me. In any case, we did ask him to be godfather to our first child, so it came out right in the end, because it was through me he met Nellie a few weeks later, and she's made him a happy man, who is now, as you know, the proud father of two daughters. So he ended up with the right woman after all. Just as I did!'

Billy sat listening to Sir John as he reminisced, but before the old man could ask any more questions as to what else had happened, Billy sat upright and asked him straight out for his permission to marry Eva, if she would have him?

Sir John's delight was quite obvious and, after sending Billy away to propose to Eva, he rang for Johnson, his trusted manservant, to bring in glasses and wine, that they might celebrate the engagement, quite sure Eva would be only too happy to say 'yes' to her handsome young Frenchman.

Of course Eva was going to say 'yes,' she'd thought of nothing else ever since Billy had come to live at Cliff House. She knew she was in love with him, but when he'd walked out of the study intending to look for her, she had no idea he was about to propose.

Billy walked up to her and, taking her hands in his, he drew her close. His face wore an expression she couldn't fathom, wondering if he was about to impart bad news. Eva felt her heart begin to race, her face paling until Billy spoke.

'Dearest Eva,' he started, nervous for a few moments, wondering if Eva was ready for marriage, 'I want to ask you an important question.'

'Yes, Billy, what is it you want to know?' she asked, thinking that there must be something seriously wrong.

'I want to ask you if you would do me the honour of becoming my wife.'

Eva couldn't speak for a while. She hadn't been expecting a marriage proposal.

'Of course I will!' she answered, her mind racing with questions, but Billy wasn't in the mood for talking, he wanted her in his arms, and that's exactly what happened. His simple question answered simply, by Eva kissing him, and him kissing her back both returning to Sir John's study to tell him Eva had accepted his proposal, at which Sir John clapped loudly, his face a picture of pure contentment.

It was decided they would marry as soon as possible, at the church on the cliffs above Polperro and, with Eva happily leaving the two men to talk of other matters, she hurried away to start and make arrangements, immediately penning letters to her friends and family, warning them invitations would soon be coming their way, inviting them to her marriage to William Sawyer!

Billy continued telling Sir John of the advice he'd received from Sir Walter, telling him of the different stocks and shares Sir Walter had advised he should invest in, as well as the government stocks that were available, and all gilt edged, after assuring Billy they would bring him a reasonable sum in dividends over the next few years and then there were the speculative shares. For some reason, Sir Walter had seemed somewhat wary of promoting these; moreover, Martin had already told him to give them a wide berth. At this, Sir John's eyes had lit up, interested in knowing which shares were being referred to. And then there were the stocks and shares in the mines and companies in Cornwall that Billy had suggested himself, but which Sir Walter had held back on, not knowing a great deal about the Cornish enterprises that Sir John had always advocated to Billy. Sir John had told him that they were worth investing in, as heavily as he could afford, for as he had said, the future, in his opinion, for Cornwall was bright. (This was advice Billy heeded, to his advantage, when, some years later, he realised his Cornish investments had indeed made him a rich man. Billy knew his father would have applauded him for his business acumen and would definitely have approved of his good fortune).

Sir Walter asked Billy to return to London in the near future, when he would take him to the Stock Exchange where he could meet and discuss his financial matters in more depth.

To this, Sir John had heartily agreed. 'Best thing you can do Billy. Why not go before the wedding?'

But on this, Billy was unsure. Eva wanted to get married soon and, since he had been away for many weeks and had only just arrived back, it only seemed right she should have her day. Once the date of the wedding was agreed, Billy wrote to Sir Walter, informing him he would return to London within a month or so of his nuptials and, with that, Sir John had to be satisfied.

Billy had to do as he wanted, and that was as much as the old man could say. He knew his own life was coming to an end and he still had work for Billy to finish before he finally gave up his life. He wanted to see the young couple married and his granddaughter settled with the young man whom he knew would love her forever.

Billy had been instructed by Eva to have a new outfit made for the wedding, a suite of clothes as befitted a young man of wealth and some standing. These were made by a young tailor in Bodmin, an émigré from an earlier rescue made by Captain Sawyer, whom Billy had set up in business when they had met on one of his travels with Sir John.

Eva's outfit, and those of her bridesmaid's, were to be designed and made in Fowey by a young lady from London, an assistant to the court dressmaker who had married a Fowey man she'd met when on a visit to the capital, introduced at a soiree given by mutual friends, where they had quickly fallen in love. The Fowey man took no time at all to persuade her to marry him and move to Cornwall, which she did, on condition that he would buy her a small salon (a dress shop) where she could display and sell her beautiful and fashionable clothes to the Cornish gentry.

After the marriage ceremony, there was to be a wedding feast at Cliff House, with the catering done by the ladies of Polperro, directed by Sally who, as substitute mother of the groom, had decided the meal should be one the locals would remember for years. She organised a cake, made into several tiers, a new idea the Royal Family had instigated the previous year and one which was quickly catching on as a 'must have' for every wedding.

And so it was, on a beautiful Cornish day, that Billy and Eva stood in front of the altar in the ancient church on the cliffs and made their solemn vows in front of their family and friends, promising 'to be true and faithful, and to care for each other in sickness and in health, until death did them part'. Then, with Billy's golden ring on her finger, nestling against the diamond ring he'd presented to her on the day she had accepted his proposal, they were joined together as husband and wife, to the delight of all those who were gathered to watch.

Sir John had given the bride away, as her father had gone on yet another voyage, unaware at the time that Billy was soon to become his son-in-law.

Marietta (newly pregnant at this time with Jonas's first child) was also in the church, as were Sally and James, as well as most of the crew of the *Boy Ben II* and many other villagers who'd taken Billy to their hearts.

The happy couple left Cliff House shortly after their wedding feast was over, showered with rose petals and best wishes from the assembled guests. They embarked upon a short honeymoon, to be spent at Heligan, where Billy had previously enjoyed a visit with Sir John, giving him the opportunity of looking over the new packing station at Mevagissey, recently built for the herring industry, as well as the new harbour that had just been completed. Then, on their way home, they were to stop at other places Sir John had wanted Billy to visit, to give his opinion on, especially the new quarry on Bodmin Moor which would, in the future, supply granite for the houses of Sir Walter's daughters.

And so it came to pass that William Sawyer (known as Billy, formerly Willelm, the son of the Marquis D'Anville) became the husband of Eva, daughter of Captain Sawyer, master mariner and owner of the lugger *Mary Anne,* and granddaughter of Sir John Inney, of Cliff House, near Fowey.

Chapter 14

Changes

With their honeymoon over, life for Billy and Eva settled into a comfortable daily routine with Eva naturally taking on the role as mistress of the house, and hostess, whenever Sir John and Billy entertained the local gentry, as well as those people of some standing with whom they wished to cultivate a business friendship. A few months later Sir John suddenly became ill and within a few days he was looking very frail as his illness and old age took its toll. The doctor had been summoned and was treating Sir John as best he could, but it was not a time when optimism abounded at Cliff House. Eva was worried about her grandfather, and so was Billy, both afraid the old man might well be succumbing to his illness, but at least Billy had mastered most of Sir John's work. He'd become Sir John's trusted assistant, as well as taking on the role of a grandson that the old man had never known. There were many in the business community of Cornwall who believed him to be Sir John's natural successor; their insight proving to be right when Sir John finally did succumb to the chest infection that had laid him low for several weeks. The end for Sir John finally happened the day before the New Year, when all the family were at Cliff House and at his bedside. By all the family, I mean, Eva and Billy, as well as Captain Sawyer who'd recently returned from his latest voyage, along with James and Sally, who had spent most of the festive season at Cliff House, with Sally trying to tempt the old man into eating by cooking what she knew to be his favourite meals, but even this didn't prolong his life and, with his beloved granddaughter, Eva, holding his hand, and with the rest of the family standing by his bedside, Sir John Inney finally gave up his life, leaving everyone bereft.

The funeral service and burial took place the following week, at the church where Eva and Billy had been married only a few months earlier; only this day it was grey and miserable, weather-wise, as well as emotionally.

It was particularly sad because everyone there had cause to be grateful for all Sir John had done for them, and of course especially Billy, who, along with Eva led the mourners into the church, along with her father, Captain Sawyer, who, out of all those present, had the most to be thankful for because without Sir John's initial monetary pay-off, he would have been unable to obtain his first ship, or to then marry his beloved Catherine.

Sir John's solicitor arrived at Cliff House after the funeral service, his case bulging with papers. Once everyone had been given drinks and refreshments, he asked that they should all be seated before he proceeded to read, in great detail, Sir John's wishes as to the sharing of his fortune and his estate.

There were no surprises: Sir John had made provision for all his servants and workers at Cliff House, as well as to certain individuals in the villages of Polperro and Fowey, as well as small legacies for those people who had done valuable service for him over the years.

The bulk of his estate, however, he left jointly to Eva and Billy, with the proviso that Billy was to take sole control of all his businesses and investments, using the income and any monies from them for the benefit of Eva and their future children.

Cliff House was to become Eva's, and then her children's and so on, in perpetuity after her demise. As for Martin Sawyer, he was given a lump sum of money, as were Sally and James, with no provisos as to how they should spend their inheritance.

That really was the gist of his will; but it was to Billy that the estate and Sir John's inconsiderable fortune was to go, for his safekeeping, a legacy Billy found a little daunting at first, until he realised Sir John must have had implicit faith in his ability to take the businesses forward into the future obviously trusting his capabilities. With that in mind, Billy relaxed about his and Eva's inheritance. With Sir John gone, Billy wanted to find his own inheritance, having put his plans on hold when Sir John first became ill.

The documents from his father were still in the chest until one evening, a month after Sir John had died, when, after they'd eaten supper, he brought them down and spread them out on the top of the desk in what had once been Sir John's old study and was now his domain.

The papers were many and various and nearly all of them related to properties Billy knew he would never see again, until he came to those relating to the chateau in Brittany. There didn't seem to be anything marked to indicate a hiding place on any one of them. He was just about to gather the papers into a pile and return them to the chest when he noticed a single sheet of parchment, obviously old from its yellowing and fragility, that had fallen out from another pile of papers relating to the house in Paris.

Billy knew from his first glance that this was what he was after. It looked to have been handcrafted, possibly by his father's hand. It was a drawing of the chateau's estate in Brittany. On it were penned numerous marks that seemed to Billy to indicate where his father might have buried the remaining family treasures.

He called to Eva to come into the room and, once she too had looked at the paper, she also agreed it seemed to be the likely place – but why did Billy want to go back to France, when they had more than enough money and land for their use in Cornwall for their futures? Was it not just greed? she'd asked him gently, afraid for his safety if he returned to France, where it was quite likely he would be recognised. If that happened, he would be sure to be apprehended and most probably slain, as were his parents.

Billy shook his head. 'Eva, you are my dearest wife. It's not greed to want what is rightly mine. I always intended to go and find my inheritance and now is the right time, before the estates are completely taken over by the Revolutionary government, who will surely make it impossible for me to gain legal access in the future to what is rightfully mine!'

Eva knew Billy well enough by then to know it would make no difference what she said because, once he had made up his mind, he would do whatever it took to get his hands on all that he believed to be rightly his. The only question now was, how he intended to return to France?

She instinctively knew it would be her father who would be the man to take him, along with Jonas, of course, who Billy trusted, and now considered to be his best friend in Cornwall.

And so it was that the next day Billy rode Penhale into Polperro, where he spoke to Sally and James, and then with Jonas, who was happily living with Marietta, heavy with her expected child. Like Eva, she was none too happy when Billy spoke of returning to France to claim his inheritance; fearing for his safety she pleaded with him not to go, and even more so when he told her he intended taking Jonas along with him to help.

It didn't matter what anyone had to say, because once Billy had made up his mind that he intended to carry out his intentions, all he needed was for Captain Sawyer to agree to take him across to Roscoff.

Once he had his agreement, he would then make arrangements for his departure. In the meantime, he put his Cornish affairs in order, sending letters to Sir Walter Lumley, telling him of Sir John's death and explaining he would be taking over any accounts Sir John had with the Bank of England, asking that they should be transferred to his name, along with a copy of Sir John's last will and testament, as well as a letter from the family solicitor confirming this.

One month later, at the end of March, when the weather was more predictable, Billy was ready to leave.

Captain Sawyer had anchored the *Mary Anne* in Talland Bay two days earlier. With the weather set fair for the following week, Billy and Jonas were ready to go in search of Billy's lost inheritance.

Eva's father could see marriage suited her and was delighted when she told him she was expecting her first baby, except that, so far, she hadn't told Billy he was going to be a father in the autumn!

Billy arrived home later that evening, after a busy few days visiting his holdings in the county and, after a celebration meal and a glass or two of one of the fine wines from out of Sir John's cellar, the two men sat and talked for hours about Billy's plans for returning to France.

That night was one of many in which Billy was to dream of his parents, and the house in the country they had loved best of all, leaving him to wonder, when he woke, just where on the estate could his father have possibly hidden the family's treasures?

Chapter 15

Brittany

Billy and Jonas stood silently on the shingle beach, patiently waiting for the ship's rowboat to take them to where the *Mary Anne* was sitting at anchor in Talland Bay, the ship having anchored there a couple of days ago, after returning from a short smuggling run to Guernsey. Once the two young men were on board her, she would then set sail for Brittany, not on a smuggling run this time, but to take Billy back to Roscoff, that he might return to his chateau home and search for the family treasures his father had hidden. Treasures rescued not only from the house in Paris, but the chateau as well. And, should he by chance happen to come across Jean-Luc, Marietta's husband, Billy's intention was to see him dead. By whatever means he could find, fair or foul. Of course he made no mention of the latter to Jonas, who he already knew to be a God-fearing man, and one who wouldn't take lightly to the idea of doing away with the one man Billy thought to be nothing short of being the scum of the earth.

Jed Pengelly was waiting on deck for the two young men to arrive, impatient to be away. By the time the two young men had climbed on board and stowed their belongings, the sails had been unfurled and raised and, with Captain Sawyer ready at the wheel, the *Mary Anne* sailed out of Talland Bay, making for Roscoff, where

Billy and Jonas were to be put ashore and collected at a later date, if and when Billy found what he was looking for.

The voyage across the Channel was fairly uneventful in the main, except for a storm that suddenly blew up to a force ten halfway across, such was its force it caused Billy and Jonas to lie in their hammocks, until Roscoff was sighted and the two young men finally found the strength to leave the ship.

Dressed as French sailors and still feeling a little groggy, they staggered off the ship and made their way across the hard towards the tavern, hoping their uniforms would allow them free passage through the small port, without any harassment or bother.

The tavern was where Billy hoped to make contact with a local man, one he believed might be able to help them, the man whom Monsieur Dupris had spoken of some months before when Billy, worried about Marietta and her family, had asked if he knew where she was?

Monsieur Dupris had assured Billy the young man would be able to help, but still Billy worried, hoping the young man had not moved away from the area, or been conscripted into the revolutionists' army. He was therefore delighted when they entered the tavern to find himself suddenly face to face with the very person he was seeking. Not that Billy knew him personally, but after asking quite loudly if anyone there knew where a Marcel Roué could be found, the young man suddenly spoke up.

It was a happy coincidence that the young man was there at all. He'd been in prison in Quimper for a minor misdemeanour and had only recently been released, returning to Roscoff because it was his hometown, where he hoped to pick up a position on a ship as he was an experienced sailor.

Billy took the young man to one side and asked if was interested in working for him for a couple of days. When Marcel nodded his agreement, Billy then asked if he could find some form of transport.

Marcel appeared to be able-bodied and quick-witted. Thankfully, Billy instinctively knew that he could trust him. Taking a chance on his instincts being correct, and knowing he had to reveal something, Billy explained quietly they had to go to the village, where his father's chateau was, to look for hidden treasure. At that point, Marcel's eyes lit up and made to leave the tavern, beckoning for Billy and Jonas to follow before all and sundry in the tavern were alerted to something going on that might be of interest to the authorities.

Knowing the area well, Marcel Roué knew Billy and Jonas needed to change out of their seamen's outfits as soon as possible and into clothing that would let them mingle with the local people. Within minutes, they were heading towards the cottage where Marcel lived, with plenty of discussions as they walked along the lane from the harbour, mainly about the way they were dressed. His chief concern was that they would quickly come under suspicion if they carried on walking to the chateau dressed as they were. It made Billy realise how fortuitous it had been to find this young man, as he seemed to have a clear mind, which Billy knew was all he needed from any man he employed; one who could make a quick judgement and act on it without making a fuss or bother.

Once they reached the small cottage Marcel called home, he left Billy and Jonas wondering what they could use to disguise themselves. Marcel, however, knew exactly what they could use and, leaving them alone in the cottage, he went into the cottage next door where his brother lived. He came back a short while later with an armful of raggedy old clothes that he threw across to Billy.

'Try these on and see if they will do the trick?' he said.

Billy sorted through them, tossing items across to Jonas, hoping there was something suitable that would make them look more like farm workers. Not that Billy cared what he looked like, but there were still areas where peasants could be hauled in front of the local magistrate for no good reason at all and, therefore, it was prudent to take any action that would prevent this from happening.

They were soon clothed in items that really should have graced a bonfire, including an old hat apiece that hid their fair hair. Before long, they were ready to set out, pushing a rickety old cart Marcel had unearthed from a barn at the back of his cottage.

It was a fairly uneventful journey, except for one mishap, when a wheel on the cart suddenly came off and they had to stop to juggle with it as they tried to push it back on its spindle. The three of them were still struggling, when a group of revolutionists suddenly appeared, stopping to ask them what was going on and where were they taking the cart, and for what purpose.

Being a quick-witted young man, Marcel told them a tale of the three of them going to help an old widow woman by moving her belongings from her old hovel of a home into a house that had recently been liberated by the excellent revolutionaries themselves. He ingratiated himself with them in such a manner that the story seemed quite believable, sufficing as an explanation; so much so, indeed, that the revolutionaries even helped to upright the wagon before sending the three young men off with a wave of their caps and shouts of 'vive la France!', much to Billy's amusement that he tried hard to conceal.

Eventually they came to the main entrance of the chateau, which Billy ignored. Instead, he led the way down the side lane that he'd used on his first visit, wary of meeting anyone who might recognise him. He had no need to worry; there were no signs of life on the estate. Nor did it appear that anyone had been in the main house, or in the stables, since his last visit, as there were no visible signs of footsteps in the dust on the floors.

Billy left Jonas and Marcel in the stables while he walked through the rooms of the chateau once more, just to make sure the house was as he'd left it. A visit that didn't please him at all. He felt as before, desolate and grief stricken that his mother and father were no longer there, and neither were their possessions. Sadly, the chateau no longer felt like his home. He tried to hold back his tears, knowing it wasn't the same as he remembered from his younger days and never would be; it was too full of the ghosts of his past, of his parents and his ancestors, who had once lived in the old chateau. His past life was over, as were his parents. He knew he had to move on, which was easier said than done, whatever age a person might be. Being stalwart and stoic, Billy just shrugged his shoulders and carried on. His life was yet to be lived.

Jonas and Marcel walked across to the chateau, intrigued and awed by Billy's home. It was a magical place to them both, somewhere they would never have entered before and, quite simply, they were both a little intimidated by its grandeur, even though it was no longer occupied or furnished as it once would have been. It was then they both became acutely aware that Billy came from a different background to theirs. A life they would previously never have been a part of. For a while, they were silent. Billy's previous life had been privileged, not that this had any effect on their behaviour towards him. As for Billy, this was no time for acting grand. His aim was to find his inheritance and then to get away from the place as fast as he could. He had no desire to linger any longer than was necessary. The chateau, like the house in Paris, was in his past and, being a practical person, he knew he had to put his sentimental attachment to the chateau to one side and accept that whatever was to be, would be; call it fate, call it destiny, or even kismet, he could change nothing. He had to accept that, although his life might have changed, he still wanted what was his!

Marcel, with some thought for their bodily needs, had brought with him some bread and cheese from his mother's larder, as well as the last bottle of wine she'd been saving, for a day when a celebration drink required it to be opened. Once the three of them had shared the food and wine, they sat and talked for a while, mainly as to where they were to start and look for whatever it was that Billy's father had hidden. At this discussion, Billy pulled the sheet of old parchment from out of his pocket, placing it down on the table in the kitchen for Jonas and Marcel to look at. There was some controversy between them as to what the marks on the map where intended to mean, with Billy looking at it the hardest, turning the parchment around several times, until he had it aligned with landmarks he recognised.

First of all, there was a sign of a cross that Billy was quite sure indicated the church, and then other marks that indicated the grounds of the estate. Others were of the outbuildings, and one other mark in particular that showed the chateau itself. Another showed where the gatehouse was located. It was from this mark that a heavily marked line showed what Billy thought to be a pathway, leading away from the chateau, towards where there used to be a cottage (this was where the housekeeper had lived with her husband, who'd previously been his father's head groom). Then it showed two crosses, on or near the stables. It wasn't clear as to where exactly they were meant to be and

Billy could only speculate as to whether these really did mark the area where his treasure was hidden.

It was then he speculated to Marcel and Jonas that his father must have had help to bury the treasure. As he thought about that, Billy knew his father must have trusted someone sufficiently to enlist their help, and the only person he knew who might have filled that role was his father's groom, a man who'd already proved himself over the years to be trustworthy and honest. Now Billy must do the same, but he also knew that the man was no longer on the estate.. (It wasn't until many years later that Billy found out that the man in question, and his wife, had been guillotined for befriending the marquis and his family, a fact that filled Billy with even more grief, already saddened that his father's trusted servants should have met with such an unseemly and ignominious end.)

With the meagre amount of food eaten and their hunger sated for the time being, the three young men set out to look for any possible clues in the grounds as to where the treasure might be hidden.

Billy started pacing out what he thought might be the first possible area, but that led to nothing of any consequence as there were no signs of the earth having been dug over in many a year. The next site marked on the map was the ground by the stables, but this also looked as though it had never been disturbed and, as most of it was cobbled with small stones, it was obvious it would have taken many weeks to be refitted had they been disturbed, Billy began to despair, knowing that too was not the place. For a while it left him feeling depressed that he would never find what he was looking for, until Jonas got down on his hands and knees and started to poke the ground with his hands, just inside the stable, where Billy had once rested Henri Masson's horse.

Suddenly, he called out to Billy to come and see what he'd found.

Billy and Marcel rushed across to join him on the floor: like Jonas, they too began scraping at the ground with their hands until Billy could feel a piece of metal. Quickly, he removed more of the dirt and could see that it was the handle of a trapdoor.

Billy looked at Jonas and then at Marcel, unable to believe what they'd found.

'Give me a hand!' he said excitedly, scraping away more dirt.

He grasped hold of the handle and tried to pull the trapdoor open, but it was stuck fast and was too hard to budge; it needed a much stronger hand than his to pull it open.

Marcel, having watched Billy struggle for some time, pushed him out of the way.

'Let me at it!' he shouted in French, which Jonas didn't understand until Marcel pushed him out of the way as well, making his intention quite clear. Grasping the handle, he pulled at it with all his might. To their utter amazement, the lid suddenly rose up in the air and there, right in front of their eyes, was an opening hiding a flight of steps that when they investigated further found it led down to a small, dark cellar under the stables. It was a place Billy had never known existed.

He was the first to go down the steps, quickly followed by Jonas, leaving Marcel to stand guard outside in case anyone arrived. Thankfully, there was neither sight nor sound of anyone else in the area.

Striking the flint box which he'd had the foresight to carry in his pocket for such an eventuality, Billy lit a candle he'd taken from the *Mary Anne*'s store. At last, he was able to see it was part of a much larger cellar.

Raising the lighted candle, Billy was amazed at what he saw before him, unable at first to believe his eyes. He heard Jonas draw in his breath, as he'd done, once they'd become accustomed to the flickering light.

To their amazement, on the dirt floor were several wooden boxes. Once Billy had prised the top off one, he could see it was full of gold bars. By the flickering candlelight, he prised the tops off several others, finding them all filled with the same thing. He was stunned, as was Jonas.

As they moved around the cellar, they could see a dozen or more leather bags, all full of coins and then, many more bags and wooden cases, all containing the treasures his mother had gathered over the years and had previously kept in the chateau.

All of which answered some of Billy's questions as to where they had disappeared.

Stacked against one wall were numerous other boxes that from his first glances he could see held some of the fine china and other precious items he knew to be from his grandparents' homes, as well as some paintings that would once have graced the walls of the family house in Paris.

Billy was astounded at the quantity and quality of his inheritance, as well as how his father must have planned for a long time how he was to hide it all, for this had been no spur of the moment action.

For Billy, the big question now was how was he to transport his find back to Cornwall without drawing attention to himself or to his inheritance, both items that the revolutionaries would love to get their hands on.

By this time, Marcel had also climbed down to see what it was Billy and Jonas had found. His eyes nearly popped out of his head, unable to comprehend the amount of valuables that lay before him.

'What are we to do with all this stuff?' he asked.

'We're going to get as much of this as we can onto the cart and take it back to the *Mary Anne*. Then it's all going back to Cornwall.'

'If you don't mind me saying so, I think we might find it difficult to get this lot anywhere near the *Mary Anne*!

'Why do you say that?' Billy asked, quite annoyed that Marcel was being so difficult.

'For a start, we will have to pass through the village, and, if we're seen with a cart full of precious stuff like this, we're sure to be stopped and questioned. I think we are going to have a rethink as to how we can get past the village, or find another way back to the port.'

Billy stroked his chin for a moment or two, deep in thought, his mind churning over as he wondered what he was to do next.

Just how was he to get his possessions back to the *Mary Anne* in one trip? He had no intention of leaving anything behind.

It was Jonas who came up with the idea of hiding the goods under a layer of manure. Unfortunately there was very little of that around, as there had been no animals on the land for some time, ever since the famine had struck, so what could they use instead?

Marcel solved the dilemma. The goods would be loaded onto the cart and covered by a couple of old ragged blankets Billy had seen earlier in the stables. Then he and Jonas would lie on top, feigning illness, while Marcel pushed the cart along the road towards the port.

Fortunately all went well for the trio. They loaded the goods from the underground cellar onto the cart, staggering under the weight of the gold. Replacing the trapdoor, they even covered the area with a light dusting of soil, hoping to hide it from prying eyes – not that there was anything left to be found – before throwing the blankets over Billy's inheritance and adding a light covering of what was left of the manure.

Billy and Jonas pushed the cart down the side lane before making their way onto the road that would take them back to the harbour and the *Mary Anne*. They were all too aware of rattling noises coming from inside the cart, from some of the stuff that was uncovered or unboxed.

It wasn't until they were nearly at the port that Billy heard the sound of men marching along the road. Stopping the cart, he signalled to Marcel to take over as soon as he and Jonas had climbed on top of the blanket, trying to make out that they were ill. Luckily for them, by the time the marching men came into view Billy and Jonas were lying on top of Billy's treasures. The band of peasants came to a halt by the side of the cart. Assuming Marcel was in charge they asked him where he was going and what was in the cart?

'There's nothing inside,' he said, 'except for these two, who you can see are sick.' In an aside to one of the group, he said quietly, 'I think it's the plague. I'm returning them to their homes as we have no need for disease in these parts!'

The group took a united step backwards at Marcel's words. They didn't want any disease near them either. They had enough trouble as it was, without taking problems back to their families.

'What sort of disease are you talking about?' asked one young peasant.

Marcel stopped the cart and went to touch Jonas. 'This one has the pox, the other I think is sickening for it. If you would like to give me a hand, we can stand them up and you can take a better look?'

'No, I don't think that will be necessary,' said the man Billy took to be the leader and who quickly stepped away. 'We can see for ourselves they don't look so good.'

Prodding Marcel with the butt of his weapon, he said, 'You'd better keep moving, young man; the sooner you get them away from here, the better!'

'Of course. I was merely taking a breather. It's hard work pushing this old cart. Perhaps you could give me a hand?' he asked, but the man just ignored Marcel's request by telling his men to march on, much to the quiet amusement of Billy and Jonas.

And that was how easy it was for Billy and Jonas to get back to the harbour, to where the *Mary Anne* was waiting. As the tide was on the rise, it was just right for the ship to sail away and so it didn't take long before the cart was quickly unloaded.

Piece by piece, Billy's treasures were taken onto the ship by the crew, mustered by Jed Pengelly to help, and placed in one of the holds, to be stored in wooden boxes the ship's carpenter had already made for something else, but which the Captain had commandeered for Billy's use once he could see how much, and the quality of Billy's inheritance was. Keenly, he watched as everything that had been piled onto the cart was off-loaded and taken below.

Captain Sawyer laughed. 'Would you mind telling me, Billy, what's going to happen to all of this stuff?'

Billy laughed. 'It's going in the hold. I fancy that if some of this were to be sold in London, if I'm not mistaken, it would fetch a pretty price. If I take some of it to Sir Walter Lumley, he's bound to know of a favourable outlet for some of my treasures. Except for those I want to take back to Cornwall for Eva and Sally to see and use!'

And so it was, with Billy's inheritance safely aboard and stored below decks, that Billy and Jonas said their farewells to Marcel, leaving him to return to home, taking the cart with him, as well as a handful of Billy's gold coins for his trouble, leaving Jonas and Billy to help the crew in preparing the *Mary Anne* to sail within the hour.

Chapter 16

London

It's time to know more about the role Sir Walter Lumley played in Billy's story, because he's the man who is going to make Billy even wealthier than he is at the moment. First of all, however, let us get to know the man himself.

We already know he's wealthy, some of it inherited, but mostly self-made by making his small inheritance work for him, thus making him one of the richest men in the City by the time he came to know Billy. Then there's his wife's fortune, an amount he's also ably increased more than tenfold over the years since their marriage.

Before Walter Lumley married Nellie Osborne, the daughter of a wealthy merchant in the City, he was already a notable presence in the Bank of England with his eyes resolutely set at the time on the woman who was destined to become Sir John Inney's late wife, Jane.

At the time of his rejection, Sir Walter had thought no other woman would ever make a claim on his heart but, within a few months, his friend and love rival had introduced him to Nellie; Sir John Inney was quite sure that Nellie was the perfect woman for Walter.

Once having met and then married Nellie, all within a few months of their first meeting, he'd found her to be a formidable woman, not the sort he'd ever reckoned on having as his wife.

To his surprise, Sir Walter found Nellie to be an agreeable person to live with, as well as having an insatiable desire for his manhood in bed, as well as her deep-rooted desire to be the wife of a wealthy man, it led to them having a perfect marriage.

Looks and personality were of no importance to Nellie in her quest for a wealthy husband, and neither was Sir Walter's lack of personality a stumbling block in their relationship. Even so, she was a wise woman, one who knew her own imperfections that she tried hard to hide, and one who also knew she desired nothing more than a husband who would be faithful to her and who would help her to achieve her primary aim of being a wife and mother, preferably of sons, although, when her first child, Lilian, was placed in her arms (after a birth that seemed to take days), she was astounded at how possessive she felt, as she looked at the red-faced infant that was the image of its father; not a particularly good look for a female child, and neither did it bode well for the child's future when it came time for her to find a husband for herself.

When the second daughter, Martha, arrived the following year, in much the same way as the first, as well as being a mirror image, Nellie and Walter's family was complete.

The years flew by, with both girls quickly growing into womanhood equally as fast. Rapidly, they became the image of their mother, in fact the very double of her, with their plump figures; their bodies were well-rounded, with delicious curves that young men seemed to like very much, especially when the view was of plump breasts, overflowing from the low-cut dresses their mother had decided they should wear at all times. Her breasts had once been a magnet for Sir Walter, who at the time could hardly keep his hands off them. She could see no reason why her daughters shouldn't get the men of their dreams, as she had done, by showing off their charms. However, her dreams were all she had left, since the sexual side of her marriage had gone into a sharp decline after only a few years of marriage, mainly because her husband had become too portly to perform as he should as a husband, and she had become much too buxom to keep him attracted.

Sir Walter had enjoyed his marriage for the first decade and a half, especially the sexual side, after the wilderness years of his younger years. As the years passed, he would have preferred his wife to be less well endowed, failing to see his own reflection in the mirror and still believing he was the young and agile stud he'd once been in his imagination.

Over the years, his life had been made comfortable by Nellie and he never had any intention of leaving her for some flibbertigibbet of a woman, who wanted only to get her hands on his wealth rather than his manhood. In the end, however, it came down to the fact that he had to have some bodily satisfaction.

When Billy had first arrived in London and had met Sir Walter, the great man had wanted Billy to stay with his family but, as time was short, Billy promised to stay when next he visited London and this visit coincided with his return from searching and finding his family treasures. Therefore, it was the ideal opportunity for him to stay with the family, to enjoy their hospitality and, at the same time, do some business with Sir Walter.

Captain Sawyer had sailed the *Mary Anne* up the Thames, depositing Billy onto the dockside with his treasures to follow later. Jonas had been charged with acting as guard, before most of it was to go into storage in a warehouse, a secure place in the city before being auctioned, and the rest being taken back to Cornwall for Billy to use, or to give to Eva and Sally, both of whom he loved and respected and knew would appreciate the items he'd chosen with them in mind.

Sir Walter, having been informed of Billy's return, had sent a carriage to take him to the Lumley house on the Heath at Hampstead, where Billy planned on staying until he'd made plans for his treasures. (This was where Sir Walter came to the fore, as he had connections with sales rooms, where valuable articles could be sold by auction to those with the money to buy them.)

Billy's arrival was the cause for much celebration, quickly organised by Lilian and Martha, Sir Walter's daughters. They were about the same age as Billy and, as Billy was handsome and well spoken, they'd both fallen in love with him the first time they'd seen him at the theatre. However, on this visit, whenever he was out of the house on business with their father, they would spend hours discussing his prowess as a potential suitor, deciding they would make a play for him.

Fortunately, Billy managed to stop any such involvement before it began by confiding his love for Eva and how he had married her some months before.

It was also fortunate that the two sisters were of a gregarious nature, and popular with their peers and therefore held no malice when he'd told them of his deep and abiding love for Eva.

As Sir Walter and his wife enjoyed entertaining the house was invariably full of friends and family each weekend, giving Billy the opportunity to meet people he would never have met otherwise. It was at one such meeting that he met someone who would have a fortuitous effect on him, but more of that later. For the time being, we must put ourselves into Billy's life as he lived it at that time, with Sir Walter and his family.

Most days Billy would travel by carriage into the City with Sir Walter, where he would spend his day walking between the Bank of England and the new arcades, where fancy shops were beginning to open, selling goods newly imported into the country from the colonies; goods Billy had never seen before.

On some mornings he would visit the coffee houses that had sprung up in the city, where members of the Stock Exchange would sit and discuss the day's dealings.

It didn't take long before Billy had introduced himself to these men and quite soon he found himself being invited back to the Exchange, where he would talk to the traders, enjoying the cut and thrust of them as they bought and sold stocks and shares.

Being quick witted and intelligent, Billy soon knew more than enough about trading to try it for himself. After a couple of weeks, he felt himself quite competent at deciding which companies he should invest his quite considerable fortune in, and those he should leave well alone. After one regrettable purchase he soon decided buying and selling stocks and shares was a business where it was as easy to lose a fortune as it was to make one. From the stories he'd heard recently from his newfound friends, buying and selling had been the downfall of many a rich man over the years.

Hearing stories such as these, he became cagey as to what he would buy and sell; so much so that, by the time it came for him to return to Cornwall, he'd managed to increase his own wealth quite considerably as well as selling some of his heirlooms he'd retrieved them from the warehouse where Captain Sawyer had sent them. Smaller items that had no sentimental value he took to one shop in one of the new arcades, set up by a friend of Sir Walter's, a place for buying and selling unwanted furniture and other goods that had come, quite legitimately, from some of the grand houses that lined the streets in the city.

Sir Walter had grown to like and admire Billy more as each day passed and wanted nothing more than for him to prosper; he also wanted to know more about his young life and what had happened in France to his family. In the evenings, when no dinner party or dance had been arranged, he would ask Billy to join him in his study after dinner, when he would bring out the best cognac money could buy, along with the finest Venetian glasses. It was then the two men would sit quietly, drinking and talking, two activities Sir Walter excelled at.

Sir Walter would light a cigar, one of many he'd recently taken delivery of from South America, that he kept in a newly purchased humidor on his desk (cigars that Billy knew would have come from a place called Cuba, in the Caribbean, where he'd recently sailed with Captain Sawyer). Not that Billy smoked; he'd tried it once and it nearly choked him. He'd decided, there and then, that smoking was not for him and, from then onwards, he never smoked again, neither did he allow anyone else to smoke in his home, much to the annoyance of his many friends and acquaintances, as smoking was quite the newest fad to have started in the city. Even Sir Walter began to cut down on the quantity he smoked when Billy was with him, but not on the amount he drank. He still quaffed copious amounts of wine at every meal, as well as swilling his good French cognac down his gullet at the end of every meal as a digestive, and at every other opportunity as well, much to his wife's disgust when he was unable to make his way up the stairs to their bed. This finally resulted in them sleeping in separate rooms, which in turn meant Nellie's conjugal needs were no longer being met. This left Sir Walter free to have his sexual needs provided for by any young women he happened to see and fancy while driving in his carriage through the London parks.

Women, such as the attractive streetwalkers, who roamed the area and who were prepared to let him entice them into his carriage with the promise of a handful of gold coins, where he would grope them, before taking them back to a small hotel, newly built at the edge of the park, where he would hire a room for a reasonable sum of money.

By the time the women had serviced him, not caring that he was portly or that his breath was rank or that his body was brandy fuelled, they would take the gold he offered and Sir Walter would be satisfied, at least for another week before the urge overtook him again and he went for another drive,

A few years later, on another visit to the Lumley household, Billy found out what had happened to Lilian and Martha.

By then, they were both married with children of their own, having managed to snare a husband each.

Lillian's husband had once been a young buck about town, an officer in the Hussars, a handsome young man who, after he'd danced with her at one of her mother's evening soirees, had found her to be irresistible and just the type of woman he desired.

To his delight she'd been quite happy to reciprocate his caresses with some of her own, kissing him in such a way it left him trembling and wanting to possess her, which of course wasn't going to happen until his ring was on her finger and a date for their marriage had been announced in the *Gazette* and the invitations to the wedding had been sent out by her parents.

Martha didn't fare quite so happily as her sister with her choice of a husband to be, which in some respects for the young man in question was perhaps as well! The young man she was introduced to was not a rich man. He was, though, quite handsome in an effeminate and boyish way, as was the style those days. Blond hair, blue eyes and clean shaven, as well as being quite tall and slim, in direct contrast to Martha who was short and plump, with an abundance of curves that enticed most men into wanting to make love to her. She was a very desirable young woman and one this particular young man had no intention of losing.

He was, of course, quite intelligent, Unfortunately, he had few aspirations to find gainful employment once he left the King's service as he had an income, albeit a small annuity from the estate of an aged relative. This was more than enough for a single man, but not for one contemplating marriage, a point he made to Martha right from the outset of their romance. But he too had fallen in love, which was exactly the reason that Nellie decided he would make the ideal husband for her younger daughter, money or no money.

Knowing he would be without employment once he was out of the army, it was Nellie who persuaded her husband to find an occupation for the young man, so that Martha might at least marry someone who could provide for her. It was also Nellie's persuasive powers, and Sir Walter's money, that was to make life even easier for the young couple, by allowing Nellie to buy and furnish a house for them nearby. She managed then to persuade her husband to settle an allowance on Martha, one sufficient to keep her and her new husband in some luxury as it was Nellie's ambition to see both her daughters happily wed and then, afterwards, to quickly become mothers, which, in due course, is exactly what happened.

With his business in the City completed, Billy knew it was time for him to return home to Cornwall, to Eva.

The *Mary Anne* had long since left London and was on her way to Cornwall. As there was a new coach service running from London to Plymouth, Billy arranged to be on board at the end of the following week, sorry to leave his London friends but promising to return in the future, promising that he would then bring Eva with him.

On the day appointed for his departure, the entire Lumley family escorted him to where the coach was waiting. After a tearful farewell from Lilian and Martha, and from their mother, Nellie, Billy finally shook hands with Sir Walter, promising to convey his best wishes to all who knew him in Cornwall.

With his newly purchased carpet bag stowed aboard the coach, the driver blew his post horn to signal the coach was leaving. Billy raised his new beaver hat and mouthed his goodbyes through the window, wondering how long it would be before he saw them all again.

Chapter 17

Jean-Luc Dupont

In the meantime, what had happened to Jean-Luc? He had no idea when he returned to the house that Marietta and his son would not be waiting for him. He knew his marriage to Marietta had been a big mistake, but his lust for her had far outweighed his conscience. As the months of their marriage passed he'd grown to be angry with her all the time, mainly because she showed him nothing but scorn; physically fighting him whenever he got near, determined never to give in graciously to his demands, or to give him anything other than harsh words. His work in the militia demanded him to be hard with those he captured and took before the magistrate, and he was the right man for doing just that. Neither was there any compassion in his heart for his young wife, or his child, had there been just a small amount of kindness in his heart, Marietta might well have forgiven him and learnt to live with him, but it's very doubtful that she would have ever learnt to love him. He must have had some good points, but without a shred of care in his body, Jean-Luc was, in Marietta's eyes, her enemy and had to be got rid of, truly believing her life to be in mortal danger every time he walked into the house. How his demise was to be achieved she had no idea, until Billy and Jonas arrived. She could hardly contain herself as she heard Willelm calling her name, believing at first it was her imagination playing games with her, or even that she was hearing spirit voices talking to her, until she heard glass breaking at the back of the house, and suddenly Willelm and another young man appeared, come to rescue her, to take her away to a new life. She was even more astounded when Willelm told her they would be going to live in Cornwall.

Jean-Luc arrived back at the house a few hours later to find everywhere quiet and still. There was no sound of life at all when he entered, no candlelight, not even the sound of his son crying for attention. He called out, but there was no reply and, unable to understand what had happened, he suddenly realised Marietta and his son had gone, vanished from the house, as well as their belongings. He searched every room, only to find the house empty and with no idea where she might have gone, not having seen her on the road as he rode home. He started to panic until common sense prevailed and he realised she must have had help to leave, never thinking for a single moment that Willelm D'Anville might be responsible, believing him to be either dead or living in England. He assumed it must have been someone Marietta knew in the nearby hamlet, or perhaps someone in her family – but who could it have possibly been? Knowing her mother was dead and that she had no brothers or sisters to call on, Jean-Luc suddenly knew the only other people who might know her whereabouts would be his own mother and father.

Determined to find Marietta and his son, Jean-Luc decided to search for her that night. After saddling his horse again, he set off for his parent's house but, when he arrived, it was only to find they'd not seen their daughter-in-law and grandson for several days, and had no idea where they could be. By this time, Jean-Luc was furious, refusing to eat or drink with them in his eagerness to find his lost wife and child.

By this time it was nearly midnight. He'd left his parent's house and ridden back to the house Marietta thought to be her prison, but this time he searched the rooms more thoroughly, walking through them all, until he came to the small room downstairs, no bigger than a cupboard really, used only for storage and where Jonas had broken the window to gain access. Seeing the broken window, Jean-Luc knew someone must have broken in and taken Marietta and the child. But had she gone willingly? He shook his head in bafflement, wondering if she had been abducted. And why? That was his quandary.

His only hope was to ride back to his headquarters and report that his wife and child were missing, and rally some help from his colleagues, but this was going to be a disappointing time for Jean-Luc. His colleagues knew him to be a bully and were not surprised to find Marietta had vanished. They all tried to tell him she must have gone away to visit someone, perhaps a family relative or a friend, but Jean-Luc was not going to believe that. He was quite sure she'd run away and that someone she knew must have helped as she would have found it difficult to cope with a small child and the amount of baggage, which he was sure she'd taken, from his first glances around the room she'd slept in.

Meanwhile, Marietta and Nathaniel were by this time already safely on board the *Mary Anne* and sailing away from France. As no one had seen her escape, there was no one to inform her by now frantic husband of what had happened. Her escape was finally completed to the jubilation and satisfaction of Billy, and the enamoured Jonas.

The next morning, Jean-Luc decided he would extend his search and, after informing his commanding officer of the previous day's failed events, he went back to Marietta's old home.

As her father was still in command of the militia and otherwise occupied, he too was not at home when Jean-Luc rode up to the house. He left his horse tied up outside to wait while he went to complete his errand.

The only servants at the time in the house were a cook-cum-housekeeper, who looked after Marietta's father, and a man who did most of the outside work, with a village boy to help him, as well as a kitchen maid, who'd been put in charge of cleaning the house. There were no other servants and the ones there were quite happy to tell Jean-Luc that his wife had not been seen in the house since her mother had died.

By this time Marietta's father had arrived home. Seeing Jean-Luc waiting and hearing his story, the two men ate a meagre supper, prepared and served in some haste by the housekeeper, who was keen to get back to her own home to relate the conversation she'd overheard between the two men. She would tell her husband that the beautiful daughter of the house had at last escaped from the clutches of the awful man she'd had the misfortune to marry, information that was soon circulating throughout the local countryside where Marietta was well-known and liked.

Of course this leaked information did not bode well for Jean-Luc in his quest to find Marietta, as a wall of silence grew around the area, preventing him from finding out any information as to her whereabouts, even had the villagers known where, and with whom, she'd gone.

After supper, Jean-Luc decided he would continue his search the next morning, after Marietta's father had suggested he should stay the night and go to the chateau, where Marietta's friend Willelm lived the next morning on the off-chance she might be staying there, not realising at the time that the Marquis and his wife had already been betrayed and guillotined in Paris, or that Willelm had already evaded the same fate by escaping to England.

Many times during the next few days, Jean-Luc despaired of ever finding his wife and child, especially after he'd arrived at Billy's old home, only to find the chateau not just deserted, but empty of the family's possessions. He went from the chateau to the small village, to ask the old servants if they knew where the family and their possessions had gone. Of course, he drew a blank.

It had been some time since the chateau had been occupied and the family's old servants had no knowledge of where any of the family might be, except for hearing rumours that the family had all been murdered. Believing the rumours, Jean-Luc had no option other than to return to his own home, a defeated man, and one in despair, having lost the only woman he knew he would ever love.

But this was not the end of Jean-Luc's search for Marietta and his son, who'd had the good fortune to escape to a better life; it was his life that was about to take a turn for the worse!

When he arrived back at his father-in-law's house to report the failure of his search, he was told there were orders waiting from high command; he was to travel to Paris, where he'd been transferred. It was a posting Jean-Luc had no love for and for which he would eventually give his life, being brutally attacked en route. Fatally injured by an unruly mob for no apparent reason, other than the lust for blood from a group of peasants rampaging through the city, killing anyone for no other reason than they didn't like the cut of his clothes or the look of his face.

Taking the law into their own hands, they'd attacked and killed him, which seems ironic now, especially to those that knew Jean-Luc delighted in betraying and harming innocent people. Marietta was not to know what had happened to her husband until several years later, when she happened to meet some new émigrés newly arrived in Polperro who, hearing her French accent, spoke with her. It was during this conversation she finally learnt of the demise of her husband, leaving her free at last to marry Jonas who, by then, was the father of not only a daughter, but also two other children as well, both sons, with another baby due in a few months time.

Chapter 18

London re-visited

Billy had left the *Mary Anne* at the port of London dock, leaving Jonas and Captain Sawyer in command of his inheritance. It was at Billy's request that the Captain arranged for some of it to be transported to a secure warehouse, where Sir Walter had assured Billy all of his possessions would be kept safe until other arrangements could be made.

Billy had already chosen several items that had once belonged to his mother for Eva, as well as several for Sally. These he asked for the Captain to deliver in person when the ship finally returned to Cornwall.

A carriage took him directly to the home of Sir Walter Lumley, where he was expected, and where he planned on staying a while, as he intended to conduct some business in the city.

There were many things on Billy's mind during his ride to Sir Walter's grand house on the Heath, but only one he considered to be a problem, and that was how to arrange for the demise of Jean-Luc, now that Marietta was happily living with Jonas.

It seemed at the time to be the only problem he would find hard to solve. But of course, he had yet to find that money could buy almost anything, even the services of someone who would kill for a price; an amount of gold that would have bought a row of houses, he later found out.

As instructed by Sir Walter, Billy approached one of the many ne're do wells recommended, one that lived in one of the dark and dismal hovels, a place where no reputable person would visit uninvited and where villains lived in impunity, with no questions asked as to whether their help was right or wrong.

Sir Walter had come up with the name and address of one such a man, advising Billy to tell the man he needed someone to travel to France, find the man in question (Jean-Luc), then to slit his throat. Failing that, if need be, a quick shot in the heart or head to finish him off. The man he approached was indeed one of the most disparate Billy had ever come across. He listened to Billy, then ruefully declined the offer of a handful of gold Billy held in front of his eyes; when asked by Billy why he'd refused, the ruffian replied it was the thought of going to France he didn't like!

Sir Walter had greeted Billy with a beaming smile and a firm handshake, and then a fatherly hug, pleased to have a male companion in the all-female house again.

Billy spent some of his time with Sir Walter at his office at the Bank of England, discussing what he should do with his inheritance, until the day came when he knew he had made as many arrangements as he could. The time had come for him return to Cornwall and Eva.

His last night with the family was spent dining with several of Sir Walter's business friends, all of whom were sorry to see Billy leave, but who'd given him their assurances that his investments with them would show a good return within a few months. Hoping this would be so, Billy said his farewells and retired to his room, to prepare himself for the next day and his journey home to Cornwall. Thankfully, this time was not to be on horseback, but in one of the new coaches that travelled between London and Plymouth, a business which he'd also had the foresight to have invested in some months earlier.

The next morning, escorted by Sir Walter and his family, Billy boarded the coach for his journey home. It was going to require several stops before the coach finally lumbered its way into Plymouth, where he would have to make other arrangements for his onward travel to Polperro.

With this finally executed, and with his baggage loaded onto a carrier's wagon, Billy hired a horse and set off for the journey to Polperro, first of all crossing the Tamar by ferry. It was this journey that set off a train of thought in Billy's mind that would one day improve travel for those who wished to go from Cornwall into Devon, and even further. However, not being an engineer himself, it was to be several years before he was to meet another engineer who had the same vision, when, finally, travel out of the Duchy was revolutionised.

At last, a tired Billy reached Polperro and Hope House.

It was good at last to see Sally and James again, and to enjoy one of Sally's home-cooked meals, but Billy didn't wish to linger that night; he wanted to get back to Eva.

Leaving his baggage to be collected later, he walked the two miles along the cliffs to Cliff House taking his fill of the Cornish night air, straight into the waiting arms of his beloved Eva and a loving reunion.

It wasn't until the next day that he told Eva all that had happened in Brittany and London, making light of his experiences at the chateau with Jonas and Marcel, except to tell her they'd found his inheritance, and then the events he'd enjoyed in London afterwards with Sir Walter and his family.

Since he'd been away, Eva had been busy as well, organising the household to her own liking, making her own mark on how the house should be run now that her grandfather was no longer the master, and especially as she knew Billy liked to live and work in an atmosphere of order and calm.

With his quest in France successful, and now that he'd returned home safe, Eva held her husband tight, pleading with him not to go away again (her pregnancy making her unusually emotional) and at the same time telling him he was going to be a father.

Billy was delighted with her news and tried to assure her he had no intention of leaving her again, but, in his heart, he knew he might have to travel back once again to France, especially if the assassin he'd contacted in London to do his bidding to get rid of Jean-Luc failed in his mission.

To Billy, it was imperative for Marietta's happiness that her husband should be found and got rid of. Not that Marietta and Jonas were very concerned, for they were already living happily together, even without the blessing of the church!

Marriage was something they looked forward to, but it wasn't essential for their happiness and no one in the village – apart from Billy, Eva, Sally and James – knew any different.

One day, several years later, Marietta met a newly arrived émigré from France, by then under the rule of Bonaparte, from whom she learnt the truth during their conversation about the death of her husband. It was a shock at first to find out her husband had died a brutal death not long after she had escaped with Billy and Jonas. It saddened her, until she realised she was now a free woman and could marry Jonas, who'd more than proved to be the kindest man she'd ever met... apart, of course, from Billy.

Epilogue

This has been the story of a young man's timely escape from revolutionary France, and the new life he made for himself in Cornwall, which to him was a foreign country. But the story does not end there, because, like all stories about families, in reality it will never end. This story will continue, until there are no more descendents of Willelm D'Anville and his beloved wife Eva still alive.

Many things were to happen in Cornwall and in France over the years. Of France we know from history that wars and the Revolution continued, and that Bonaparte ruled in France. That the Battles of Waterloo and Trafalgar took place, as well as other wars, and one in particular between England and France, during Billy's first years in Cornwall. It was as if the world had gone mad. Wars were fought in the belief they were a cure-all for all the ills throughout the world, when in fact they were then, and are now, merely symptoms of a worldwide ailment that continues to this day. The principle symptoms being avarice and religious intolerance, with no care by those in power for the rights of the common man or woman to enjoy a good standard of living for themselves and their children, and to live with no fear or oppression.

Willelm D'Anville was not a man who lived this way. His friends knew him as William Sawyer, or Billy, a man greatly respected as a human being. His wealth enabled him to become an entrepreneur, renowned throughout Cornwall as not only a financier but also a man who did good works for the benefit of his fellow men and women. He was a Christian man who lived through his beliefs, encouraging others to do the same.

The reign of terror in France, leading to the Revolution, was to change France forever. The King was executed, as was his wife, and life changed for the French populace, but this, or so it appeared, seemed to be what most of the people wanted and therefore nothing could be said or done that would alter what had happened.

Eva and Billy's lives continued in much the same way as before, once he'd returned to Cornwall, after finding his hidden inheritance, except that they became parents to a son, called Henry, born that autumn in a bedroom of Cliff House and then the following winter, a second child, a daughter, named Catherine, after Eva's mother was born.

Over the years, the family's fortunes improved vastly, which Billy used to improve the living and working conditions of the people of Cornwall. Apart from all the businesses he was already involved in, he bought a newly built schooner, the first of several that he was to add to his fleet, primarily to sail the oceans in search of exotic fruits and spices, which would then be transported back to London with great speed. Then there was the success of these same vessels travelling across the Atlantic, bringing back trade goods from the Americas.

These were just a few of the many ventures Billy became involved in, but there many others. Some involved mining, in Cornwall as well as abroad. Then there was engineering. He was one of the first enlightened men in the country who pioneered the new mode of travel by train, as well as bridge making and building roads. Certainly, nothing happened in the county of Cornwall, or even beyond, without Billy Sawyer being involved in some way, as history was to prove.

He had many other interests as well. Investments in silver and copper mines in both Mexico and South America, as well as mining interests in other countries; searching for rare minerals and gems, all of them profitable, with some leading on to other projects.

And so Billy's businesses have carried on.

Henry, Billy's son and heir, went into the family business as soon as he was old enough, but only after he'd finished his education, which involved him going away to school, and then onto university, the first of Billy's children to do so. Once Henry had taken his degree, he too travelled the world, before finally settling down to have a family with a local Polperro girl, giving Billy and Eva their first grandson. Finally, he took over the business from Billy, who by then was getting old and wanting to spend more time with his beloved Eva. The two of them re-designed the gardens at Cliff House, which by then had been renovated and modernised. They often took short holidays in Hampstead Heath with Lilian and Martha; by then, Nellie and Walter Lumley had both died.

Billy never did get to live in his Chateau in Brittany again, which he sometimes regretted. At times he would rant and rage at the French Government for stealing his property but, as he grew older, he became more philosophical, knowing his present life in Cornwall was the one that has given him great joy.

He could often be found looking out to sea from the cliff path – was he looking towards France, with wishful thoughts in his head for what might have been? Probably, but who knows? He might just be looking out for the Excise cutter to come round the headland, as it did many years ago, looking for goods that had escaped paying tax.

No longer did he have fears of waiting for a ship to return to Talland Bay with a load of contraband goods to be hidden in the village, as smuggling was no longer a necessary evil in Polperro.

I would like to say this is how this story ends. One man saved from the guillotine in France by another who risked his life to save him and others, who all wanted to escape from a country torn asunder by a revolution. A country where, even since those dark days, wars and revolutions have killed many a kind and gentle person, not necessarily those tainted at birth by their ancestry But that's life, or as the French say with a shrug of their shoulders, *c'est la vie*!

Catherine, Billy and Eva's daughter, married into a Cornish family who had aspirations for her husband to become the next Sheriff of the county and so she became a lady, one who then made it her life's work doing 'good deeds', which amused Billy no end.

Eva continued to love Billy as she had always done, endeavouring to give him the stable home life he craved after the loss of his parents and his heritage. It was a happy marriage that lasted until Billy died at the age of seventy-five. Eva followed him the next year. Some say of a broken heart, which I cannot dispute, knowing how much she loved him. Their children continue to live and thrive in Cornwall, as Billy wanted, although they do all speak French, at his insistence, with the fond hope that one day, maybe one of them will try to get back the properties taken from the D'Anville family during the 1789 Revolution.

So what happened to Henri Mason?

It seems a long time since Henri Masson was Billy's tutor and much must have happened to him. Did he evade capture?

To Billy's surprise, he had news of Henri when he was in London, nearly forty years later, while staying with the Lumley family. He had spent the day at the Stock Exchange, as was normal practice for him at that time, being a big investor, when suddenly a voice he recognised spoke to him. When he turned to see who it was, standing next to him was none other than Henri Masson, his old tutor.

Henri bowed, as was his way when meeting an aristocrat, which he still firmly believed to be Billy's status. Taking hold of Billy's hands, he drew him into his arms, in a loving embrace that old friends always do, delighted to see his young student once more. Although startled at seeing Willelm in such auspicious surroundings, Henri was not surprised to see him looking as prosperous as he did, knowing his former young student's superior intelligence.

'Henri, it's so good to see you again!' Billy had said, his voice cracking with emotion. 'How did you manage to get to England? And what are you doing now you are here? And how is your mother? I presume she came with you!'

'No, I am afraid not, my mother died a long time ago; old age and ill health finally took their toll on her just as we reached Calais, when we had a chance to escape. Sadly, she is no longer with me.'

Billy had no idea how to answer, sad for Henri in his loss, merely patting his arm in sympathy.

Henri, seeing Billy's distress, continued to tell him what had happened after Billy had ridden away on his horse to meet with Captain Sawyer.

'My mother and I knew we would have to get away as well. Like some of our friends, we knew our names would also be on the list of those to be arrested and, once they had us in custody, we knew we would be guillotined. Not for being aristocrats, because everyone knew we were not of that sort of family, but because our sympathies were known through our association with your family; anyway, it was obvious our time was running out.

'Once I'd persuaded my mother we must leave straightaway, I sold your good horse that we might use the money to aid our escape. I then managed to find a man with a cart, a good man from the village that I knew quite well, one who was prepared to take us, and a few of our possessions to Calais. I knew, once there, we would be able to get a passage to England, so your money paid for all that, for which I must thank you.'

Billy wiped a hand across his eyes, wiping away some tears.

Henri continued. 'All the time we were travelling, my mother begged me to leave her and save myself, but I couldn't do that. She meant everything to me and I was determined she would see freedom in England. Unfortunately she was taken ill and died a few days later. Thank goodness that by then we had been taken in by kind friends of one of my previous employers, good people, who saw to it that she had a decent burial after a service that was brief but memorable at the church at Calais. I am sure she would have liked that.

'Once I was alone and could do as I wished, I managed to get a passage within a day or so to Dover and was soon in England, where I made my way to the French quarter in London. I knew I would be able to find employment and, sure enough I did, with a friend of Sir Walter Lumley who, I believe is a man you know well?"

'So why are you here today?' Billy asked.

'I'm here because my employer once asked that I learn all there is to learn about stocks and shares, knowing mathematics was a subject I excelled in. He thought I might be a good person to advise him. It's been a strange experience for me, but I've managed. Since that first time I now understand how the exchange works and will advise my employer later today, as always, as to what I believe he should invest his money in this month and then we will have to wait and see if my ideas come up to the standard he expects from me. It's been most interesting for someone like myself, who in the past, had been responsible for teaching young men, like yourself. As far as I know, all have gone on to work for the Government or into banking!'

'Unfortunately, I never made it into banking or in the government!' said Billy rather ruefully. 'With my father murdered and our homes possessed by the Revolutionists I had to find other employment.'

'And what sort of employment did you go into?'

'I journeyed to Cornwall with Captain Sawyer and there I met his father-in-law, Sir John Inney, a businessman, and became his apprentice!'

'An apprentice? That seems to me to be a menial sort of job for someone as educated as yourself!'

'You may think so, but I took to it very well. Indeed, I ended up doing most of Sir John's work and he trusted me. Finally, he gave me full responsibility for running his businesses after he died. Also, I fell in love with his granddaughter, Eva, and married her. We've been married now for several years and have two children: a son, Henry, named after you and my father, of course, and a daughter, named Catherine after Eva's mother. So you can see, life in Cornwall has been good for me and I hope to continue living there, spending my inheritance improving life for us both, for the rest of my life.'

'Inheritance? How did you manage to get hold of that?' Henri asked, delighted his young student's life had turned out so well.

'My father had entrusted a wooden chest filled with gold and coins to Captain Sawyer for safe-keeping, some weeks before he and my mother were arrested. When we landed in Cornwall, the Captain made sure the chest went with me. Since then, I've found more of my inheritance hidden in France and that also has been taken to Cornwall, so I'm quite wealthy and, really, I have no need to work. But I do, as I believe the Devil makes work for idle hands!'

Henri Masson laughed and clapped him on my back.

'Well done, Willelm!' Henri said.

'That's another point!' Billy said. 'My name is no longer Willelm D'Anville. I am now known quite simply as William Sawyer, or Billy for short. That's the name I will take to my grave!'

Henri and Billy talked for much longer until, eventually, they went their separate ways, both of them delighted to have met each other once again and even more delighted to learn that each of them was happy to be living in England. Henri told his former pupil, before they parted, that he'd recently met a young lady and had at last fallen in love. He was planning to marry her within the next few months, which was good news. After they'd made plans to meet again before Billy returned to Cornwall, Henri left to go about his business while Billy continued with his plans for the day, which were very similar to Henri's; that of attending the Stock Exchange to see how his stocks and shares were faring.

Captain Sawyer, sadly, fared less well in the future. He continued to sail the *Mary Anne* for many years until he sold it to another young master mariner who wanted a tried and tested ship. He could have no better. The Captain replaced his ship with a schooner that he named *The Lady Catherine* (after the love of his life), a ship he hadn't had to gamble for.

All went well until the day he landed at one of the ports in the Caribbean and found himself involved in a fracas that was not of his making. Unfortunately, he was mortally wounded and was buried in a grave that would forever rest under the sun of a foreign country. Billy was sad when he learnt of his death, as was Eva, but they were both sure he went to meet his maker with no regrets, having lived his life as he'd wanted; sailing across the seas of the world, seeing sights that were to enthral and inspire him. Had Catherine, his lovely wife, lived, then his life might well have been different, but that was not to be. In the last few years of his life he would often visit his daughter, Eva, whenever his ship was in English waters, but not in the *Mary Anne*, as by then she had long gone. Was it his great-grandfather who'd been responsible for Martin's gambling addiction in the first place? For he was the man who had lost what would have been a fortune many years ago, his only legacy to the family being an oil painting that James and Sally had hanging on the wall of Hope House, one item from the past that will forever remind them not to gamble away their hard-earned money. It was the painting Billy always admired, until he was told the circumstances of their acquiring it. All he could say to that was: that's life!

Marietta became the mother of five children; Nathaniel, her first son by Jean-Luc Dupont, and four children by Jonas Matthews; two sons, Marcel and Claude, and two daughters, Michelle and Marie-Louise, named after her mother and her grandmother.

Nathaniel Dupont became an exalted explorer, travelling the world, as had been predicted by Ned Pengelly many years ago. His work was find rare plants that he sent back to Cornwall to be planted in the gardens of the gentry of the county. The other children all lived and died in Polperro, marrying local young men and young ladies and in time becoming parents to children, who, in their turn, made Marietta a grandmother and a great-grandmother, a role she knew she'd been born to.

As for Jonas, he never stopped loving Marietta. He'd always wanted to marry her but, until they had written proof Jean-Luc Dupont was indeed dead, they were unable to legalise their union. That was of no great importance to them, as they loved each other and would do so until the day they died. As far as anyone knew, they might have made it through the pearly gates without being legally married because they'd lived and loved honestly, and devotedly, for more than forty years; no better recommendation could be found for entry into heaven than that. They did marry, eventually, with their children and grandchildren at the service, which made them all laugh. How many couples get married with their children seeing them wed?

Others we mustn't forget are the rector of the parish and his daughter Louise. The rector met an unfortunate end. He was attacked in the church vestry while locking away the silver chalice that had been used for serving wine during the communion service for a hundred years. His assailant managed to get as far as Bodmin Moor before he was apprehended and brought to justice. He confessed to that crime, which he couldn't deny as he was found clutching the chalice in bloodied hands. He was found guilty for it, as well as for several other attacks throughout Cornwall. He was sentenced at the assizes to be hanged in Bodmin for his crimes. On the day of the hanging, several thousand people travelled to watch the ghoulish spectacle.

Louise, the rector's daughter was as course heartbroken at this sorry event. Thankfully, she had Eva and Billy to help her in her time of need, giving her a home until she could get her thoughts together as to what she should do with her future. She was to find lasting happiness, and had several children, when the new rector was appointed, who just happened to be a single man.

Much taken with Louise, and with the blessing of all in the village, they married within a few months of him taking charge of the parish, with Billy giving the bride away, and his young son and daughter acting as page and bridesmaid to the happy couple. And so life goes on in Polperro, one of the prettiest villages in Cornwall.

Here ends the story of a young man, one who had been born to a different life; destined at birth to be an aristocrat but, by a quirk of fate, had escaped from the tyranny that raged in France during that time, surviving the threat of the guillotine, unlike his parents, whose tragic deaths left him devastated. Billy, as he came to be known, travelled across the Channel to safety and a new life in Cornwall, a place he came to love and where he was to meet Sir John Inney, who became his great mentor and friend, and who was the grandfather of his beloved wife, Eva.

Billy never forgot his beloved parents. He built a memorial to them in the grounds of Cliff House, a place where he would go and sit when he needed guidance and assurance. He was sure his father's spirit listened, as Billy's own fortunes increased, so who could possibly doubt that his father was not guiding him? Was this not the truth?

Billy and Eva's graves are in the cemetery of the church on the cliffs, where they were married, and where they are still maintained by their children and their grandchildren and great-grandchildren and will be, ad infinitum!

And finally, as it is said in France when one must go away; *au revoir*, until we meet again.